DON'T LOVE A LIAR

NEW YORK TIMES & *USA TODAY* BESTSELLING AUTHOR

CYNTHIA EDEN

PROLOGUE

Someone had tucked her doll in bed. Eight-year-old Kennedy smiled as she skipped forward. She'd been looking for her doll all morning. She called her Kaylie, and Kaylie was her absolute *favorite* doll. Because Kaylie looked just like her. Her mother had gotten the doll made especially for Kennedy.

She stopped by the side of the bed, the pink comforter brushing her arm as she leaned forward, but just before she touched her doll, Kennedy stilled. Something was wrong.

Her hand flew away from the doll as Kennedy's breath left her in a fast rush.

Kaylie's pretty blue eyes...her eyes were gone. Two gaping sockets just stared back at her. Kennedy opened her mouth to scream.

The floor creaked behind her. She whirled around even as she felt tears slide down her cheeks.

Her brother stood here. His hands were fisted at his sides. His head was slanted forward, and his dark hair tumbled over his forehead. Not looking at her, he said, "I'm sorry about your doll."

Her knees were shaking. She'd *loved* that doll, and he knew it. "What did you do?"

His head tilted back. He looked at her — his eyes exactly like her own. "I don't think it hurt her. She never made a sound…"

CHAPTER ONE

Her dress was blood-red. A fitting choice. She glided into the ballroom, the red dress hugging her figure, then swirling out near her long, long legs. A thousand white lights glittered around her, making her seem to shine. To fucking sparkle as she lifted her chin high and acted as if she owned that whole room.

There were whispers. Of course, there were whispers. She was Kennedy Clarke, *the* scandal of the hour, and even though she'd been the one to spearhead this charity party, half the folks there hadn't thought that she'd actually show for the big event. Not with all the dark and twisted drama surrounding her missing brother Kyle.

The killer.

But Kennedy just strolled right through the crowd, pausing only to pick up a slender champagne flute. She had to hear the other voices. Remy St. Clair could sure as hell hear them, and he was standing alone near a back wall.

"Kyle killed his fiancée, did you hear? Tortured that poor girl…"

Kennedy paused to watch the band.

"I don't think they found his body. Do you really believe he killed himself rather than go to jail?"

Her head tilted back. Her long, black hair trailed over her shoulders. She took a sip of her champagne and then went to study the giant Christmas tree that sat in the middle of the room.

"There could be other victims. The police think there are more."

She smiled as she stared at the tree. At all of the presents underneath it. The charity gala was to raise money for the local children's hospital. All the guests there had donated hefty sums, *and* they'd brought in presents for the children.

"Do you think she knew? Did she help him to vanish?"

Her delicate shoulders stiffened. Her head turned, but she didn't look at the gossiping woman with the overly loud voice. Instead, she looked—

Straight at Remy.

Bright, bright blue eyes.

Eyes that seemed to hit him with the force of an electric shock.

He'd seen pictures of her before. He always studied his prey carefully before he moved in. Remy had known that Kennedy was beautiful. Rich, gorgeous, smart. Sexy.

Dangerous.

He'd prepared for all of that, and yet…

Seeing her in person somehow made him feel caught off-guard. He didn't look away from her. Didn't even force a fake smile. He couldn't. All he could do was stare into her eyes and realize that he wanted the beautiful and dangerous Kennedy Clarke.

He felt the lust burn through his body. Felt the white-hot attraction that *would* be a serious problem. But he just went with it. He let the desire burn for her, and he knew it would show in his eyes.

It would show, and the next step would be up to her.

For a moment, she seemed to hesitate. Her chest rose and fell too quickly, but then Kennedy headed toward him. A waiter passed her, and she put her barely-touched champagne flute on his empty tray. Her gaze stayed locked on Remy. And when she was close enough, he caught her scent. Strawberries. She smelled like sweet strawberries.

He'd always loved them.

"Hello." Her head tilted. Her gaze held his. "I don't think we've met."

No, they hadn't.

She offered her hand to him. "I'm Kennedy."

His fingers took hers. And when he touched her, a deep, hot awareness flooded through him.

A primitive attraction that he knew would prove problematic.

Her hand was small in his, soft. Delicate.

"I'm Remy. Remy St. Clair."

She didn't try to tug her hand free. Just kept studying him. "Thank you for coming to the gala tonight. It's a very important cause, and I appreciate your support."

Ah, was that why she'd come across the room? Because this was her event, and she was doing her society princess bit and thanking him for —

"Would you like to dance?" Kennedy asked him.

The question surprised him. He blinked.

Then she tugged on her hand. "Or not." Her smile came and went, a flash that never made it to her incredible eyes. "Sorry, I didn't mean to —"

"I would love to dance with you." His hold tightened on her hand. He wasn't letting her go that easily.

Some of the tension seemed to leave her shoulders. But then she bit her lower lip and glanced over her shoulder. "Are you new to this town?"

Not even close.

"Do you know who I am?"

"You're Kennedy. You just introduced yourself to me." He finally let a faint smile curve his own mouth.

When she glanced back at him, her gaze went to his mouth. She stared for a moment, seeming to gather her thoughts, then her gaze lifted to meet his. Her stare sure packed one hell of a punch.

"Let's have that dance," he murmured, and, keeping his hold on her delicate hand, Remy led them onto the dance floor. Like the other men at the ball, he was dressed in a tux. High-end. Too damn expensive. He'd even put on the bow tie, though he hated the thing. Made him feel like he was choking. But he'd needed to blend.

Kennedy wasn't blending, though. The woman was shining bright.

The band started playing a slow, sexy tune. Just as he'd bribed them to do. Because, yes, he'd intended to dance with Kennedy that night. Only he'd thought that he'd be the one to approach her.

Nice change of plans.

He curled one hand around her slender waist and brought her closer to him, so that their bodies brushed. She moved easily in her heels, her steps matching his perfectly.

"You're a good dancer," she whispered.

He was passable. She was polite. He inhaled her delectable scent and wondered if she'd feel the growing hard-on that he had. "People are watching us."

She put her head on his shoulder. Didn't look at the people around them. "Yes."

"Want to tell me why?" He knew why.

"Because everyone loves a good scandal."

No, not everyone.

His hand moved toward her back, and he realized—shit, there *was* no back to her daring red dress. His fingers touched her silky, bare skin.

She shivered.

"You're a beautiful woman, Kennedy."

"Beauty is only skin deep. Beneath the surface, I could be a monster."

Yes, she could be.

But then, so could he.

Oh, wait. I am.

He kept dancing, moving her easily, and enjoying the feel of her in his arms far too much. As far as jobs went, this one didn't suck.

At least, not yet.

"I guess men don't usually care, do they? Sometimes, it's just about what you see." Now she lifted her head. Gazed into his eyes. "What do you see when you look at me?"

"A gorgeous woman with lips made for kissing and eyes I won't ever be able to forget." All true.

Her tongue swiped over her lower lip. "You don't see the right thing." Her words sounded like a warning. But then she whispered, "Would you like to come home with me?"

Holy fuck. She'd just asked him to take her to bed? Okay, Kennedy had just thrown his game plan to hell and back. "Uh, Kennedy…"

She pulled away. "I can't believe I just said that." Her eyes squeezed closed. She stopped dancing and just stood in the middle of the dance floor. "I can't believe I'm here. I can't believe he's *gone*."

Oh, shit. The woman was—

Her eyes flew open. A mask had slipped over her face. She stared at him with the cold, expressionless mask of—of a doll. "Thank you for the dance, Remy St. Clair. Good night."

Then she lifted her dress a few inches—the better to run from the dance floor and head for the door. For a moment, he just stood there, feeling too much like Prince Charming must have felt when Cinderella cut out in the middle of their grand ball.

Only he wasn't Prince Charming.

And she wasn't going to escape from him that easily.

He immediately turned to follow her, only to find a tall, curved blonde in his path. She wore a dress of emerald green, one that matched her eyes perfectly, and she put a well-manicured hand on his chest. "Want to dance?"

He wanted to find Kennedy. His gaze darted over the blonde's shoulder. Kennedy was sure moving fast. She was already at the door.

The blonde followed his stare. Gave a light, mocking laugh. "Trust me, I am saving you from a fate…" Her voice dropped dramatically. "*Worse than death.*"

His gaze slid back to her. "Don't remember saying I wanted to be saved."

Her lips parted. She blinked.

"And thank you for the offer of a dance, but I have other plans for the night. I'm sure a woman as lovely as you will have an easy time of finding a partner." He gave her a nod, stepped around her, and left her there with her mouth gaping.

He hurried across the floor. The whispers were louder now.

"Can't believe she came here."

"Do you think she's like him?"

"Sickness can run in a family."

He was almost at the door.

"Twins. They say twins share…everything."

Anger hummed through his body as he shoved open the door. The ballroom was located in an elegant New Orleans hotel. A curving staircase — one lined in lush, red bows — led down to the first floor. Kennedy was already stepping off the stairs.

He hurried after her.

She was fast. Impressive, in her heels.

She turned onto a narrow corridor. One filled with small Christmas trees and pale, white lights. She rushed forward, her dress trailing behind her with a rustle of silk.

"Kennedy!"

She hesitated at his call, pausing only a moment, and he saw that a doorman waited nearby. When Kennedy looked back at him, Remy could have sworn he saw tears on her cheeks. Impossible, of course.

Kennedy Clarke was supposed to have a heart carved from ice. She couldn't be crying. Not there.

Kennedy whirled away from Remy and hurried for the door. The man there opened it quickly, holding it for her as she disappeared into the night.

Oh, hell, no.

A moment later, Remy shoved past the doorman, too. He burst into the night air — air that held only the faintest chill. The holidays might be coming, but this was still the Big Easy. Temperatures barely dropped at all in December.

Kennedy was hurrying toward a waiting limo, one that sat near the opposite street corner. She was moving so quickly —

So quickly that she didn't notice the car speeding toward her. A car with too bright lights that was moving helluva fast.

"Kennedy!" he roared.

She froze. Seemed to get caught, like a deer in the headlights, as she gaped at the car hurtling toward her.

Move, Kennedy, move!

She leapt forward, but that car — it changed positions and shot toward her.

The driver is aiming for her.

Not on his watch. Using all of his energy, Remy raced for her. He grabbed Kennedy, and they both flew forward as he shoved them toward the limo. They hit the ground, and he grabbed Kennedy, hauling her behind the rear of the limo, getting her out of the way just as the crunch of metal filled the air.

That sonofabitch had just hit the limo. The other vehicle hit the limo and careened down the road.

That sonofabitch had almost killed Kennedy.

Tires squealed, and the smell of burning rubber filled the air as the vehicle raced away.

"Jesus, baby…" Remy's hold on her tightened. "Are you all right?"

A tear slid down her cheek.

CHAPTER TWO

Her heart thundered in her ears. Her palms were bleeding because they'd scraped over the ragged pavement, and Kennedy could barely suck in a breath.

"Kennedy?" He pulled her to her feet, and held her tight. The gorgeous stranger she'd met at the ball. The man who'd held her like she was some kind of fragile treasure on the dance floor. The man who hadn't looked at her like she was the freak of the week.

The man who'd just seriously saved her ass.

His slightly callused fingertips ran over her arms, as if he was checking her for injuries. She didn't have any injuries — well, other than the scrapes. Nothing serious, though, because of him.

"*Who are you?*" The words just blurted from her.

His eyes — dark chocolate — gleamed. "Already told you, I'm Remy St. Clair."

He acted like some kind of superman. He'd moved so fast. And — "You could have been killed." She shoved against him. "You need to stay away from me." She swiped at the tears on her cheeks.

His lips parted in surprise.

"*Kennedy!*" She recognized the worried voice of her driver. Henry had been with her family forever. He wasn't just a driver. He was an advisor, a part-time bodyguard, a friend — hell, he *was* family. Pretty much the only family she had left. Henry rushed around the limo, his face showing his fright as the light from the nearby street lamp fell on him. "Are you okay?"

No, not at all. "I'm fine."

Henry's gaze raked over her. He was close to sixty, and as fit and strong as a man half his age. He worked out religiously, and the guy took her safety as his main priority. "Is that blood on your hands?"

Yes, dammit. She shoved her hands behind her back. "I'm fine, really."

Remy growled. "She was nearly killed. Fine isn't even *close* to what she is."

She ignored him. "Are you all right, Henry?"

"I was on the other side of the vehicle." His breath heaved in and out. "Saw the guy coming. Saw him *aim* for you."

Yes, she'd rather thought the vehicle had aimed for her, too. Her gaze fell on the limo — the left side had been dented — the frame crumpled in and bore the hard marks from the impact with the other vehicle.

"The video cameras will have caught the driver, don't worry." Remy's voice was a deep, oddly delicious rumble of sound. She shouldn't be finding it sexy, not while they were standing on the side of the street, being gawked at by everyone around them. Not when she'd just come inches away from getting an up-close and intimate hit from an SUV.

Remy yanked out his phone. "I'm calling the cops."

Cops. Right. Yes. That was what they should do. Call the cops. Answer all the questions that the authorities asked. File a report. Not like she could just leave the scene of a crime.

Or rather, she wasn't *supposed* to leave the scene. But...

Her chin lifted. "Will the car still drive, Henry?"

He blinked. Cocked his head as he seemed to consider the matter. "The hit was pretty close to the tank. I don't smell any gas, but I'm not sure we should risk—"

"You're *not* leaving." Remy sounded shocked.

She wanted to run away as fast as she could. Unfortunately, it looked like fate had other plans for the night.

As if on cue, a siren wailed in the distance. Maybe one of the gawking onlookers had called in the hit and run.

"Give us a moment, would you, Henry?" Kennedy murmured.

Henry shuffled away, moving to better inspect the limo.

She pulled in a deep breath. Then another. Then —

Remy pulled her hands from behind her back. He turned them over and stared at her palms. "You *are* hurt."

His fingers feathered over her skin.

A shiver slid over her. "It's nothing." Her voice was way too husky. She cleared her throat. "Thank you. Truly, you saved me from what could have been a serious injury, and I just want you to know how much I appreciate your help."

He stepped even closer to her. "Your driver was right. That SUV *aimed* at you."

The police siren was louder. The cop must have been close by when he got the accident report. When she turned her head, she could see the flash of blue lights coming up the street.

"Someone just tried to kill you, and you seem as cool as ice."

Ha. He had no idea. "Appearances can be deceiving." Her stare cut back to him.

Remy's eyes narrowed. "What's going on?"

More drama than the handsome stranger needed to hear. "I'm trouble you don't want, okay?" She should have stayed away from him in the ballroom. But when she'd looked up and she'd found his eyes on her, when she'd seen a man staring at her with interest, with *need,* she'd weakened. She was just too tired of people staring at her with accusation in their eyes.

"Maybe I like a little bit of trouble in my life."

He had a white knight complex. She got it. She'd even seen the type before. A guy who wanted to save the day. Nice of him. But didn't he get it? White knights...they often wound up getting hurt. Badly.

Not that he really *looke*d like the white knight type. If anything, Remy St. Clair appeared like the dark and dangerous villain. He wore his expensive, black tux with easy grace. He was tall, powerfully built, with thick, dark hair that shoved back from his high forehead. His features could have been cut from stone. A strong, hard jaw — one that was covered in the faintest of stubble. A long, straight blade of a nose, and high, sharp cheekbones.

But it was his eyes that had first captured her attention. Those deep, chocolate eyes. Eyes that seemed to burn with emotion.

This guy...he made her think...*what if?*

Too bad they hadn't met in another life.

She gave him a quick smile. One of the real smiles that she didn't offer to just anyone. "Thank you," she said again, and, giving into an impulse she absolutely should have resisted, Kennedy pushed onto her toes and put her mouth against his. The kiss was intended to be light and quick, but—

His hands locked around her waist. He pulled her closer.

Her lips parted, and his tongue thrust into her mouth. He gave a rough, animalistic growl. And then he just took her mouth. Claimed her. Kissed her with a white-hot, burning desire. A desire that rocked her straight to her core. Her breasts ached, her hips arched toward him, her whole body became super sensitive, and she wanted to sink into him.

Wow. Wow.

His lips broke from hers. He didn't let her go. "Yes."

The one word seemed to fall heavily into the air.

She licked her lips and tasted him. *The man packs a very powerful punch.* "Yes—what?"

"Yes, baby, I'm coming home with you tonight."

Shock rolled through her. "What?"

"You did ask, didn't you?" He smiled at her. A sexy, confident smile. "But then you ran away before I could give you my answer." His gaze drifted over her. "It's a hell yes, by the way. An, oh, fuck, yes. Because, really, what sane man would tell you no?"

A man who knew who she was. A man who understood that she was dangerous.

The patrol car screeched to a stop. The blue lights flashed in a sickening blur. She'd come to the gala because it was *her* event. She'd organized it for the last five years. She ran her own party planning company, but this gala — it was always done for free because she cared so much about this cause. The children mattered to her. She'd been determined to hold her head high against the gossip. But then she'd nearly been run down.

Nearly been killed.

Worse, she'd almost gotten an innocent man killed, too.

So, she shook her head, quite sadly, and said, "You don't want me."

He gave a rough laugh. "You're very wrong there."

"I'm not a safe lover. You should stay away from me." But she was the one to back away from him. "Far away."

She turned her back to him. Hurried toward the young cop.

"*I don't think so.*"

Remy's words followed her.

***

Remy watched his prey as she hurried toward the fresh-faced cop. Her dress was torn. Her hands were bloody.

And her kiss was pure wildfire.

He sucked in a deep, calming breath. Then he backed away from the wide-eyed crowd. He pulled out his phone because he was freaking pissed, and this situation needed to be handled *immediately*. Hunching his shoulders, he headed for the mouth of a nearby alley. His call was answered on the second ring.

"What in the hell was that about?" His voice was little more than a low snarl. "She could have been seriously hurt. We wanted her to turn to me, but not to—"

"*It wasn't us*," the frantic voice on the other end of the line assured him. "That shit didn't come from our end. We saw the attack, we're already checking the vehicle's tag, and shit—hold on, I got a hit."

He pinched the bridge of his nose and prayed for patience.

"It's a stolen car. It was jacked about two hours ago."

His heart drummed hard in his chest. Remy spun around, and his gaze unerringly found Kennedy as she stood with her head tilted toward the young cop.

"Kennedy Clarke has plenty of enemies. You knew that going in," the voice blasted in his ear. "Use this to our advantage. You just saved her— *use this*."

Yeah, he knew exactly what the guy really meant. *Use her.*

"Find that damn driver," Remy growled back. "He could have killed her. Get the asshole and lock him up!"

Kennedy glanced over her shoulder, and her gaze drifted over the crowd until she found him. For a moment, her bright stare lingered on him.

The cop said something to her. She shook her head.

Remy shoved his phone into his pocket, and he began marching straight for them. With each step he took, he saw her body stiffen a little bit more.

"We'll try to find the driver, ma'am," Remy heard the kid say as he closed in, "but do you have a way to get back home tonight? Do I need to call a cab for you?"

"I'll be taking her home," Remy announced.

She stiffened. "That's quite all right. My driver will—"

The driver—she'd called him Henry—stood just a few feet away. His hard stare was on the smashed limo. But as Remy stared at him, Henry coughed and turned his attention toward Kennedy and the cop. Nodding, he said, "I just got to wait for the tow truck driver. Once the limo is secure, I can take Kennedy back to her place."

Remy reached for Kennedy's hand. Being careful of the scratches on her palm, he folded her hand in his. "I'll see her safely home."

The cop looked at him. Henry squinted at Remy suspiciously. Kennedy just stared at the ground. She seemed lost. Vulnerable. *Not* the woman he'd expected.

But then, a hit and run could rattle anyone.

The cop finally asked, "Uh, who are you, buddy? Are you, um, her date or — "

"I'm Remy St. Clair. I'm a PI."

Now Kennedy's head whipped toward him.

He kept his focus on the cop. "The SUV that you're looking for is a late model vehicle, black, with one busted tail light." He rolled back his shoulders. "I didn't get a look at the driver. I was more interested in making sure that Ms. Clarke survived. But I did peer back in time to get the tag number." He rattled it off as the cop scribbled the number down in his notepad. "The traffic cams should have caught the guy. Get an APB out for him and start checking all of the local garages because he may decide to dump the vehicle. Hopefully, you can get the jerk within the hour."

The cop hurriedly backed away as he got busy on that APB.

Remy turned his attention to Kennedy.

She was staring at him with what could have been hope on her face. "You're a PI?"

He shrugged.

"Did you just move to the city?"

"No, I've been here a while."

Her brow furrowed. "How do I not know you? How do—"

"I used to work for Kace Quick. I've recently gone out on my own." Remy waited for the name to register. It only took a few seconds.

She took a quick step back. "The crime lord?" Her voice had turned into a whisper.

"I don't think Kace likes labels. Neither do I." He shrugged once more. "I was his bodyguard, and I was his fixer. Things have changed in his life, things have changed in mine, and I decided it was time to start my own business." That was a very short and sweet summary.

"You…you know who I am."

Were they back to that? He tried not to smile as he said, "I believe you introduced yourself to me as Kennedy."

Kennedy gave a hard, negative shake of her head. "That's not what I mean. If you live in New Orleans, then you know who I am. Everyone down here knows. My family is the scandal of the hour."

"Do you really want to talk about that…here?" He motioned toward the crowd.

Her chin lifted. God, the woman was gorgeous. All sharp cheekbones, bedroom eyes, and sexy lips. Even in the middle of hell, she looked like a super model.

"Cameras are rolling," he murmured. "I'm sure you're going to be on every news story in the area tomorrow morning."

She didn't look toward the cameras. She didn't look away from him.

"Let me get you the hell out of here," he urged her quietly. "I'll take you home. You'll be safe." He actually meant those words. He could protect her. Well, from every threat but himself.

"I'm never safe." She swallowed. "And I don't think I can trust you."

You can't. Not ever.

"You just confessed to working for a criminal, and—"

"I would think that you—of all people—would know better than to believe everything that you hear."

Her lashes shielded her eyes.

"I know better than to do that," he continued carefully, because he did not want to blow this. He'd put too much time and energy into her already. "That's why I don't believe the stories about you and your brother."

Her lashes rose. She stared at him. Seemed to be trying to see through him.

Oh, baby. Look as long and as hard as you want. You won't ever know if I'm dealing in truth or lies.

He kept his voice low and easy as he added, "My ride is waiting in the parking garage. I can have you out of here in less than two minutes."

She bit her lower lip. The same lower lip that he'd kissed. He wanted to be the one biting it, but first, he had a job to do. She was the job.

"The cop knows my name. People *see* you with me. I'm not going to take you away and hurt you. Hurting you isn't on my agenda. I'm the guy who saved you, remember? That's all I want to do. I want to keep you safe." His hand lifted and the back of his knuckles slid over her soft cheek. "That's something I happen to be really good at doing, by the way. Protection is my business."

He saw the flicker in her eyelashes, and he knew she was going to take the bait even before her lips parted.

Maybe he should feel like a bastard for manipulating her, but…

"Take me home. Please."

That last word, the soft *please*…it made him feel strange. His chest ached, and he realized that he felt…fuck. Guilty? Nah. Couldn't be guilt. He'd lost his conscience long ago.

He answered a few more questions and chatted with the cop while she said goodbye to Henry. He heard Henry tell her that he'd take care of the limo and see her soon. From his research, Remy already knew all about Henry Marshall. Henry lived in a guest house on her property. An ex-Marine, the guy had worked for the Clarke family since Kennedy had been a kid. Remy could see the affection between them.

Kennedy gave Henry a tight hug before she slipped back over to Remy.

Remy caught her elbow in his hand and carefully steered her toward the parking garage. He was acutely conscious of the eyes on them.

Not that he gave a damn. But Kennedy sure seemed to tense. Soon, they were in the parking garage, and he opened the passenger side door of his Benz for her. She slid onto the leather seat, and the scent of strawberries teased him once again.

Lust hit him sharply, a hard knife to the gut. *Not now.* Wrong time and wrong place. He'd have to deal with his desire for her. It couldn't get in the way of the job.

Remy shut the door and hurried to the driver's side. A faint noise stopped him in his tracks, and Remy's head turned as he scanned the cavernous parking garage.

Silence.

He waited a beat, his eyes darting toward the dark shadows. Getting her away from the scene and back to her home was priority one. Forging his bond with her was priority two but...

Battle-ready tension slid through his body. He could have sworn someone was in that garage. Watching. Waiting.

He wanted to search every inch of the place, but if he did that, he'd be leaving Kennedy unprotected. If he walked away from her there, hell, by the time he came back, the woman could be long gone.

He did another visual sweep of the garage, just in case, and then he climbed into the driver's seat. As he cranked the engine, her hand flew out, and her fingers curled around his wrist.

Her touch electrified his whole body. *Yep, definitely going to be a problem.*

"You just stopped behind the car. Like...something was wrong."

His head turned. In the dim interior of the parking garage, it was hard to see her clearly.

"Was someone there?" she asked, voice breathless.

He wouldn't lie about this part. In fact, the truth would serve him better. He needed her a bit afraid. God, he was such a bastard. "I think so." But it could have just been a reporter. Or someone from the gala, or —

"I think someone is always there." Her fingers slid away from him, and for some reason, he didn't like that. He'd been enjoying her touch.

He reversed the car. "Maybe that's a problem I can handle for you."

"What do you mean?"

He slanted her a smile. "I'm a PI. Like I said before, protection is my business."

***

He didn't know who the man was. The guy's hand had lingered on Kennedy. His body had been too close to hers as they walked through the garage, and now, they'd just driven away together.

Kennedy didn't have lovers. She didn't share her secrets with anyone.

But that man — that stranger — had just driven away with her as if it were the most natural thing in the world.

He eased back into the shadows of the garage, sliding around one of the heavy, stone columns. He'd wanted to get close to Kennedy that night. Wanted to see her. Wanted to talk with her.

But the stranger had changed everything.

Who in the hell are you?

He would be finding out.

CHAPTER THREE

As he drove through the heavy, wrought-iron gates, Remy gave a little whistle. He could see the house that waited up ahead, at the end of the long driveway. *If* you wanted to call it a house. The thing looked more like an antebellum version of a castle to him. Lights shone from within it, blazing brightly into the night.

"Some place you have," he murmured.

"It's my family's home." She didn't sound overly thrilled.

He drove toward the house. Braked in front of the curving, white steps that led to the entrance. Then he killed the ignition of his car.

"Thank you for the ride. And, um, for saving me." Her voice was strained but still sexy. He found pretty much everything about her to be sexy. "I'll just go —"

"No." Flat. Simple.

Her head turned toward him. "What?"

The bright lights from her house partially illuminated the interior of his car. "Don't just go. Invite me in."

He heard the sharp inhale of her breath. "I don't know you."

"You invited me to come home with you when we were on the dance floor. You definitely didn't know me then." He leaned toward her and tucked a lock of her hair behind her ear. "Didn't seem to slow you down any."

Her hand rose, and her fingers curled around his wrist. "I invited you home because I *didn't* know you."

The woman was making zero sense.

"You looked at me—you weren't like the others. I thought I saw desire in your eyes."

Believe me, you did. Kennedy in her red dress—a sight sexy enough to make a grown man drool.

And yearn.

"For a moment, I wanted to escape. Escape isn't exactly easy for me these days. I can't trust people. My friends have turned their backs on me. They all think I'm a monster—"

"Sounds like you picked the wrong friends." She was still touching him. He was definitely still liking her touch. "Maybe you should try someone new." *Try me, baby. I'm right here.*

"I shouldn't have approached you. You just made me feel…" Her words trailed away.

He was dying to know how he'd made her feel.

"I'm dangerous," Kennedy blurted.

"I heard that story in the media." He still didn't look away from her. "Like I told you before, I know better than to believe everything I hear." He smiled at her. A slow, sensuous smile. "You don't look dangerous to me."

Her hand fell away from him. She unhooked her seatbelt. Straightened. "My brother is a suspected serial killer. Kyle is either dead or he's hiding, and the world wants someone to blame for his actions."

She wasn't telling him anything he didn't know.

"The hit and run tonight isn't the first time I've been caught in the cross-fire."

The surge of rage he felt caught Remy by surprise. "Someone is targeting you?"

"If you can't get to the enemy, then you get to the person closest to your enemy. I'm the person closest to Kyle."

Fuck. "You need protection."

"I need to find my brother. But every PI I've gone to in this town — they've all been useless to me."

"I can find him for you." The words came out of his mouth smoothly because they were exactly what he was supposed to say. He was playing a role. Doing his part perfectly. Dangling the bait to attract his prize. To attract *her*.

She didn't speak.

"I'm a damn good PI. And I've got some references that might just surprise you." He gave a bitter laugh. "There are a few powerful people in this town who've used my services before. They owe me, and they can vouch for me. Hell, they're the reason I was at your fancy gala tonight. They're helping me to branch out with my clientele." He had her on the hook. He knew it. "But when I got inside and I found you...hell, I forgot everything else. I could only see you."

He knew how to charm. Knew how to say all of the right words. He knew—

She opened the passenger door and slid out with a rustle of her red dress.

She was leaving? Well, shit. So much for turning on the charm with her.

Remy jumped from the car and rushed around to her. He intercepted her just as she was climbing up the steps. Time to try another tactic. "You shouldn't be alone here. Not if people are targeting you."

"I've got a state-of-the-art security system. And Henry stays in the guest house. He'll be back soon."

But until then, she was alone.

"Let me check the house," Remy offered. "Just to make sure you're okay. Just to—"

"I'd like that list of powerful people you mentioned. I want to review your references." Her voice was very careful. Her body held too stiffly. "And if they say you're good, then I want to hire you."

Hire him…not fuck him.

She'd wanted to do that back at the gala, but now—now everything seemed different.

She stood there, looking so beautiful that she made him ache. He wanted to wrap her in his arms. Wanted to kiss her. Hold her tight.

But…

"You seem so perfect," Kennedy whispered. "The white knight who appears and saves the day. You saved my life tonight, and now I find out that you're a PI. So perfect."

He waited.

"But I don't believe in perfect. I know what a lie it is. After all, I lived that perfect lie for the last twenty-five years. So, thank you for the ride home. But until I can check your references, we're done, Remy St. Clair." She turned her back on him. Walked to her door. An obvious dismissal.

Well, hell.

"Want to give me your number?" he asked. "So I can send those references to you?"

She'd stopped in front of her door. But as he watched, she took a careful step back. "It's unlocked. I left it locked. I know that I left it—"

He bounded toward her, wrapped his hands around her shoulders, and immediately yanked her back.

"It *should* be locked," Kennedy whispered. "The alarm should be on. The door should be locked. And not all of the lights should be on. There are too many lights. Why didn't I notice that sooner? It should be—"

He didn't say another word. He scooped her into his arms and ran back to the car. In a flash, he had her in the passenger seat. He grabbed his gun from the glove box. "Lock the door," he ordered flatly. "Stay here until I get back."

Her gaze jerked from the gun in his hand to his face. "Remy?"

"Stay here. Lock the doors," he repeated.

She gave a quick nod.

He whirled away and raced back for the house. This night was sure as hell not going how he'd anticipated. A hard wave of adrenaline pulsed through his blood as he bounded up the porch steps. Remy shoved open the front door and went in with his gun up and ready to fire. Lights blazed inside of the house, and there was a heavy stillness that seemed to consume the place.

His feet slid over the marble tile in the foyer. He could see a spiral staircase to the right, one that led to the next floor. His gaze darted toward the stairs, but he didn't see anyone there. The stairs were empty. They were—

He stilled. *Something* was on the stairs.

He stalked closer to the stairs and saw the item that had been carefully placed on the bottom step. "Fucking hell."

***

He was coming back to her. Kennedy's breath left her in a quick rush when she saw Remy running back toward her. He still had his gun out, and he held it with an easy confidence. He came to her side of the vehicle, and she frantically unlocked her door and shoved it open. Kennedy surged to her feet. "Did you see anyone?"

"I searched the whole house. No one is inside." He glanced back over his shoulder, staring at the hulking manor that was both a home and a prison to her. "Your security system had been disabled, and, uh, something was left behind."

Something? She didn't like the sound of that.

"We're calling the cops. They need to get out here. Search for fingerprints."

"What did you find?" Her hands twisted in front of her.

"Probably some kids just being dumbasses. You know how they are."

"What did you find?" Why wouldn't he just tell her?

A muscle jerked along his jaw as Remy focused on her once again. "Some bozo left a doll on the stairs."

Oh, God. She could feel her skin icing. Her hands clenched into fists. "What's wrong with the doll?"

He blinked. It was strange. Almost…robotic. Remy's head tilted as he studied her. "What makes you think something is wrong?"

Seriously? "Because some freaking psycho broke into my house. And you just said he left a *doll* on my stairs. Something has to be wrong with it." Something was wrong with the whole scene! Her voice was rising. Kennedy forced herself to choke down her fear. "Is it the doll's eyes?"

He gave one slow nod.

"What happened to the eyes?" *Please, please don't say —*

"They were gone."

CHAPTER FOUR

Most of the cops had come and gone. They'd searched her house. Looked for their clues. Collected their evidence.

And taken away the child's doll that had been left behind. A doll with missing eyes.

A sick game. A joke that wasn't funny.

A message.

Kennedy stood on her porch, her arms wrapped around her stomach, as she watched another patrol car drive away. The uniforms were just doing their jobs. But...

"You think it was a message from your brother?" Detective Amanda Jackson's voice was low.

Amanda Jackson had been working her brother's case from the very beginning.

Kennedy turned her head so that she was staring at the other woman. Amanda was tall and slender, with dark red hair. She wore a suit jacket and long, black pants. Her trademark style. Every time Kennedy had seen her, the detective had been wearing similar clothing. Her hair had been cut to frame her face, a face that was delicate, something Kennedy suspected the tough detective hated.

"I thought you believed my brother was dead," Kennedy remarked quietly.

Amanda hesitated. "His body hasn't been recovered. Only the fiancée's body was found."

Like she needed that reminder. Kennedy would *not* flinch. Keeping her emotions under tight control, she replied, "His car went into the Mississippi River. Kyle's body could be in the Gulf of Mexico by now. We may never find it."

Amanda just stared at her.

And so did Remy. He'd stayed with Kennedy, stayed the entire time while the cops had been conducting their investigation. He'd been a silent, strong shadow. Why did she feel better having him near? He was a stranger to her. He was—

"You were the victim of a hit and run tonight, Ms. Clarke. And now someone has broken into your house." Amanda lifted her brows. "Sure makes it seem as if you are the killer's next target."

"The killer?" She knew exactly what—no, *who* – Amanda was talking about.

The sick sonofabitch who'd murdered two women in New Orleans. The man who'd abducted Jeanine Jacobs shortly after Valentine's Day. The man who'd kidnapped her, kept her, tortured her…and eventually killed her. When her body had been found, a blindfold had been placed over her eyes, and her neck had been slit open. The newspapers had said poor Jeanine Jacobs looked just like a broken, bloody doll.

The Broken Doll Killer.

And then the killer had taken his second victim. Stacey Warren…her brother's fiancée. She'd been kidnapped, and Kyle had nearly lost his mind. Kennedy had seen him breaking apart before her eyes. He'd searched and searched for Stacey. Then one day, he'd said that he understood, that he'd *found* her. He'd rushed away—

The next day, Stacey's body had been discovered on the muddy banks of the Mississippi. She'd been naked. Like the first victim, her neck had been cut open. A blindfold covered her eyes. Another broken doll. And Kyle…

His vehicle had been dragged out of those muddy waters, but he hadn't been seen again.

The Press had gone wild, and her brother had been pegged as the perp.

"Could be a copycat."

Remy's deep voice made her jump.

"Could just be some asshole trying to scare Kennedy," Remy added as he seemed to think things through in his mind. "Sure as shit doesn't have to be her brother."

But the detective merely sighed. "I didn't see any sign of forced entry. The alarm was turned off. Hardly the work of someone who isn't familiar with this home. More likely, it's someone who *knows* Ms. Clarke. Someone who has easy access to her place."

Her heart lurched in her chest. "It's *not* my brother."

Amanda stepped toward her. "Are you afraid of him?"

"I *know* my brother. And I don't think he's a monster." Her trembling fingers were clenched into fists.

Amanda just gave a sad shake of her head. "Who are you lying to? Me or yourself?"

Remy stepped closer to Kennedy, his arm brushing hers. She could feel the warmth of his body reaching out to her. She hadn't realized just how ice-cold she was, not until that moment.

"How much longer until the scene is clear?" Remy asked. His voice was brisk, rough.

The detective turned her head and narrowed her eyes on him. "I don't get you two." She motioned toward them. "What are you doing, Ms. Clarke? Getting a taste for the dark side?" A pause. "Because this man isn't some safe new boyfriend for you. I *know* about Remy St. Clair."

Before she could speak, Remy moved in front of Kennedy.

"She's been through one hell of a night. From where I stand, Kennedy is the victim." His voice was even rougher. "Now, how much longer until she gets her house back?"

A man carrying a black box walked out of the house.

Amanda grunted. "We're done. That was the last tech." Then she headed after him, moving toward the porch's steps. But at the bottom of those steps, she turned back and glanced at Kennedy. "If we turn up anything, I'll let you know."

The detective hardly sounded reassuring. Her words seemed to be more of a threat.

Kennedy slid to the side so she could get a better view of the other woman.

"Lock your doors, Kennedy," Amanda warned her. "Maybe use some of that trust fund to get yourself a real bodyguard, not just Henry. Because someone sure as hell seems to be gunning for *you*."

The detective headed toward her waiting car. A few moments later, it was just Kennedy and Remy on the steps. The night air felt especially cold to her. Maybe it was the wind — it seemed to carry a distinct chill.

"So much for police protection," Remy muttered. "Guessing you don't have the best relationship with the local PD."

Serious understatement. Her gaze darted toward her front door. The lights still shone from within the house.

"Kennedy?"

Her shoulders straightened. "You didn't have to stay. I...I know I must have kept you very late." Jeez, one dance at a charity ball had turned into a serious nightmare situation for him. That would teach him to flirt with strangers. *Did you learn a lesson, Remy?*

His hand slid under her chin, and he tipped back her head. "Did you think I was just going to leave you with the cops?"

Yes, that was exactly what she'd thought. "You don't know me. You've gone out of your way to be helpful—"

His rough bark of laughter cut through her words. "Oh, sweetheart. Ask the people who know me well, and they'll tell you, I'm not the *helpful* sort."

She shivered. "You have been to me."

His dark gaze darted over her. "You're cold." He shrugged off his coat and wrapped it around her shoulders.

A gentlemanly gesture. So kind and protective.

"You should go inside," he added with a worried frown. "It's warm in there."

No, it was always ice-cold in the house. Or at least, that was the way it seemed to her. But he wouldn't understand that if she told him. No one had ever understood.

No one but Kyle.

But Remy was obviously trying to do some brush-off routine. The guy had stayed with her *forever*. It had to be nearing two a.m. Henry had returned home when the cops were there. After checking in with her, he'd gone to the guest house. She could see that his light was already turned off.

It was time for her to get inside. Lock her doors. Pretend that she wasn't freaking the hell out. And it was also time for her to say goodbye to Remy.

His hand was still under her chin. His head was close to hers. It was an intimate position. So perfect for a kiss. But...

Kennedy cleared her throat. "Good night, Remy. Thanks for being my knight in shining armor."

She caught the faint narrowing of his eyes.

Then she pulled away and headed for her door.

"You going to be all right tonight?"

"Of course." She didn't look back at him. "The cops searched the house thoroughly. The place is safe. I'll lock up. Set the alarms."

"I'd advise you to get a *new* alarm system. Someone got past the security once already. It can't happen again."

No, she didn't want it to happen again.

"What if you'd been here?" Remy pressed. She heard the squeaking of the porch's wooden floor as he advanced toward her. "What in the hell would you have done then?"

Her spine straightened. "I keep a gun in my nightstand. I would have defended myself."

She could feel him behind her.

"A professional bodyguard isn't a bad idea. You were almost run down tonight, and now this—"

She finally turned toward him. She was barely holding her shit together. He probably had no idea just how terrified she really was. She wore a mask all the time, and she was so tired of it. "Protection is your business, isn't it?"

His head tilted toward her. "Yes."

"How would you keep me safe?"

"I'd stay with you. I'd be with you all night. You wouldn't have to be afraid. I'd be so close that no threat would get near you. Fuck, in order to get to you, the bastard would have to go through me first."

Wouldn't it be wonderful to actually have someone that she could depend on? Someone who wouldn't flinch from the darkness that came her way?

But...

"Good night, Remy St. Clair. Thank you for saving me. Thank you for all of your help tonight." And she did lean toward him. She did push onto her toes and press her mouth to his. The kiss was soft and brief, and she yearned for so much more.

But she was used to not having what she wanted.

She pulled away and slipped inside the house. Her fingers were trembling as she locked the door. Reset the alarm. And then she stood there, feeling the cold sweep around her.

This house…she *hated* this house and all of the ghosts and pain that were trapped within its walls. Trapped, just as she was.

***

Remy strode back toward his car. His muscles were tight, and a slow rage burned inside of him. Kennedy had been afraid. He'd seen the fear in her eyes. She'd been terrified, but she'd still turned away from him. She'd still gone into the house alone.

He climbed into his car. His hand slammed into the steering wheel. *Fuck.* He'd wanted to go in after her. No, what he'd wanted was to kick in that damn door. To grab her and to take her the hell away from that place. He'd wanted her safe. He'd wanted her with him.

In his arms.

In his bed?

Shit. This case wasn't supposed to be about mixing business and pleasure. But Kennedy — she was throwing his plans straight to hell.

She was afraid.

He hadn't realized just how much he'd hate for Kennedy to be afraid of anything.

He cranked the car, jerked it into reverse, and got the hell out of there. There were eyes on her house. He'd made sure of it. He'd called in a man to watch while the cops had been investigating. He wasn't leaving her unprotected. Hell, no. She wouldn't know his guy was there, but the fellow would be keeping a very close watch on her home. On her.

First thing in the morning, he'd text Kennedy a list of his references. She hadn't given him her number — like that was going to be a problem. She didn't understand who she was dealing with.

Remy drove back to town as quickly as he could, but he didn't head to his place. Instead, he drove down to the river front. When he parked, he jerked off his tie and threw the annoying thing in the backseat before he yanked at the buttons on his shirt. Then he was hurrying forward in the dark. The rundown restaurant — his destination — would already be closed to normal customers, but he wasn't there for some late-night snack.

The back door opened as he approached.

"She didn't let you stay, huh?" Detective Amanda Jackson asked as she held the door open for him. "So much for an easy in."

"What in the hell was tonight's shit show about?" Remy demanded as he entered the seafood restaurant. His gaze swept the team assembled there. Homicide detectives and FBI agents. *All* under his command because the FBI had taken over the Broken Doll case.

"Hold up, boss," Joshua Morgan said as he lifted his hands. "That hit and run wasn't us. Shit, we found the car. Wiped clean of prints and abandoned near Jackson Square."

"Tell me one of the traffic cams caught the driver," he growled.

But Joshua shook his head. Tall and lean, the African-American agent was a pro when it came to making profiles for the FBI. Serial killers were his specialty.

"And the doll?" Remy demanded. That fucked-up doll. "Someone want to tell me what that twisted crap was about?"

The cops and agents were dead silent.

Not a good sign.

"We're going to run the evidence collected," Amanda announced with a firm nod. "Maybe it *was* just some punk kid playing a joke. Maybe it was someone who wanted to scare the hell out of her."

Or maybe it was someone who wanted to hurt her.

"You need to get close to her." Joshua tapped a pencil to his chin. His gaze had turned thoughtful. "So close that she doesn't kick your ass away when trouble comes." He paused. "And in order for that to happen, we might have to break some rules."

Remy had broken plenty of rules in his life. He'd done it before, and he'd do it again. Lies were his stock in trade. They spilled from his lips far easier than truth ever did.

"Kennedy is the key to this investigation," Amanda continued as she grabbed for the crab claws that were on the table before her. "She's been holding back from the beginning, and if we're going to get closure, we have to find out the truth from her. Her brother isn't dead, I'd stake my badge on that. She knows where he is. She's hiding him. Hiding him, but she won't be able to control him. That man *will* kill again, unless we can stop him."

And that was where Remy came in. Because his new job *was* Kennedy. He had to break past the wall of ice that she used to surround herself. He had to earn her trust. Learn her secrets.

Then he had to rip her world apart.

Just another day in the life of Remy St. Clair, straight-up bastard.

CHAPTER FIVE

When Kennedy strolled into his office at one p.m. the next day, Remy made sure not to let any expression cross his face. Kennedy was dressed in a soft, black sweater and an elegant pair of black dress pants. Her heels, though, they were red. Sexy as all hell, too.

She approached his desk as his assistant shut the door behind her. The assistant was a new hire. The office was new, too. The place gave him a killer view of the river.

"Your references checked out. Thanks for texting them to me, though, um, not everyone was exactly thrilled to get my call." She rolled one shoulder and winced. "Story of my life these days."

He stood behind his desk, with the river at his back. Remy motioned to a nearby chair.

After a moment, she sat, crossing her legs and lightly kicking one of her high-heeled feet.

"I've gone to other private investigators since my brother's disappearance. They've all turned up nothing." A pause as she studied him. "How can I know that you'll be any different?"

Handle with care. "I can't promise that I will find your brother. I'm not here to lie to you." Yes, he actually was.

She bit her lower lip. Seemed to consider things, then said, "I think there's some confusion about why I'm here."

Remy crossed his arms over his chest.

Her long lashes shielded her gaze. "Finding Kyle would be wonderful, but…" A slow exhale. "I want proof."

"Proof?"

"Proof of Kyle's innocence. The cops already have plenty to say he's guilty, but I know my brother. He wouldn't have committed these terrible crimes."

He waited.

"So, this case — me hiring you — it isn't about if Kyle is dead or alive." Her lashes lifted, and she stared at him with her too-bright gaze. "I'm not hiring you to find him. I tried that, over and over. Right now, I need proof that my brother didn't kill those women."

He strolled around the desk. Propped his hip on the edge and stared down at her. "I'm guessing those other PIs couldn't give you the proof of his innocence that you needed."

"They couldn't find him, and they thought he was guilty as sin." Her tongue swiped over her lower lip. "But they were happy to take my money anyway. Take my money and turn up nothing."

His gaze slid over her face. She'd carefully applied makeup. A sheen of red to make her lips look plump and slick. The right touch of blush to make her cheeks look even sharper. But...

He reached out and curled his fingers under her chin. "You didn't sleep well last night." He could see the shadows under her eyes.

"Hard to sleep after someone breaks into your house, *and* you're nearly run down in the street. Those kinds of things will give a girl nightmares."

"Why the hell are you still in New Orleans?" The question burst from him. But it was one that he just didn't get. When the shit had hit the fan, why hadn't she vanished? She had enough money to do so. She could have started over anywhere else. Run from the reporters and the gossip. Gotten the heck out of Dodge.

"New Orleans is my home."

He waited. Realized that he was caressing her. She had the softest skin.

"Guilty people run," she whispered. "I thought if I stayed then I'd show them that I'm not a monster. Kyle isn't, either."

"But what if he is? What if your brother is the monster? Aren't you worried that he'll come back to hurt you?" And he had to push because it was the job. "Aren't you worried that *he* left that doll for you? That your brother could be planning to kill you next?"

Her gaze didn't waver. "He wouldn't kill me."

Don't be so sure of that. But he only said, "How do you know he's not at the bottom of the Mississippi?" His hand slid from her skin. She didn't want him to find her brother. With that new information he realized...Shit, the local cops were right. Kennedy probably *knew* her brother wasn't dead. She might already know where he was.

He saw her throat move as she swallowed. "We're twins. He was born two minutes before me. Two minutes. We've shared every secret that we ever had our whole lives."

Did you share the secret of his murders? Of his sickness?

Her hand rose and pressed to her heart. "You'll think I'm crazy, but...when we were sixteen, Kyle was in a car accident. The vehicle flipped. Kyle was hurt, tossed from the car, and I could *feel* it. I felt his pain and his fear, and I knew that he needed help."

He stared down at her.

"I *feel* him, okay? He's not dead. I'd know if Kyle had left me. I'd know it deep inside."

So, he was supposed to buy the twin connection thing, huh? No. No way. But he would certainly act like he believed her lies, and when it was time, when he'd broken down her walls, Remy would get her to admit the truth to him.

The local cops believed that she was somehow still in contact with her brother. That she'd found a secret way to get messages to him.

They also thought the bastard might have another woman. That he might be holding her right then. Torturing her. Because the guy had a pattern. He wasn't just going to stop his crimes cold turkey.

Time was of the essence.

"He's innocent," she said as she gazed at him with her bright blue eyes.

Innocent, Remy's ass. But he didn't say anything.

She gave a determined nod. "Once we have the proof that he's innocent, then we can go to the cops. We can clear his name."

And what? Her brother would pop out of his hiding spot? Remy had to shake his head. "Sweetheart, you're missing something very, very important."

She stared up at him, her lips slightly parted.

"Innocent men don't hide. You said it yourself. The guilty run." It sure looked to him like Kyle Clarke was running fast.

Kennedy flinched.

"You need to prepare yourself for the fact that your brother *is* a killer. That he tortured and murdered those two women and that he could spend the rest of his life locked away in a prison cell."

"Not if we have proof." Kennedy rose from her chair and stood before him. "Proof keeps Kyle out of prison."

His eyes narrowed on her. "I don't play games." Yes, he did. All the time. With everyone. Especially with her. "You talked to the references I sent you this morning." He paused a beat. "What did they say?"

"The judge said that you made his problems vanish. I-I didn't think he'd talk to me. I mean, not with all that's going on, but—"

"I told him to talk to you. I told him to answer your questions honestly. Same thing for the divorce attorney, and the tech CEO. I told them to tell you everything you wanted to know."

She nodded. "They said you weren't afraid to get your hands dirty."

Dirty, bloody, whatever it took.

"They told me you would get the job done."

"I will. *If* I take the job."

Now surprise flashed on her pretty face. "What? What do you mean *if*? I thought—"

He had his own conditions that he was going to lay out for her. He had to make the scene look authentic, after all. "I need honesty from you. That's what my clients have to give me. Total honesty. I can't work off bullshit."

"I'm not offering you bullshit!"

"And I need all access. If you want me ripping into your brother's life, then that means I have to rip into *your* life, too. I get access to every part of your life because it's *your* life, your link to him that will give me the clues I need."

Kennedy shook her head. "The other PIs didn't need—"

Remy laughed, cutting through her words. "You already told me those bozos turned up jack and shit, so I don't think we need to compare my services to theirs, hmmm?"

Her luscious lips thinned.

"I want full access to you. Access to every secret in your life. You hold back on me, and I'll walk. But you trust me…you give me what I need, and I'll find the proof for you. *If* it's out there." His muscles had tightened. "You need to be aware, though, that I might just find more evidence of his guilt. Your brother could be a killer. A sadistic murderer. And that is all the world will ever see."

"He's more than that."

Not to his victims, Kyle wasn't. "An all-access pass to your life," Remy murmured. "That's what I want."

She was desperate. If she wasn't desperate, she wouldn't have come to him.

But she didn't agree to his terms.

Kennedy hesitated.

So... *Push her.* "I'll want to be close to you."

Her eyes widened. "What?"

"I told you before, protection is my business. It fucking burned in my gut to leave you last night. Someone is playing games with you. Someone is jerking you around—"

"I spoke with the cops this morning. They said the hit and run—the car involved in that was stolen. They found it, abandoned. They think the driver didn't aim for me. I was in the wrong place, at the wrong time."

Did she really buy that? *I saw the car aim for her.* "Doesn't explain the doll," he growled. "Doesn't explain the fact that someone was *in* your house. And if you're my client, I'm not letting that shit happen. I'll put a new security system in for you. *I'll* make sure you're not alone at night. I'll be right there."

He saw red cover her cheeks before she blurted, "This isn't about sex."

It had been about sex last night. When their bodies had pressed together on the dance floor, when she'd looked up at him and asked him to come home with her...

"I wasn't talking about sex." His words were little more than a fierce growl. Too hard and angry. "I'm talking about your safety. Some bastard was in your house. I thought about you until dawn. I couldn't get you out of my head, and yeah, I even left a freaking guard near your place, just because I had to know you were all right."

"What?"

He'd revealed that truth to push his advantage. "I want to be close. You need me close. You're in deep, and you aren't turning to the cops for help."

"Because they don't want to help me." Their bodies were almost touching. Her scent surrounded him. He craved strawberries. "They think I could have been involved with my brother's crimes. They think I helped him — or that I'm helping him now."

Yeah, the word for that was…*accomplice*. The cops thought it. The FBI thought it. No one had proof. Yet.

"I can't trust the cops. I can't trust anyone."

His back teeth clenched. "You can trust me," he gritted out.

And he saw it. The hope in her eyes. The woman was desperate. She hadn't slept probably more than a few moments the night before. She was at the end of her rope. She needed an ally. She needed a protector.

He was right in front of her.

Turning on the charm—because he could be charming, under the right circumstances—he gave her the words that Remy knew she needed to hear. "I protect my clients. I do my job. I'll keep you safe, and if proof of your brother's innocence is out there, we'll find it."

She stepped back. Seemed to gather herself. She smoothed her already smooth hair. Her dark locks were twisted in an elegant bun at the base of her neck. The style accentuated her features. Made her look even more beautiful.

"How much are your services?"

"I'm not cheap."

She nibbled on her lower lip.

He smiled at her. "But I'm sure you can afford me." The woman had money to burn. He knew all about her finances. Born with a silver spoon in her mouth. All that money and a psycho for a brother…Remy lifted his brows. "Do we have a deal?" He offered his hand to her.

She stared at his extended hand. Then her gaze lifted back to his. The hope was there again. So was relief. Both lit her eyes. Kennedy thought she'd found a champion.

Her fingers closed around his. "Deal."

Oh, sweetheart. You think I'm saving you. When will you see…I'm going to destroy you?

"I want to be with you, though," she said quickly.

His hold tightened on her hand.

"I want to be involved with the investigation. I want to see what you find. I want to know it all, every step of the way. No surprises."

He couldn't promise that.

"Kyle isn't a monster," she told him. "*I'm* not a monster."

"If he's not guilty, then you understand — that means someone else is hiding in the shadows. Someone else who could be watching you. Targeting you."

Her delicate nostrils flared.

"You prove your brother's innocence, and we're going to prove someone else's guilt. That someone will direct his fury at us."

"Two women are dead," she returned, her voice a bit unsteady. "It has to stop. No one else can die."

Remy nodded. "You'll let me in? Give me full access to your life? Allow me stay with you? Protect you?"

"Yes." She tugged on her hand.

He let her go. "Then I guess we need to get to work."

Her shoulders sagged a little. He could see the relief sweep over her features.

"Where do we start?"

"We start with the last victim." The dead fiancée. "We're going to Stacey Warren's place. You own it, right?"

Kennedy gave a fast shake of her head. "Not me. Kyle bought the condo for her."

But now that Kyle was in the wind…

"I have a key, but the cops have been over that place, time and time again."

They had. True enough. "But they weren't there with *you*."

Her brow furrowed.

She didn't get it. She *was* the key here. She knew her brother better than anyone else. So, she'd be able to see the things he'd left behind. The clues that might be for her alone.

"Your brother was living with Stacey at the time of her disappearance, wasn't he?"

"Yes."

"Then we start there. We look, *you* look. He might have left something for you, something that only you would notice. We begin with her life. We find out *why* she was the victim, and then we work backwards from there."

"Okay." She turned away.

His lips curled down. "It's not going to be easy."

"I didn't expect easy." She was almost at the office door.

He was going to have to shock her. Have to terrify her. Have to turn her against her brother. Have to pull every dirty, low-down trick he had.

But he'd get her to flip her allegiance. Get her to trust only him.

Then the nightmare could end.

***

Kennedy unlocked the door to Stacey's condo. The air seemed a bit stale, and the interior was so dark and cold. She hurried inside, flipping on the lights, sending the shadows vanishing.

But the cold lingered.

Remy's footsteps thudded softly behind her. "This place is...familiar."

"Yeah, it's on every haunted tour in the city." She stopped in the middle of the den, her gaze on a picture that sat on Stacey's mantel. Stacey was in the picture, a wide smile on her face. A man stood behind her, his bright blue eyes laughing as he held her. Kyle.

Kennedy had taken that picture of them, right after their engagement.

She cleared her throat. "The condo — the whole building — it's supposed to be haunted. A doctor went crazy and murdered three of his patients here in the 1800s."

Silence from behind her.

Kennedy turned slowly to face Remy. His dark eyes seemed particularly hard. She lifted her chin. "Most of the places in the Quarter have a haunted reputation, I'm sure you know that. But this place is — "

"Who decided to buy the condo? Did Stacey want it? Or was it your brother's decision?"

"My brother. Stacey was an artist. He thought she'd like the light." She pointed to the right, to the giant windows that stared out at the city. "Stacey didn't like the stories about the building, but once she saw the view, she fell in love. She told me that stories didn't matter. Stacey didn't believe in ghosts."

He walked toward the window. Gazed down at the street. "Maybe she should have believed."

She followed him to the window. A carriage was below them—the driver had stopped to tell his riders about the building. She saw him point toward them. The tours came through the Quarter all of the time. The haunted tours were particular favorites with the tourists. "Stacey hated the tours at first. People always staring, but then…she started to like them. She said it was fun to pop up at the window and give people a show."

Stacey. God, she'd been such a bright light. So fun. Always seeming to burn with energy. She'd pulled Kyle out of his shell. He'd shed the darkness he always seemed to carry and finally, *finally* seemed happy.

Until she'd vanished.

Until he'd changed.

"Her bedroom—*their* bedroom is to the right." She rubbed her chilled arms. "Like I told you before, the cops came through and searched thoroughly. They took the computers and, well, I don't even know what else." Kennedy could have sworn that she was now smelling Stacey's perfume. An expensive mix that Kyle had brought from Paris. To Kennedy, it had always smelled like roses and wine.

Remy turned and headed into the bedroom.

She lingered by the window. The tour guide was still talking. The people in the carriage were snapping pictures.

Kennedy knew that the stories about that building had changed, now. It wasn't just the mad doctor and his patients who supposedly haunted the place. The locals were saying that Stacey was trapped there, too. The woman who'd never be a bride...

Kennedy's fingers slid to the right and curled around the white curtains that rested at the edge of the window.

The curtains could almost look like a dress. Especially if you were looking up from the street. So, sure, she could see where people had taken to saying the dead bride stood in the window. But...

Stacey shouldn't be some ghost story to scare tourists. She shouldn't be gone. Shouldn't be in a cold grave at the cemetery. Stacey and Kyle had planned to get married on New Year's Eve. They'd had so many plans.

The floor creaked behind her. "I need you to come with me."

She swiped her hand over her cheek.

"Kennedy?"

She didn't want him to see her crying. She was so tired of crying. So tired of doing all of this alone. Pretending that she was fine when she wasn't. Nothing was fine. She was tired of lifting her chin and straightening her spine when she heard the brutal gossip. So damn weary of keeping her mask in place when the cops questioned her.

Her parents were long gone.

Her brother — no, she wouldn't go there. It was just her.

All alone.

Alone.

The floor creaked again.

She spun toward him. "Coming." She hurried forward, bracing herself before she entered the bedroom. But...

The sheets and covers had been stripped from the bed. Right. The cops had taken them. *DNA collection.* Her gaze jerked around the room. The whole place felt cold and so stark.

"Where is this?" Remy stood near the wall, his right index finger pointing toward a large, framed photo.

She could see the small cabin in the photo, the little pond behind it. Stacey was smiling, grinning from ear to ear as she held up a fish. "That's my family's fishing cabin. It's, um, about forty-five minutes away from town, and—"

"How often did your brother take Stacey to the cabin?"

"They went there every weekend."

His gaze narrowed on the photo. "Isolated…"

Her shoulders stiffened. "It's not some kill site, okay?" The words tore from her.

His head turned toward her.

"I know what you're thinking. It's the same things the cops thought, too, when they went to the cabin and searched it. They even took their cadaver dogs out there, thinking my brother had killed other women and hidden them on the property." She drew in a shuddering breath. "But they found nothing. The dogs didn't turn up anything. There was no new evidence. My brother *didn't* kill those women. That's just my family's old cabin. A place I visited when I was a kid. A place my brother still loves." *Loves.* Present tense.

"I'll want to see the cabin."

Just like he'd wanted to see the condo. She glanced around the bedroom, feeling like an intruder. Hating it. Hating—

"Was anything missing, Kennedy? Any of Stacey's personal belongings that you weren't able to find?"

Her stare slid right back to him.

"Serials keep trophies. This guy — he would be the type to enjoy the trophies. I can tell by the way he's killing his victims. The way he's *keeping* them. He wouldn't just want to forget them when they died. There would be something that he kept, something that he savored."

"Her engagement ring." She rolled back her shoulders. "It was never recovered. Stacey was wearing it when she went missing. She always wore it. But when I — when I viewed her in the morgue…" *Don't think about that place. The antiseptic smell. The white sheet draped over Stacey's body. The thick slice in her neck…* "The engagement ring wasn't part of her belongings. It wasn't there."

He crossed the room to her. "Did you tell the cops?"

"Yes." But Amanda had just shared a telling glance with another detective. "But the detective just insinuated that my brother had taken the ring. She'd said that maybe he and Stacey fought. That he'd killed her because she'd been cheating on him and Kyle took the ring back." She ran a hand over her neck. "No matter what I said, the cops blamed my brother."

He stood in front of her. "Was she cheating?"

"No." But… "I don't think so. I mean, I don't know, okay? Kyle never said anything to me about her cheating, but it's not like he *would*. He just seemed happy. Kyle was finally happy, and I thought everything was okay."

His eyes narrowed. "Finally?"

Crap. She needed to be way more careful. "I mean he was happy, the way couples are when they're planning for the future."

His jaw tightened, but Remy turned away. Went to the door on the right.

"That's her studio," she called.

He opened the door. The hinges gave an ominous groan. Then Remy strode inside. She followed him, her steps much slower. Much, much slower. There wasn't anything to find in that condo. And being there felt like an invasion. Stacey was dead and buried, and going through her place felt like an invasion.

"I'm surprised the home hasn't been cleared out yet," Remy announced as he began to look at a stack of canvases on a table.

"I…was putting it off. Hoping…" But her words trailed off. *Hoping that Kyle would be back.* "It's Kyle's place. His memories of Stacey are here. I didn't want to throw anything away, not without him."

Remy paused to look at the easel. A canvas sat on an easel, but it was covered by a paint-stained cloth.

Her head tilted as she stared at that cloth. That was…odd. "I don't remember that."

His shoulders stiffened.

"I, um, I was here when the cops came by for their search. I don't remember the canvas being on the easel." She inched closer to it. "Maybe they just moved things around," she muttered. Yes, that made sense. They'd been searching through everything. Maybe they'd just moved some of the canvases and this one had gotten placed on the easel but...

Her hand reached for the cover. She tugged it—

"What in the hell is that?" Remy snarled.

She couldn't look away.

It's me. It's me. It's me. The refrain echoed in her head. She was staring at a painting...a painting of a woman with long dark hair, pale skin, a heart-shaped face. A woman who wore a black blindfold and who had a necklace made of blood.

Remy's hands closed around her shoulders, and he spun Kennedy around to face him. "This wasn't here before?"

What? "N-no." She craned her neck, horrified, as she gaped back at the painting once more. Her gaze fell to the bottom right corner. She saw the signature there...*SW.* Stacey Warren. And the style, the colors, the brush strokes—all of that *was* Stacey. But it was impossible. Stacey wouldn't have painted that. She *couldn't* have painted that.

"The painting wasn't here when the cops searched the place?"

She shook her head.

He kept one hand on her shoulder and his other reached for his phone. "You know what that means?"

She did. Her stomach was in knots. *That's me.*

"The fucking killer came back here, Kennedy. And he left a message for *you*."

CHAPTER SIX

"She's the next victim," Joshua Morgan said as he peered through the one-way glass at Kennedy. She sat inside the interrogation room, her hands balled into fists on her lap, her head tilted down.

Her pose was that of a woman who was afraid, and it made Remy feel...

It's fucking ripping me apart.

He wanted to be in that room with her. Wanted to be at her side. Wanted her in his arms. The horror that had been on her face when she'd seen the painting...Jesus, was she that good of an actress? Because he didn't think so.

"Whose idea was it to go to the condo?" Detective Amanda Jackson asked from behind Remy.

He exhaled slowly, made sure that he'd schooled his features, then he turned toward her. "Mine."

She lifted a brow. "But she *hired* you, right? Came to your office, told you her sob story about her brother being set up. I mean, it only makes sense that you'd start the investigation by going back to the dead fiancée's place." She motioned toward the one-way mirror. "I get it. Kennedy Clarke is a beautiful woman. Even an agent as supposedly street smart as you are can get pulled in by her."

Joshua coughed. Choked.

And Remy laughed. "Detective, I think you have the entirely wrong idea about me."

But she just shared a smirk with her partner, a balding guy with a spreading paunch. Mayo. Brock Mayo.

"She graduated summa cum laude with a degree in business from Tulane," Brock offered with a shake of his head. "The woman is smart. Smart enough to play even the FBI."

"This isn't a pissing match." They should be very clear on that. He wasn't there to take their bullshit. "You two still raging because the FBI took control of your case? Sorry. Deal with that shit. You couldn't get the case closed, and FBI Brass ordered me to step in because my special skills were needed." Someone higher up the FBI's food chain had pulled strings and voilà, there he was. "And, Detective Jackson, don't worry about me falling for a pretty face. I never get distracted from my cases. I never lose sight of what matters."

Her brows lowered. "Kennedy set you up. Took you in there to find that canvas so you'd think she was the next victim. She's throwing you off, she wants—"

"Wants what? Her new PI to think she needs protection?" Didn't Amanda understand? "It doesn't matter what I think. I would do my job regardless."

She slid around him and moved closer to the mirror. The better to watch Kennedy. "She probably planted the doll at her place, too. She wants the world to see her as a victim and not as an accomplice to these crimes. When you're the victim, you get pity. Sympathy. Everything can be forgiven." She motioned vaguely in the air with her left hand. "Kennedy wants her place back in society. I mean, her party planning business is pretty much in the gutter right now, and she has to be desperate. Why else would she go to that gala last night? Kennedy Clarke is setting the stage, and she thinks we're all falling for her act."

Once more, Joshua coughed. "Or *maybe* she's just in danger."

Everyone stared at him.

He yanked at his collar. "Hear me out, okay?"

Remy crossed his arms over his chest. He wanted to be in that room with Kennedy. Two more minutes. That was all he was willing to wait. And then he'd be in there with her.

Joshua had rolled up his sleeves. "We don't know when Stacey Warren painted that piece—"

"*If* she painted it," Remy cut in. "It's possible someone just signed her initials to it. We'll get the FBI to do their magic. Get an expert to compare it to her other work, brush strokes, technique, all that shit." They wouldn't jump to any conclusions.

"Uh, yeah," Joshua pulled off his glasses and polished them on his shirt. "And if that expert says it is her work, then we need to figure out *when* Stacey painted it."

Tension snaked through Remy.

Joshua slid his glasses back into place. "Kennedy's brother could have gotten Stacey to paint that piece ages ago. Before the *first* victim was found. Because maybe, just maybe, Kennedy has been his main target all along."

When it came to profiling, Joshua was considered one of the best at the Bureau. That was why Remy had brought the man in for this case.

"But you don't go after your real target first." Joshua's voice had turned considering. "You practice first. You get better."

The FBI certainly thought the killer had been practicing. The public believed there were only two victims but…

"Uh, this is BS," Amanda snapped. "You're saying Kyle Clarke got his girlfriend to paint a picture of his sister in a blindfold with a bloody neck? Really? And she just did it? No questions asked? I don't buy it. I don't—"

"We don't know the nature of their relationship." Joshua rocked forward onto the balls of his feet. "For all we know, Kyle Clarke was the dominant in the relationship. Maybe Stacey gave in to his demands. I've seen her other work—it's all of a darker, more violent nature. This type of piece would have been right up her alley. If he'd pressed her, she would have done it for him." Joshua shrugged. "Of course, there's one person who can tell us for sure about their relationship. And she's sitting in that chair…"

Remy's gaze darted back to Kennedy. She looked up, turned her head toward the glass, and he felt the impact of her bright stare like a punch to his gut.

"She can tell us what the relationship was like between Kyle and Stacey," Joshua added. "Kennedy is the key. Victim or accomplice—she holds everything we need to know."

"Yeah, but the trick is to get the woman to actually *talk*." Amanda sounded disgusted.

Her partner grunted his approval. "You think we haven't gone at her, again and again? She acts like she's cooperating, but gives us nothing."

Maybe because they hadn't approached her the right way.

Amanda rolled back her shoulders. "I'll go in and see what the hell she will say. We've got a history together now, right? Who knows? Maybe she'll actually give me some truth this time." She whirled for the door.

"I'm coming, too," Remy announced flatly.

Amanda stiffened. Then she threw a glare over her shoulder. "Coming in as what? Her PI? An FBI agent? Or the guy who wants to screw her?"

All of the above, thanks. He kept his expression blank. "I'm coming in as the senior agent on this case. The guy who was sent down specifically to oversee the investigation. That good enough for you?"

Her eyes showed her frustration.

He smiled and told her, "So I'll be in that damn room. Thank you very much."

***

The door opened, and Kennedy's breath left her in a relieved rush when she saw Remy step inside. She knew he'd been questioned separately. Wasn't that always the MO of the cops? Question folks separately, make sure the stories matched up.

But this shouldn't be some kind of interrogation.

I'm scared. That was me. I know it was me in the painting.

Detective Jackson marched in after Remy. She pulled out her chair, sat down across from Kennedy, and looked extremely unhappy.

Yeah, join the club.

Remy pulled out the chair next to Kennedy. His leg brushed against hers as he took the seat. Then he reached for her hand. His fingers curled around hers. Squeezed. "You okay?"

She focused completely on him. He'd insisted they call the cops, and, yes, she got why. "It was me." Kennedy shook her head. "How? I *know* Stacey's work. That was her painting. How could she do something like that? And where was that painting for all of these weeks, where—"

"*If* Stacey Warren created the painting, we don't know *when* she did it." Amanda's voice was flat. "For all we know, her abductor could have made her create the, uh, work of art. He could have made her do it while she was spending all of that time in captivity. We have no idea what happened to her during that lost period of time."

Kennedy slowly moved her head so that she was staring at Amanda.

"Or maybe," Amanda continued as her gaze locked on Kennedy. "Maybe Stacey made that painting long before she was abducted. Maybe her fiancé asked her to create it for him. Tell me, just what was their relationship like?"

Kennedy licked her lips. "Kyle wouldn't…why would he want a painting like that?"

"Would you say they were partners?" Amanda pushed, not answering Kennedy's question. "Or was one of them more dominant in the relationship? I spoke with Stacey's friends, and they all agreed that she was pretty easy going. The mellow-type, if you will. But your brother, he had a reputation for being demanding. Perhaps a little controlling, perhaps—"

Kennedy leapt to her feet. "Stop it."

Amanda stared up at her. "Did I say something to upset you?"

Everything about this nightmare was upsetting. "*My* face. I know my own face. My face set to look like I'm one of the killer's victims. This isn't some game. It's my life, and I'm scared to death, and all you can do is sit there and make more accusations against my brother." She'd pulled her hand from Remy, and now she slammed both of her palms flat against the table top. "It's not him. Kyle didn't do any of this. But someone else is out there and that person is targeting *me*." This talk with the detective was going nowhere. Kennedy shoved away from the table. Disgusted, frustrated, her gaze cut to Remy. "I told you the cops were useless. Let's go."

The chair legs shrieked as he shoved his chair back.

Kennedy rushed straight for the door.

"You don't trust the cops…" Amanda's voice stopped her. "But you trust *this* man? Do you even know who he really is?"

Kennedy stiffened.

"Until recently, he worked for a crime boss." The detective just dropped her statement like a bombshell.

Kennedy didn't give her the pleasure of a reaction.

Amanda wasn't done. "Did you notice that he holds his shoulder a little stiffly? Because he was involved in a *shoot-out* a little while back. The guy isn't safe. He's not the one you want to put your trust in."

Kennedy's head turned, and she saw the fury flashing in Remy's eyes. So much rage. And that rage was directed at the detective.

But he crossed to Kennedy's side. Once more, Remy reached for Kennedy's hand. His slightly callused fingertips were careful against her skin. "I'll keep you safe," he promised Kennedy. Then his head angled toward the detective.

A sneer was on Amanda's face. Kennedy knew the detective didn't like her. Amanda had made that clear on more than one occasion. More like, *every* occasion. Amanda thought Kennedy was a monster, just as much of a murderer as she believed Kyle to be.

"I *will* see you again, detective," Remy rasped. "Count on it."

With her free hand, Kennedy yanked open the door. Remy stayed at her side as they navigated through the police station's corridors, past the bullpen and the little array of Christmas lights that illuminated the space, and then out of the front entrance. Her breath came too fast. Her heart raced in her chest, and she just wanted to get away from that place. She could feel the prying eyes on her.

They hurried down the white, stone steps in front of the station. She glanced back, her stare darting to the two large wreaths that hung on the station's main doors. For a second, she was worried that the cops would follow her. That they'd force her back inside.

Remy's fingers tightened around hers. "Easy."

She whirled toward him. "There is nothing *easy* about this." She pulled from him. Glared back at the station. "That detective doesn't want to help me. None of the cops in there want to help me. They think I'm some kind of crazy killer. Me and my brother. Doesn't matter that it seems like I'm being targeted, it doesn't make a difference to them!"

"It makes a difference to me."

His voice was calm and deep, and, in contrast, Kennedy felt as if she was screaming. Wait, maybe she was. So what? Her life was so broken and out of control that she just wanted to scream. She wanted to throw back her head and scream as loudly as she could.

"Let me take you home, Kennedy."

"Home is the last place I want to go." Night had already fallen. Because she'd been kept in that station for too long. And she didn't even know what the cops were going to do with the new "evidence" — hell, probably nothing. She turned from him and rubbed her arms. "I need a drink."

Actually, she could use more than one.

"Then let me get you one."

Her head whipped toward him. Careful now, more in control, she said, "I don't want to go where everyone knows who I am."

"Good luck, in this town…"

She stepped closer to him. Going with her gut, she entreated, "Take me to Fantasy."

He stiffened. "You sure about that?"

She wasn't sure of anything. Not even her brother's innocence, even though she'd been fighting so hard, hoping *so desperately,* that everyone was wrong about him. But there were secrets she'd kept, secrets that would have to come out, eventually.

Could she tell Remy her secrets? Maybe.

"Fantasy is Kace Quick's club." He studied her, raking his gaze over her body. "You feel like stepping onto the wild side tonight?"

"Absolutely." Her voice was brisk and cool. A total lie. Inside, she was shaking and thinking that she was in way, way over her head. But she wasn't about to hit one of the fancy bars where her *ex*-friends liked to mix and mingle.

She wanted to be a face in the crowd. She wanted darkness. She wanted anonymity. Kace's clubs always promised that. All of that — and more. *I need that more tonight.* And Remy was her pass inside. "It's exactly what I want."

He caught her hand in his. Brought her fingers up and pressed a quick kiss to her knuckles. "Then just remember, you asked for this..."

***

"Think you were a little hard on her?"

Amanda turned at the question, her eyes narrowing. It was another one of those FBI agent assholes. She was tripping over them. It had been *her* case. She'd been handling it just fine with her partner, and then the NOPD had gotten pushed to the side.

Joshua Morgan lifted his hands in an I-Surrender pose as he widened his eyes. "Hey, don't look at me like I'm the bad guy. I'm not. We're on the same side."

Bull. She stormed around him and snagged her jacket from the back of her desk chair. He followed. Unfortunately. She turned and almost plowed into him. His hands rose and curled around her shoulders, as if to steady her.

She didn't need steadying. "Get your hands off me."

His hands immediately dropped. "I…listen, detective, I think we got off on the wrong foot."

"I don't like you." She wasn't in the mood to mince words. "And I don't like your partner."

"He's not my partner. Remy is the special agent in charge, he's —"

"He's a fucking criminal, as far as I'm concerned." The bullpen was empty so she didn't bother monitoring her words. Her partner had cut out just a few moments before. "You think I didn't do my digging on the guy? He spent the last year embedded in Kace Quick's world. You want me to buy that he never crossed lines with Kace? Or with any of his other undercover cases? Baloney. Sell that shit somewhere else." She'd gotten access to Remy St. Clair's files. Sure, she'd broken rules to do it, but she'd wanted to know who the asshole was who'd taken over her case. "He plays a good chameleon, maybe he plays the role too well. An FBI agent shouldn't be getting so up close and cozy with a suspect, not when —"

"You are not fully aware of everything that is at play with this case. There are some very specific reasons why Remy was chosen for this job." His face was hard, and his voice had turned icy.

That just made her madder. They were keeping her in the dark too much. Her hands fisted. "If I'm not aware, it's because you two won't brief me on my own case!"

"Those orders come from—"

No. She was done. Enough. "Just get the hell out of my way. I'm finished for tonight." Her temples were throbbing. Fury rode her hard.

A muscle jerked in his jaw, but Joshua gave a grim nod before he stepped aside. She brushed past him.

"She could be a victim."

Amanda stilled. Her head craned toward him. "The woman has a pretty face. She sheds a few tears, looks helpless, and you buy her story?" A sigh of disgust blew from her. "Get with the program. Kennedy Clarke is lying. She's hiding her brother. She's planting evidence, and she's playing us." She took an angry step away from him.

"That's not what her body language says."

He was going to make her scream.

"She was afraid when she was sitting in the interrogation room. The painting *scared* her."

Okay. Fine. "Yeah, it scared her. Because she just realized her brother—her sick, twisted twin—might be coming after her. Bet she's regretting helping him elude the cops now. What goes around, comes around." She dug her car keys from her pocket and marched for the door.

"How can you be so cold?"

Cold? Is that what he thought she was? Now Amanda spun back to face him. "I've seen husbands kill their wives. I've seen teenage boys shoot their mothers. I've seen shit that gives me nightmares. You don't trust anyone after that. Not anymore. You learn to block the world out because you have to put up a shield in order to survive." *Cold.* Furious, her gaze raked him. "You're a Fed. *You* should know better."

She was done wasting time with him. She clocked out and got her ass out of there. Five minutes later, she was stalking through the dark parking garage and wishing she was at home, with her feet up and this bitch of a day behind her. Amanda still gripped her keys tightly. She hit the fob on the keychain when her coupe came into view, and the tail-lights flashed. The red lights shined in the darkness of the parking garage. Car horns sounded in the distance, and she rolled back her shoulders as she approached the vehicle. Her gaze darted to the backseat, an old habit she'd picked up even before she'd run her first beat as a green uniform. As a kid, she'd watched some scary movie where the killer had been hiding in the backseat. Since then, she'd *always* checked her backseat.

It was empty. It was always empty.

She climbed into her car and let out a long, slow breath once she'd secured the locks. Her shoulders slumped, and her mask fell away.

God, she hated this case. Hated seeing the images of the dead women. Hated that their killer wasn't caught. Hated that she was *failing* those vics.

She reached up and adjusted her mirror. And for just an instant, she could have sworn that she saw a dark form darting behind her vehicle. Her heart jerked in her chest. Immediately, Amanda unlocked her car and jumped outside, pulling her gun.

But no one was there…

***

"Stay close to me," Remy directed as they approached the long line of men and women who were waiting to get inside of Fantasy. He didn't bother with that line, though. Instead, he went right toward the bouncer blocking the club's entrance.

The guy inclined his head when he saw Remy and immediately waved him inside.

"I *am* close to you," Kennedy muttered back, and she was.

He'd wrapped one arm around her waist, and as they moved, he kept her body flush with his. There was no way he'd lose her in that place.

Fantasy. The club had been an actual murder scene just before Halloween. And the building had even been torched. But Kace Quick had rebuilt almost overnight, and when the club had opened again, the lines to get inside were even longer.

Kace had once said that the folks in New Orleans were obsessed with death. Remy knew the guy was right. Darkness called to people in the Big Easy. Too many answered that call.

The band was playing. Pounding out a hard, loud beat.

"Am I dressed okay?" Kennedy asked, leaning up toward him.

She was fucking fine. Looked killer in her black sweater and pants. Some women in that club wore jeans that fit like a second skin. Some wore leather coats. Some wore see-through dresses. But to him, no one looked sexier than Kennedy. And that was going to be a problem. He was supposed to be maintaining his control. He wasn't supposed to be getting lost in *her.*

"You're perfect," Remy told her simply and that was the truth. He had to play this scene carefully, though. She'd asked to come to Fantasy and refusing her would have raised a red flag. But, hell, he and Kace hadn't exactly ended things on the best note. If the guy was in the club, there was no telling what he'd do.

No, wait, Kace *wouldn't* blow Remy's cover. Because the guy owed him.

Remy steered Kennedy toward the bar. Let her order her drink, but he just shook his head when the bartender turned to get his order. He wasn't drinking that night. He wanted to stay focused and alert. Some SOB was gunning for Kennedy.

You won't get her on my watch.

"I want to see the show." Kennedy downed her drink quickly. Too quickly. "When does the show start?"

Fantasy was Kace's latest brainchild. On the weekends, he had cirque-style performers come out and perform for the crowd. The place ignited, and everyone was swept right up in a new world. A sensual, seductive world.

Sometimes, it was too easy to fall for the fantasy.

"It starts at midnight. We're way too early for it now." He turned his head. Saw other men eyeing Kennedy. Did they recognize her? Some had to. Sure, she might believe she could blend into a crowd at a place like Fantasy, but he didn't think she'd blend anywhere.

The woman stuck out, she shined too freaking bright.

He tugged on her hand. "Come on."

"But I need—"

He jerked his head toward the club's second level. "We're going to the VIP area." He wanted her out of the crush. In the more secure VIP space, he could control who got close to her. Already, too many bodies were pushing in on them, and when one dumb SOB with too carefully styled brown hair brushed his body against hers and tried to pull her toward him—

"*Get the fuck back,*" Remy ordered him, voice lethal.

The guy blinked a few times. "Wait? What? I was just gonna dance—"

Remy pushed Kennedy behind him. "Her dance card is full. And you grab another woman without her permission in this place, and you're going to find yourself with a broken hand." The guy must be new to Fantasy. "Learn the house rules, buddy, before you land yourself in the ER." He motioned with one hand, and the bouncers watching—guys he recognized from his time at Fantasy—closed in. "Take care of this one," Remy snapped. "Make sure he *fully* understands the rules."

He turned back to Kennedy. She stared up at him with her wide, bright eyes. She stared at him like…

Shit, she's starting to trust me. Because she was looking at him like he'd just saved the day. No, saved *her*. And he hadn't. He wasn't there to save her. He was there to destroy her world.

"Just a dumbass," he muttered. "Forget him." His fingers threaded with hers. They'd get to the VIP area. She wouldn't have to worry about people watching her. She could drink, relax, and maybe, *maybe* she'd reveal her secrets to him.

They were almost to the stairs that would take them to the VIP level when Kennedy stopped. She tugged her hand free of his. "Will you dance with me?"

The music was a bit softer. Not romantic, not by any means. This wasn't that kind of club. But the couples on the massive dance floor now had their bodies pressed together as the music beat in a slower rhythm. Their arms were looped together. Their bodies twined tight.

"Just for a few moments," she added, voice husky. "Please?"

Remy found himself walking onto the dance floor. He'd *never* danced there. He pulled her close, locked his arms around her waist even as she put her arms around his neck. Her head pressed to his shoulder, and her sweet scent filled his nose. She surrounded him. So soft and sexy. And —

Over her shoulder, he caught sight of the silks that dangled from the ceiling. Part of the show. An aerial performer would use those silks later in the night for her act, but…right then, he had a memory of another time. Another woman. His body stiffened as he stared at the silks, and he remembered the one he hadn't been able to save.

Another killer, another night. Violence that just wouldn't stop. Monsters who hid in plain sight. Monsters he'd sworn to stop.

"What is it?" Her head lifted from his shoulder. "Remy, what's wrong?"

Everything. He forced his jaw to unclench, and he realized that he was holding her too tightly. "I can't save you, if you're not straight with me." His voice was a growl because the anger inside of him was real. "I don't want you winding up dead on my watch because you were keeping secrets."

He heard the catch of her breath. Her long lashes flickered.

"That was you in the painting, Kennedy. And right now, you're running scared. Running to the dark side of town because you don't want to face the man who's after you."

She stared up at him. "You're right. I am afraid."

"I'm going to take care of you." He would *not* let her get hurt. "But you have to be straight with me. You have to tell me everything, you have to—"

"*Remy St. Clair.*" The rough, deep rumble came from behind him. A familiar rumble. A rumble that he knew belonged to Kace Quick.

Remy stiffened. He kept his eyes on Kennedy's face.

"Remy, you damn liar." Kace drew closer to him. "What in the hell are you doing in *my* club?"

CHAPTER SEVEN

Amanda kept one arm around the bag of groceries she'd picked up, and she kicked her apartment door closed. She spun around, flipped her lock, then she made her way to the alarm panel that waited near the door. Reaching up with her free hand, she pressed in the code so the incessant beeping would stop.

Silence. Blessed silence.

Exhaling heavily, she squeezed her eyes shut. Home. Finally. She was going to toss a pizza into the oven and forget the whole day. She was going to —

She heard the squeak of her wooden floor.

The sound made a little shiver go over her. Amanda couldn't help but tense. After all, she was a cop. And she knew every single bad thing that could happen to a person — mostly because she'd seen all of that terrible shit firsthand. But her apartment was on the second floor of a historical building, one first erected back in the 1800s. The place groaned and squeaked and heaved all of the time. Settling, or at least, that was what the rental agent had told her when she first checked into the place.

She should have grown used to all of the sounds by now.

She hadn't. And maybe that was why her whole body was stiff when she peeked around the foyer wall and looked into her den.

Darkness waited in there. With a quick jerk of her hand, she flipped on the lights.

Nothing.

These cases—they were getting to her. When you saw too much darkness for too long…you started jumping at shadows. Shaking her head, Amanda headed for the kitchen.

The floor groaned beneath her feet.

***

Remy kept his face expressionless as he spun to confront Kace. "You sonofabitch…" He narrowed his eyes in warning on the man that was both friend and sometimes enemy. "It's been too long."

Kace Quick. Ex-crime boss. Current billionaire. All-around pain in the ass. The guy flashed a broad grin at Remy. "Some would say not nearly long enough."

Yeah, he had a feeling Kace might feel that way about him.

But then Kace stepped forward and locked Remy in a hug. "Slumming, are you?"

Fantasy hardly counted as anyone's slum.

But Kace's murmur had been just for Remy's ears. The guy had already pulled back, and he'd turned his assessing stare on Kennedy.

"Well, well…" Kace's blue gaze swept over her. "What do we have here?" Two guards stood just behind Kace, clad in suits and with their gazes carefully sweeping the crowd. They'd already made sure that everyone else was several feet away from Kace.

Kace didn't let anyone get too close. One of the reasons why it had been impossible to bust the guy.

"We have a who, not a what," Kennedy replied. She offered her hand to Kace. "I'm Kennedy."

His fingers closed around hers, and a pleased smile curled his lips. "Thought I recognized you."

She slanted a worried glance back at Remy.

So much for not being recognized. He could have told her that earlier, but, well, she'd wanted to run.

And he'd let her.

Kace hadn't released her hand yet. And he was still smiling. Two very bad signs. "How about we take this upstairs?" Kace invited, all charming and affable host. "Because I would love to learn more about you, my dear."

Shit.

Kace tugged Kennedy forward. The guards closed in behind them, and Remy was left to pull up the rear. He heard Kace say, "Are you enjoying my club? Oh, my apologies, in case you didn't know, I'm Kace Quick..."

Of course, she knew. Kennedy knew she was holding hands with the man who'd once been the most wanted criminal in the Big Easy.

And she was as cool as could be.

Moments later, they were upstairs, cosseted away in the second-floor VIP area. The tinted windows allowed those in the VIP lounge to view the show downstairs — to view the crowd, the band, to view everything behind a shield of privacy.

Kace hadn't brought in his guards. A sign he didn't want them to hear this little chat. But the guy *had* finally let go of Kennedy.

Remy moved quickly to stand by her side.

Kace smirked, his gaze laughing. "Found someone new to play with, did you, Remy?"

"I'm not playing," he fired back. But, obviously, Kace was.

The guy could be such a dick.

He won't blow my cover. However, Kace would certainly enjoy torturing him a bit.

"I hired Remy," Kennedy confessed quickly.

One dark brow rose as Kace seemed to consider her words. "Did you? Interesting."

She nodded. "I need him to help me find my brother."

Kace strolled toward the bar that was positioned on the other side of the room. A very well-stocked bar. Normally, a personal bartender would be in the lounge, eager to help whatever VIP was holding court. Since no one else was there, Remy knew Kace must have given orders for the space to be cleared out.

The better for their private chat.

"Your brother." Kace stared into a glass of whiskey. "That wouldn't be the man who is suspected of those murders, now, would it?"

The guy knew it damn well was.

"He's innocent," Kennedy announced, squaring her shoulders.

Kace put the glass down, not drinking the whiskey. He turned back to face Kennedy and gave a sad shake of his head. "You can't choose family. That's a real bitch, isn't it? Since we can't choose them, then we're forced to pretend they aren't monsters."

Her cheeks flushed. "My brother *isn't*—"

Kace cocked his head to the side as he studied her. "You're afraid."

Remy stayed at her side. "She doesn't need to be. I'll keep her safe."

But Kace—the bastard—just laughed. "If you're at her side, maybe she should be *more* afraid."

Remy's jaw locked, and his hands clenched.

"After all, you could bring all sorts of…" Kace's lips quirked with a smile that never reached his eyes. "Trouble, to her door."

Kennedy's fingers curled around Remy's fisted left hand. "Remy is keeping me safe."

"Is that what he's doing?" Kace's smile stretched. "Ah, now I see."

Seriously, Remy might have to punch the guy, just for old time's sake.

But Kace's mocking smile faded as he seemed to really study Kennedy. "Remy is very good at his job."

Sonofabitch. Don't play games with —

"Don't ever forget that," Kace warned her.

Her head turned toward Remy as she frowned.

"You and your brother have the same eyes," Kace announced. "Very distinct. One look, and I knew who you were."

Just that fast, her head whipped back toward Kace. She let go of Remy's hand and took a step toward the other man. "You know my brother?"

Know, not knew. Because she hoped he was still alive? Or she *knew* with certainty that he was?

Kace flashed his smug grin. "You aren't the only Clarke to enjoy a walk on the wild side." He motioned vaguely in the air. "Your dear brother enjoyed spending time in this very room. He visited right after our big grand opening. Of course, that wasn't the only time he came to one of my clubs. I've seen him more than my fair share of nights over the years."

This was news to Remy — and he'd *worked* with the guy.

"Have you…have you heard from my brother since his disappearance?" Kennedy asked, her voice breathless with hope.

Kace studied her, sweeping his gaze from her head to her feet and then back up again. "I think he'd be more apt to contact you than me. Twins, I believe? I've heard there's nothing stronger than that bond."

"I *haven't* heard from him, and I'm scared. I need to find him. I need — "

Kace stalked toward her. "You're scared." He seemed to consider that. "Scared of what you'll find out about him?"

She cast a desperate glance over her shoulder at Remy. She looked scared and uncertain, and she was turning to him for help.

That was what he wanted, right? So, even though his gut was clenching, Remy let this scene play out.

"Or are you scared that your dear brother will *hurt* you?" Kace pressed her. "Is that why you've hired the man who guarded me for so long? Because you worry the brother you love is the maniac you should fear?"

Her hair flew over her shoulder as she focused once more on Kace. "You didn't answer my question. Have you heard from Kyle?"

A beat of silence passed. Finally, Kace responded, "No. I thought he was dead."

She flinched.

"But if I should hear from the guy's ghost, I'll be sure to give you a call...or rather, I'll call the *PI* you've hired." His stare drifted to Remy. "How about a private word, old friend? Outside?"

It wasn't a request. It was an order. The guy had always been good at orders.

Remy slipped toward Kennedy. His head leaned toward her, and he rasped, "Stay here. I'll be right back." His breath blew lightly against her ear, and she shivered.

He knew Kace would catch the small movement. The guy caught everything.

That was how he knew I was a Fed. I thought he didn't suspect me, but the guy knew the truth all along.

Remy followed Kace out of the VIP lounge. But they didn't head downstairs. Instead, Remy inclined his head, and one of his guards moved to block the door they'd just exited.

"Vaughn will make sure your new, ah, client remains safe." Kace motioned vaguely with his hand. Then he turned to the right, moved down a small corridor, and entered another private room.

Remy glanced back, making sure no one was following them, and then he stepped into the sound-proof room with Kace.

"What in the hell…" Kace began, his voice a growling demand, "are you doing?"

***

Amanda pressed the button on the bottom of her e-reader, turning it off for the night. She slid beneath the covers, adjusted her pillows, and for a moment, she simply stared at the ceiling.

There was no husband, no boyfriend, no lover in her life. She'd had a fiancé, they'd been together for almost a year before she'd broken it off. She just…

She'd stopped trusting him.

Not because of anything he'd done. Dewayne had been great. Or at least, he'd seemed great.

But how many men had *seemed* great? How many men had she learned were liars and abusers? Killers? She'd needed space. Needed to think. She'd told Dewayne she wasn't ready. And he—

He hadn't waited for her to *be* ready any longer. He'd said he'd waited long enough.

Her lashes closed. She could have sworn that she felt wetness on her cheeks. This case. This damn case…

An image of Stacey Warren flashed through her mind. Stacey had been engaged. And Amanda would bet — she'd stake her life — on the fact that Stacey had trusted the wrong man, too. She'd made a fatal mistake.

It was better — so much better — not to let anyone get too close.

Danger was everywhere.

The floor squeaked in the other room as the apartment settled around her.

***

"I'm doing my job," Remy defended as anger churned through him.

Kace laughed. "Is that what you're doing with the sexy Kennedy Clarke? Because I saw you on the dance floor, my friend. I saw how you held her. I saw how you danced so close to her. I saw how you *looked* at her." A pause. "And I saw the rage when the other jackass dared to touch her."

Kace had probably been watching them from the minute they stepped into Fantasy. Figured.

"Why did you bring her here?" Kace wanted to know. As if he felt real curiosity and wasn't just jerking Remy around.

"Because she asked to come here. She wanted to escape — "

"So, you brought her to my darkness? Not worried I'd let the truth slip about you?"

Remy deliberately rolled his shoulder. The injury had healed, but the roll was a reminder for Kace. "I figured our debts weren't quite settled yet."

Kace's eyes went flat and cold. "No, not yet." He rubbed the bridge of his nose. "So how about I start to settle things?"

"Fine by me."

"You didn't realize her brother came here."

"No."

"Not surprising. During your time here, I made sure you didn't see some of my more…important customers."

"Kyle Clarke was important?" Now real surprise was flaring inside him.

"Very important. You see, Kyle Clarke was a silent partner in my business."

Well, damn.

"Like I said, he liked to walk in the darkness."

What the hell? The FBI should have uncovered—

"He was a dangerous man." Now Kace was staring at him, his gaze hard and direct, all traces of humor long gone. "A man with plenty of secrets. He was a fighter, did you know that? A boxer."

And Kace enjoyed his sparring, too. Just how close had the two men been?

"Kyle was cold. Calculating. In fact, I'd say he really only cared about one thing in this world. The one thing that he told me — on the very first day we met — would always be off limits to me."

Remy waited. Though he suspected —

"His sister. The man seemed to have no emotion for anyone else. But he told me once that if I ever touched Kennedy, he'd kill me."

Someone had threatened Kace Quick? And lived to tell the tale?

Kace paced closer to him. "In Kyle's mind, no one would ever be good enough for his sister. She was the perfect princess, and it was his job to keep her safe from the rest of the world." A sigh escaped him. "I can't help but note, you were touching her *plenty* on my dance floor. And I do wonder, just what would her dear brother think of that?"

"I don't give a shit what he thinks. The man is a suspected serial killer, he's — "

"One drunken night, he made a confession to me that I never forgot."

"What?" Remy wanted Kace to just spit that shit out, he wanted —

"He told me that he would destroy anyone who ever hurt his sister. He said...Kyle said she was the only good thing in his world. And without her, he was sure the darkness would swallow him whole." A laugh, one that held no humor. "Guess that darkness finally swallowed him, huh?"

What. The. Fuck.

"But that's the thing…he was always trying to keep her safe, always keeping her *out* of the danger in his world, and yet, here she is." A furrow appeared between Kace's brows as he seemed to mull something over. "Kennedy asked *you* to bring her to me?"

Yeah, and now it seemed suspicious as hell. "To your club, not to you."

The furrow deepened. "Perhaps she knows a whole lot more about her brother's darkness than I realized. Twins share everything, don't they? Your lady might have the same wild and dangerous needs burning inside of her."

"She's not *my* lady."

"No?" And with a blink, Kace was back to appearing all innocent. Total BS. He'd never been an innocent. "My mistake. Guess I got the wrong idea when she was plastered to you downstairs." He sauntered around Remy and headed for the door.

But Remy wasn't done. "Do you know more?"

Kace laughed without looking back.

Seriously, the SOB needed to —

"I don't have more to offer you about Kyle Clarke. I really haven't seen him, and if I did run across him, well, haven't you heard? I'm a law-abiding citizen, engaged to an FBI agent. If some wanted criminal comes to my door, I'll be telling my lovely fiancée all about him. Bree would be the first to get the call." He glanced back over his shoulder, and there was no humor in his expression. "Because I would never risk my Bree. I only knew what Kyle wanted me to know. The man was good at his lies. If he comes around me, you can rest assured I'll never let him be a threat to me or anyone who belongs to me."

And Bree very much belonged to Kace. She'd entered the club determined to take down Kace. She'd left the club owning the guy's heart and what was left of his soul.

"Good talk," Kace muttered. "Now you can see your ass out of my place."

Just like that, Kace was gone. Remy exhaled slowly, squared his shoulders, and then headed back for Kennedy. He glanced over the balcony and saw the packed crowd below. The music was louder. The drinks flowing as the night wore on.

The guard was still stationed in front of the VIP lounge. When he saw Remy, the fellow stepped to the side. Remy opened the door. Kennedy stood at the bar. A quick glance showed him that she'd poured herself a drink, and she held the half-full glass in her hand.

Kennedy peered over her shoulder at him, then looked back at the drink. "I lied."

Baby, tell me something I don't know.

"I suspected that my brother knew Kace Quick. That was the whole reason I wanted to come here tonight. Not because I thought I wouldn't get recognized. Screw that." She slammed down the drink. "People know me wherever I go in this town. That's my curse now. But I was afraid Kace wouldn't talk to me, not unless I came in with you."

She'd used him.

Why did that piss him off?

He was using her.

He crossed the room. Closed his hand around her shoulder and spun her toward him.

Her eyes were so bright and clear, and, God, that gaze of hers seemed to burn right through him. "I heard him talking once," Kennedy confessed. "Kyle thought I didn't hear him. He was talking about Kace and the clubs, and…I noticed money went missing. A *lot* of it. I thought he was on drugs. What else could it be? I confronted him. I wanted to get Kyle *help* – "

You can't help some people.

"But it wasn't drugs. Kyle swore it wasn't. He said he was just a private partner with Kace. Kyle made it clear he wanted me to stay out of this part of his life. He swore it wasn't dangerous. Swore he had everything under control." She bit her lower lip. "Then the money was repaid a year later. I thought everything was done. I thought our world was normal again and then…"

Then her world had exploded.

"Kace doesn't know where he is," Remy told her flatly. A hot anger coiled in his gut. She'd played him, fucking *played* him, and he hadn't even realized it. What in the hell? Was he losing his edge? His hand tightened on her shoulder. "You don't lie to me."

Her chin notched up. Her gaze shot fire at him. "It wasn't a lie."

"Bullshit. You withheld information. You led me to believe—"

"I needed to talk with Kace Quick. You were my in."

Sonofabitch. "You used me."

"What do you want me to say? That I'm sorry? I'm not." Kennedy shook her head and didn't look a bit sorry. She simply looked gorgeous. "My life is on the line here. My brother's life is. I will do anything to protect him. Don't you get that? Haven't you ever had to lie or—"

"I know all about lies." He forced his jaw to unclench. He was spilling lies every time he spoke with her. "But you can't lie to me. If I'm going to help you, you have to be truthful. I need to know all of your secrets."

She laughed. A bitter sound. "I know nothing about you. I'm supposed to bare my soul to you? I'm supposed—"

He let her go. "We're done." It was a gamble, but he had to roll the dice. Remy turned his back on her. "I'll take you home. You can find another PI."

"Remy?" Shock had her voice rising.

"I don't work for clients who feed me only half of the story. You think I'm some thug who will cover your criminal brother's lies? Cover *your* lies?" He marched for the door. "You don't know me."

"Wait!" Her steps rushed behind him, and Kennedy grabbed his arm. He let her spin him around. "I need you."

"Yeah, sweetheart, you sure as hell do. Because *someone* is after you. Your face was in the painting. You were dead. But you don't seem to get that you're in danger. You're running around town, looking for your brother, when he could be the one after you. You need me," he said again. "I'm the one who can keep you safe. I'm the one who can guide you through this nightmare, but not if you lie to me. Not if you hold back. It's all or nothing. It's everything…or I walk."

Her gaze searched his.

Would she call his bluff? Tell him to get the hell out? Or—

She rose onto her toes. Her mouth pressed to his.

His whole body stiffened. "No, baby, no." And it took all of his control, but he pushed her back. "You're not seducing me in order to get my help."

Her cheeks flamed dark red. "That's not what I—"

"No?"

"Dammit, *no!*"

"Then why the kiss? Why now? Why—"

"I don't know, all right? I just—" She blew out a hard breath. "I'm not trying to seduce you into helping me. I'm sorry I misled you. I don't know what I'm doing. I'm trying to hold my self-control together while I'm freaking out. I'm desperate, and I'm scared, and I've never trusted anyone completely—no one but Kyle."

"Kyle isn't here any longer," he gritted. *And, Kennedy, you're trusting the wrong man.*

"I need you." Her stare held his. "And I want you. I wanted you from the first night that we met. And the kiss—it was just about us. Not about me trying to trick you or use you or..." She shook her head. A few tendrils of dark hair had escaped from her twist, and they slid against her cheeks. "I'll tell you everything. And I won't kiss you again. I get it—hands off. You're not interested in me that way. My mistake. Blame it on the drinks or the adrenaline or my really shitty day. We'll go back to just being business partners. Nothing more."

"The fuck we will." He hadn't meant to say that out loud. Had he?

She blinked. "Uh, Remy?"

"You tell me everything. I'll keep you safe. That's my job." More than she realized. "But as far as me not being interested…" Now he moved forward and caught her in his arms. He carefully positioned her, caging Kennedy between his body and the door. His palms flattened on the wood behind her. "I am very, very interested. I've wanted you from the beginning. And the desire I feel has *nothing* to do with the job."

Her breath came quickly. Her scent surrounded him. Her lips were red and parted, and he wanted her mouth.

So he took it.

Her kiss had been soft and tentative. His wasn't. His was deep and rough and wild. He took and he claimed, and he wanted everything that the woman had to give him. Maybe this was a line that shouldn't be crossed. Maybe he should keep his hands and mouth off her. But…

She'd said she wanted him.

He'd been burning up with desire for her.

And Remy let that desire loose. He tasted and he savored, and her hands rose to curl around his shoulders. Her nails bit into his skin as she moaned into his mouth. If she'd been another woman, hell, he might have taken her right there. In the club, with the music pounding downstairs. He could have her naked in seconds. He could take her up against the door. Or on the couch, or —

Not here.

Because she wasn't just another woman. She was Kennedy. This was a case. And, shit, he wasn't going to fuck her for the first time in Kace's club.

His dick shoved hard in his pants. He wanted inside of her. Wanted to make her moan and come. And he *would*. Just not there.

Not then.

With an effort — a freaking super human effort — he lifted his head. His hands were still on the door. Like the rest of the room, the wooden door had been painted black. Her lashes lifted and Kennedy stared at him.

"We're going to be together," he promised her. "It will have nothing to do with the case." She had to understand that. When this mess was over, he didn't want her ever thinking that —

That what? That I'm a damn liar? A bastard? He was.

"I agree. It has nothing to do with the case," she whispered back. "Nothing."

He wanted to kiss her again. "Let's go home, Kennedy."

But she shook her head once more. "I don't want to go to my place tonight. Please. Can we go to *your* home?"

There was fear in her eyes. Remy didn't like that. He didn't want her afraid, not of anything or anyone. His protective response to her flared without warning. "Of course," he told her. "My place."

He felt the relief slide through her.

***

Amanda's eyes flew open. Something had woken her up, and she didn't know what it was. A bad dream? An alarm? An—

A hand flew over her mouth.

Adrenaline poured through her system, and she surged up, ready to fight whoever the hell was on top of her.

Electricity hit her, volt after volt plunging through her body. She knew what was happening. She'd been tased before. Every cop *had* to be tased, it was part of training, but the volts flew through her body, making her twitch and shudder, rendering her helpless as the bastard above her grabbed her hands. When the shudders stopped, he flipped her over, shoved her face down into her pillow, and cuffed her hands behind her back.

The handcuffs were cold and hard, and her pillow shoved into her mouth. Amanda gathered her strength as she reared back to —

The bastard hit her with the electricity again. Every nerve in her body shuddered in agony. The metal handcuffs bit her wrists.

What was he going to do? He was trying to make her helpless. Was he going to rape her? Kill her?

He yanked her onto her back once more. She felt something sticky press to her lips. *Tape.* Duct tape?

"No screams, sweetheart."

She didn't have the strength to scream right then. And there was a damn chunk of tape over her mouth. If she could have just gotten her gun from the nightstand…

I would've had a chance.

"Don't worry." His fingers slid over her cheek. "You can scream later." His voice was a gruff whisper of sound. "I like the screams. Before I'm done with you, you'll scream and scream for hours. But no one will be there to help you."

Her room was covered in darkness. She couldn't make out his features. Just felt the hot stir of his breath against her cheek. And —

He slipped something over her head. Over her eyes. Her lashes fluttered behind the fabric when he secured it behind her head. *A blindfold.* Oh, dear God, a blindfold!

The Broken Doll Killer. No, no. She gave a desperate scream, but the sound came out as a weak whimper, smothered behind the tape.

He lifted her into his arms. Slung her over his shoulder. He was big, strong.

Kyle Clarke was big and muscled. From his file, she'd read that he was six-foot-two, two hundred pounds. The bastard—he'd come into her house. He'd *gotten* her.

She had to get away. She twisted and heaved and—

"I have your gun. Move again, and I'll use it on you."

If she left that apartment, she was a dead woman. Amanda knew it with certainty. He'd torture her, and he'd kill her, slowly. She had to fight. While she still could. Her muscles were weak, still trembling and jerking from the taser. But she fought to twist herself against him, fought to get out of his arms—

She hit the floor. She didn't know if it was because she'd jostled herself loose or if it was because he'd dropped her. She had a chance now, she had—

Something hit her in the head. Rough and hard and there wasn't even a whisper of sound. Her body slumped as pain swamped her. She was going to pass out. Amanda knew it, and there was nothing she could do to save herself.

When she woke up, she'd be in hell.

CHAPTER EIGHT

She was cold. Kennedy wrapped her arms around her stomach as she headed into Remy's den. He'd taken her to an older house in the Quarter, one hidden behind a high gate and nestled in the darkness. The ceilings were high, swooping over her, and a large, stately fireplace waited in the corner. He knelt in front of the fireplace, and as she stood there, flames lit his face.

"Bought the place about two months ago," he explained as he rose, brushing off his hands. "Gonna remodel it. Or at least, that's the plan. The second floor is pretty much a disaster area right now, so it's better if you just stay down here for the night." He angled toward her. "The bedroom is down the hallway. I'm sure I have a t-shirt you can use, if you want to switch into something else."

Her gaze slid around the cavernous den. A couch, two chairs. No pictures. No paintings. Nothing personal at all. "You don't have a Christmas tree."

He looked around, as if surprised. "Ah, yeah…" He rubbed his hand along the stubble that covered his jaw. "Didn't seem much point in getting one, not when it was just me."

Just me.

She hadn't put up a tree at her place, either. It had seemed so wrong with everything that was happening. When her brother could be dead at the bottom of the Mississippi. She crept closer to him. "Has it…um, has it always just been you?" She knew nothing about his family. "Do you have any siblings, any—"

"No brothers. No sisters. And my parents died a long time ago."

Her heart squeezed in her chest. "I'm sorry."

"Like I said, it was a long time ago. My parents were killed in a robbery when I was seventeen."

A robbery?

"A guy broke into the house. My dad tried to stop him. My dad—he was shot. So was my mother." His hand fell to his side. "I was spending the night at a friend's. Didn't even know they were gone, not until I got dropped off the next morning. I walked in, and they were dead."

She stopped creeping and just rushed to him. "I'm so sorry!"

He swallowed.

Kennedy wanted to hug him. She forced her hands to stay at her sides. "Did the cops catch the person who killed them?"

"Yeah. They did." His lips twisted into a humorless smile. "A kid who was seventeen, just like me. Only he was strung out on drugs. He didn't even remember shooting them, but he had their blood on him when the cops arrested the guy. Their blood, my mom's jewelry. And he still even had the gun he'd used on them."

She *had* to touch him. Kennedy wrapped her arms around him. Remy stiffened in her embrace. "I'm trying to make you feel better," she muttered, holding him tighter. "I hate you lost them." She ached for him. For the boy who'd come home and found his whole world just gone.

"My grandfather raised me. Took care of me through high school and college. He had a heart attack a year after I graduated."

Maybe they were more alike than she'd realized. Kennedy pulled back and stared up at him. "Your life hasn't been easy."

"We're not promised easy lives. We have to fight for what we want."

Yes.

She was still touching him. Instead of hugging him, her hands had flattened on his chest. Behind him, the fire crackled, sending shadows dancing across the room. Not a gas fire place. He'd put the logs in the fire and started the blaze himself. The scent teased her nose.

"Your parents died when you were young, too," he murmured.

Kennedy flinched. "It was a fire. Kyle and I were fifteen. Our parents — their boat caught on fire, and they were trapped inside."

His hand lifted and curled around her jaw.

"Kyle was on the boat with them," she added, voice soft as the fire crackled. "I, um, I was sick so I stayed home. He had to jump in the water, and he was out there, all alone. When he came back, he didn't talk to me for days."

"And your grandfather raised you, didn't he?"

"You've been researching my family, huh?" If he knew everything, why ask? And when had he started digging into her life?

"I'm looking for your brother. I wouldn't be a good PI if I hadn't started probing." His lips curled down. "I knew you'd be coming to my office, so before your one p.m. appearance, I looked deeper into your life."

Not like some of the grizzly details were hard to find.

"But," he added gruffly, "reading the cold facts are different from hearing you tell me what happened."

His hand was warm against her, pushing away the chill she'd felt. She swallowed. "Yes, I was also raised by my grandfather. Guess we have that in common." Kennedy tried a weak smile. "Wonder what else we have in common?"

When she'd smiled, his gaze had fallen to her mouth. She saw his stare linger. Heat.

Remy shook his head. His hand slid from her and he moved away, taking a few steps that put him close to the couch. "What was it like, for your brother, after your parents died?"

"He was sad. We both were. But we had each other." She'd always had Kyle. In the worst of times, he'd been there for her. "He always tried to protect me."

Remy's head cocked. "What did he protect you from?"

Now that he wasn't touching her, a chill skated down her spine once more. *Don't tell him. Keep those secrets.*

But wasn't she supposed to reveal everything? She moved closer to the fire, extending her hands toward the blaze. "I'm a liar." It was easier to say those words when she wasn't looking at him. God, why could she never stop pretending? Maybe because she'd been doing it for so long. Maybe because it had been drilled into her.

She couldn't do it any longer. She didn't want to do it.

Her grandfather had always told her to keep the secrets. To go along with the stories. To keep the fake smile pasted on her face because the world would love nothing more than to tear down the Clarke family.

Her grandfather had seemed to miss the big picture. The outside world didn't need to tear them apart. They did a good enough job of destruction without anyone else's help.

She stared into the flames, watching them twist and turn.

Remy had said he'd only help her if she gave him the truth. At this point, what did she have to lose? Everything was already gone, and maybe if she'd spoken up sooner, things could have been different. "I wasn't sick."

She heard him take a step toward her. Kennedy didn't look back at him, it was easier to just stare into the flames.

"My ribs were broken." Her hands were shaking. "I stayed home because I was hurt."

"How the fuck did your ribs get broken?"
Perfect families are perfect lies.

The fire danced. "I was pushed down the stairs."

"What?" His hand closed around her shoulder.

She flinched. "If you keep touching me right now, I'm not sure I'll be able to tell you everything."

His hand tightened, but then he let her go.

"It's hard." A stark confession broke from her. "Because it still hurts." The memories always would.

"Who pushed you down the stairs?"

"Kyle and my father were fighting. I tried to stop them. I stepped between them. It was an accident." She hadn't wanted her father's fist to hit Kyle.

But Kyle had shoved her back, and she'd slipped on the rug at the top of the stairs. *Down, down, falling too fast.*

"Who. Pushed. You?"

"It was an accident." The fall had been an accident. "Kyle was trying to get me out of the way so that I wouldn't be hurt." The flames flared higher. "My father never hurt me, you see. He saved that for Kyle." She could see him in the flames. "But I was tired of my brother being hurt."

"I want you to look at me."

She didn't want to look at him.

"Baby, please."

"Why do you call me baby? Your voice goes soft when you do it, and it makes me think you care." She shook her head. Stiffened her spine. "We might become lovers, but it's too soon to care. It's too soon for pretty lies. Actually, I find I'm quite tired of all the lies."

"Look at me, Kennedy."

By staring into the fire, wasn't she just hiding? "It's easier to tell the story, if I don't look at you."

"And it's easier for me to see the truth if you do."

She *was* telling the truth. Slowly, Kennedy turned toward him. He stared at her, and his gaze was so deep and dark.

"Tell me," he urged her.

Her heart slammed into her chest, and when she spoke, the flat calmness of her voice surprised her. "There was a lot of rage in my house."

A muscle flexed in his jaw.

"Always on the inside, always away from prying eyes. Not for the world to see." She swallowed. "My mother was going to leave my father. Finally. It didn't matter how much money he had. Didn't matter that he told her he'd take everything from her. She was going to leave." She'd heard that fight, that last terrible fight.

No more! You won't do this to my children or me anymore!

A tear slid down her cheek. "I don't know why she went out on the boat with him, but I know the fire wasn't an accident. I heard my grandfather talking. I know he made the original arson investigation report vanish. My father…I think he started the fire. It *was* set deliberately. They were locked inside their cabin. My mother and my father. My brother escaped through a hatch because he was small back then, small enough to slide out. But he couldn't get my mother out. He couldn't get help on the radio. And all he could do as the fire raged was to jump off the boat. To tread water until help arrived. He had to watch while my father killed my mother because he didn't want her to leave him. Because he couldn't stand the idea of anyone breaking his control."

"Fuck, Kennedy, you've kept this secret your whole life?" Remy's hand lifted, and his knuckles carefully pressed to her cheek, catching the tear that had fallen.

"My grandfather didn't want the family name ruined." Like it mattered. Why did appearances matter? Her grandfather was long gone now. Dead in the ground. No longer keeping up the lie that the Clarke family was so perfect.

No, she'd been the one still doing that. Some habits were hard to break.

"You're sure that your father set the fire?"

"That's what Kyle told me."

Remy's lips thinned.

"My father valued control over everything else. He wanted to control his wife. He wanted to control his son. He wanted total power, and he would *not* let anyone leave him."

A furrow appeared between Remy's dark brows. "You said he hit your brother. Did he hit you, too, Kennedy?"

"No." She swallowed. "He always said…said that Kyle was broken. Twisted. And he had to fix him. Had to make him stronger." But her brother hadn't been broken. "Kyle was always small when we were younger. Quiet. My father didn't want that. He wanted a son who was strong and tough. He wanted to make Kyle into a fighter. He wanted Kyle…" Her words trailed away.

To be just like him.

And her darkest fear…the terror that clawed her apart at night was the worry that perhaps Kyle had become like him.

The fire crackled behind her.

"What happened to Kyle after your parents were buried?"

"If you look into his past, you'll find a trail that says he went to boarding school in Europe. That he was sent there for a year." Another story. Another lie. Sometimes, she felt as if the lies were drowning her.

"Where did he really go?" Remy asked quietly.

"He went to Europe." A pause. "To a psychiatric facility. Kyle had nightmares, you see. He'd wake up, screaming." But more than that, God, did she dare tell him?

Another tear slid down her cheek.

"Tell me everything. I can't help you if I don't know—"

"I woke up one night, and Kyle was at the foot of my bed. He had a knife in his hand."

She saw it—the way Remy's eyes changed. They didn't blaze with fury. They went cold. Flat. Hard. "No!" Kennedy surged forward, and she grabbed tight to his hands. "He wasn't going to hurt me!"

"He had a *knife*—"

"Kyle was there to protect me. He said the monsters were going to come back, and he had to be there to stop them."

But Remy's eyes didn't change.

"Kyle wasn't there to kill me." Her breath iced her lungs. "He was there...I think he would have killed anyone who came after me." Anyone who'd gotten too close to her. "Our grandfather said Kyle attached too much to me. That he got fixated. That he needed help. So he sent Kyle away. I begged him not to do it." She'd needed her brother. He'd been the other part of herself. "But one day, I woke up, and Kyle was gone." A year would pass before she'd see him again. "When he finally came back, there were no more nightmares. He never came into my room again like that. We didn't talk about our parents. We didn't talk about the past at all. We...we started living the lie that our grandfather had created." Living it until she'd almost believed it.

Perfect lies, perfect families.

The fire was warm at her back.

Remy's gaze was still too cold.

"Please, Remy, say something."

He leaned toward her. He reached for her —

And Remy pulled her against him, holding her tight in a hug that chased all of the cold from her body. "I'm sorry you went through that hell."

Her eyes squeezed shut, the better to stop the tears from falling.

"I'm sorry you were alone. I'm sorry you had so much pain."

Her arms curled around him. She held him in a desperate grip. He was warm and strong and so very solid. Not a dream. Not some desperate hope. She'd just shared her darkest secrets with Remy, and he hadn't turned away in disgust. He'd taken her into his arms. He made her feel safe. Protected.

This time, she wasn't alone. This time, she had him.

His lips pressed to her temple. "I will keep you safe, Kennedy."

God, she wanted to believe that. "It's not him," she whispered. "Please, don't let it be Kyle." Her fear — the one that terrorized her. Every single moment. Her faith in her brother — that had been the lie. Because she didn't believe one hundred percent in his innocence. With the evidence, how could she?

Her fear…

Don't be him. Don't let my brother be the monster.

Remy lifted his head. She stared up at him. She'd exposed every secret she had. All of the careful lies that the Clarke family had put in place. One after the other until they'd all ignited.

Kennedy felt gutted as she gazed into Remy's eyes. Her heart had broken — it had broken long ago. The same day her ribs had broken, and she'd tumbled down the stairs, falling, rolling over and over as her brother screamed for her. She'd landed at the base of the stairs and hadn't been able to move at all.

Her mother had rushed toward her.

My poor broken doll…

Pain consumed her. She'd spent too many years having pain as her constant companion. She wanted more. She needed more.

"You should get some sleep," Remy urged her carefully. "Rest. Take my bedroom. Know that you're safe. Nothing bad is going to happen to you here."

Bad things could happen anywhere. "I don't want to sleep."

What she wanted was oblivion. She wanted to escape the pain and the fear and everything else. Her hand pressed to his chest. "I'm not asking for tomorrow. I don't want some kind of forever commitment."

His expression was so hard and unyielding.

"Tonight," she whispered. "I'd like tonight with you."

His gaze cut away from her. "You should go to bed, Kennedy."

Oh, God. What had she been thinking? He'd just found out what an absolute train wreck her whole life was. Like the guy was going to want to hop into the nearest bed with her after all that she'd unloaded on him. Her timing was shit.

And her pain just got worse.

She let her hand fall. Her head sagged forward because she couldn't look him in the eyes right then.

"I'm trying to give you a chance," he growled. "My self-control is shot to hell where you are concerned. All I want to do is take you far away from any pain that could ever hurt you again."

Kennedy's head whipped up.

His eyes weren't cold any longer. Heat blazed in the darkness of his stare.

"I want you. Make no mistake about that. I want you naked. I want you beneath me. On top of me. Any way I can get you. I want you screaming with pleasure. Because I never want you knowing pain again." He released a ragged breath. "I want you, and if you don't get in that bedroom, if you don't get away from me, I don't think I'll be able to stop touching you."

"I want you." Wanted his hands on her. Wanted every single thing that he had to give.

"You don't want tomorrow." His gaze scorched her. "But, Kennedy, I don't think I can have you once and let go." His words were a dangerous rumble of warning. "I think I'll have you, and I'll just want more."

"Remy…"

"Don't regret it." What could have been a flash of torment appeared in his eyes. "Don't regret giving yourself to me."

"I know what I want." No regrets. Just need. "It's you."

"Go into the bedroom. You're running on pain and adrenaline. You're—"

"I want you," she said again. And she wasn't ashamed or scared or anything else. Not in that moment. She could see his need. Practically feel it in the air around her. "Tomorrow can come. It always does. We'll figure it out then, all right? Maybe the sex will be the worst of our lives, and neither of us will want a repeat performance."

"I don't think that will happen."

No, neither did she.

"One way to find out," Kennedy murmured. His hand rose. Closed around her shoulder.

She wasn't going to flee. She wanted something good, dammit. In the world where everything had gone to hell, she was going to take something for herself.

"I tried. Remember that, will you?" he rasped.

"I want to remember what it's like when you kiss me."

His head bent. His lips brushed over hers. Tantalizing. Tempting. Promising. "I'll make sure you never forget."

Remy scooped her into his arms. The move caught her off-guard as surprise rolled through her. Kennedy looped her arms around his neck, and she felt a smile curving her lips. A real smile.

He carried her down the hallway. Into the bedroom. Into *his* bedroom. There were still no pictures on the walls. No personal touches, but she saw his discarded coat on a nearby chair and the closet door was open, revealing his clothes hanging there.

He'd been prepared to give her his bedroom. Chivalrous. Kind.

There was so much more to him than she'd expected.

So much more.

He lowered her onto the bed. His touch was gentle, ever so careful. He kissed her again. A deeper, harder kiss. She loved his taste. Loved the way he made her feel. Her nipples were tight and aching, and her hips rocked up, the movement instinctive.

But he stepped back from the bed. His eyes stayed on her as he yanked off his shirt. Threw it to the floor. She couldn't look away from him.

She'd known he was strong, but without his shirt—his muscles were incredible. Rippling. Cut. Not a six pack. More like a ten pack. She looked at him and wanted to lick her lips. She looked at him and—

Scars. There were slashes going across his abs. Small, puckered red marks. One near his shoulder. Another on his left side. One under his heart.

Kennedy jerked upright, her hand reaching out toward him. "What happened?"

He tensed beneath her touch. She remembered what Amanda had said. About her not really knowing him. *Ask him why he holds his shoulder so —*

"They don't hurt anymore, Kennedy."

She touched the mark on his shoulder. "You were shot."

"A few times."

He was acting like it didn't matter.

It did.

His pain mattered.

Her hand slid down his stomach. To the thin, white lines that looked like slashes. She hadn't even noticed the scars on first glance. She'd been too busy seeing him.

"Knife wounds," he told her gruffly.

Knife wounds?

"A long time ago. In another life."

She could only shake her head. Then she bent, and her mouth brushed over the old scar near his heart.

"Baby, it doesn't hurt anymore."

Sometimes, the old pains were the ones that hurt the most.

Her lips feathered over his chest as she moved from one scar to the other. A knife wound. A bullet wound. What kind of life had he lived? How much danger had he faced? Tenderly, she pressed her mouth to each mark, wishing she could take his pain away.

"Kennedy…" His hands slid down her arms.

She looked up at him. There was a hard, stark need etched onto his face. His eyes seemed to blaze at her, and she'd never before seen a man stare at her with such fierce lust. He wanted her. Didn't care about her past or her future. He was focused on her.

And she was completely focused on him.

"Do the scars bother you?" His voice had turned guttural.

"Nothing about you bothers me."

"And everything about you turns me on." He tumbled her back onto the bed, caged her there with his body, and took her mouth. The kiss was hotter, rougher, a bit wilder as the desire they both felt rushed to the surface. This wasn't the time for more talking. Need was too fierce, desire too sharp as it burst through her.

He stripped off her sweater. Tossed it over the bed. Kissed a path down her body as he slid his fingers under her bra straps. There were faint calluses on his fingertips, and she liked that roughness on her skin. She liked his touch. Wanted more. Wanted him, *everywhere.*

He lifted his body just enough for them to ditch her pants. She'd long since kicked off her high heels. Clad in only her panties and her bra, she should have felt vulnerable there with him. He was so much bigger than her, stronger. A man with a mysterious, deadly past.

But she didn't feel vulnerable. There was no hesitation. Only a sense that being with him was right. He was right. Nothing could have stopped her in that moment.

His hand went between her thighs as he stroked her through the thin silk. She was ready, and she arched into his touch. Kennedy didn't want the silk between them. She wanted his fingers on her sex. Wanted his fingers *in* her. Wanted the heavy erection she'd felt to push hard into her body.

Pleasure waited. She needed to feel the wild rush right then. Over and over…

He unhooked her bra. Shoved it away. His mouth closed over her nipple, and she arched off the bed because the pulse of sensual sensation was so strong. He was licking her and stroking her, and a moan tore from Kennedy's mouth. Arousal heated her blood as her nails scraped down his back.

"You are gorgeous." He kissed his way to her other breast even as his fingers slipped under the edge of her panties. He could rip those panties away for all that she cared. She wanted to feel him as—

He pushed two fingers into her. She hissed out a breath and pressed toward him. His palm pushed down against the center of her need, and his fingers thrust into her. He worked her sex, driving her straight to the brink, even as he licked and sucked her nipple. The stimulation had her gasping and shuddering beneath him as her whole body tightened. Her climax bore down on her, so close. Already so close—

"Not yet." His hand pulled away from her.

Dammit! She wanted to come now! She'd been so close. So—

He eased down her body. Stripped her panties down her legs and let his callused fingertips caress her inner thighs. Then he was pushing her thighs apart. Bringing his mouth toward her exposed sex.

"Remy—"

He put his mouth on her. If he hadn't been holding her hips, Kennedy knew she might have leapt right off the bed. He licked her, sucked, stroked, and she came, a hot, pounding wave of pleasure that surged through her body over and over again.

He climbed from the bed.

She could only pant. Only feel. Only watch him and wonder —

Why are you leaving me?

He yanked a foil packet from the nightstand. Ditched the rest of his clothes and shoved on the condom. Then he was back in bed. His expression was cut into lines of hard lust. He settled between her legs, and when she reached for him, he pinned her hands on either side of her head.

Remy drove into her, one deep, hard thrust that had her sucking in a breath.

"Kennedy?"

She was tight, and he was freaking huge. "Give me…one second." It had been a while. Like, a really long while. The kind of while where you lose count of the days.

He let go of her right wrist. His hand snaked between them, and he caressed her. Remy didn't move his cock, just kept it fully lodged inside of her, stretching her, but his touch had desire pulsing through her again. Her body relaxed around him.

"Now?" Remy asked her.

She nodded against the pillow. *Now, now, now!*

He withdrew, thrust, but his thrusts were more managed now. More controlled. He positioned his body so that every move had him sliding over her clit, and the friction was incredible. Her body softened around him, she met him thrust for thrust, and soon, with her legs wrapped tightly around his hips, she was urging him on. *More. Faster. Harder.* She wanted to scream those words at him, but Kennedy bit her lower lip instead. Bit it so hard she nearly broke through.

"No." His finger pressed to her lip. "I want to hear every sound. I want *everything*. Give it all to me."

She parted her lips. Opened her mouth and took his finger inside. She licked and sucked and she was staring straight into his eyes. She saw his gaze widen. Saw the flash of primal lust.

He stopped being controlled.

So did she. "Faster."

His hips pistoned against her.

"Harder," Kennedy gasped.

The headboard slammed into the wall.

She seemed to splinter apart. Pleasure burst through her as the climax hit, and Kennedy cried out Remy's name. He was with her. His whole body stiffened, and she saw the pleasure on his face. The climax seemed to go on and on, she could feel him all around her, and it had *never* been that good. Earth-shattering, mind-numbing pleasure. Amazing.

She'd enjoyed sex before. She'd liked her lovers.

But this…

This was different.

So different.

Her heartbeat thundered in her ears. A light sheen of sweat covered them. He was still *in* her. Her breath came in rough pants as she gazed up at him.

"I was right," he said, his voice a deep, sexy growl that Kennedy swore she felt in every cell of her body. "I can't have you once and let you go."

She didn't remember asking to be let go. She swallowed — twice — then managed to say, "That definitely didn't qualify as the worst sex of my life."

His eyes narrowed.

"But I think it might have been the best."

CHAPTER NINE

He was in trouble, and he knew it.

Once wasn't enough. Once just made me want her more.

Kennedy was asleep beside him. Her hair was loose around her shoulders. Naked, her body soft and sexy, and he wanted her again. Wanted to kiss every single inch of her body. Wanted to thrust deep into her and go mad with pleasure.

Remy felt different. They'd crossed a line. There was the case, and there was supposed to be them, but, hell, he knew that was bullshit. She *was* the case, and when she found out the truth about him—there was no way she'd ever let him touch her again.

He should have kept his hands off her and kept his dick zipped up in his pants.

But there was something about Kennedy…

She gave me her secrets, and I paid her back with lies.

Would she have hated him less if they hadn't slept together?

Would he hate himself any damn less?

Fuck!

Remy slid from the bed, being careful not to wake her. Kennedy needed her sleep. She'd had one hell of a day.

And things were only going to get worse.

After dragging on a pair of jeans, he headed out of the bedroom and made his way upstairs. Most of the upstairs area *was* under construction, but one of the bedrooms up there was his office — his work room. He climbed the stairs without making a sound. At the top of the stairs, he glanced back.

No sign of Kennedy.

A few moments later, he opened the door to his office and slipped inside. His laptop was closed as it sat on his desk. He eased into the desk chair and pulled out his phone. It was close to midnight, but if you couldn't wake up your partner at midnight, then who the hell could you call?

Joshua answered on the second ring. "You okay?" he immediately demanded.

"Got some intel for you." He was a traitorous prick. He'd worked undercover on more cases than he could count. He'd been specifically requested by the higher-ups for this job…because he didn't let pesky things like a conscience get in the way.

Do the job. For the greater good.

Only nothing about this job felt good.

Kennedy didn't know yet — this wasn't just about the two women who'd been murdered in New Orleans. There was so much more to this case than met the eye.

"Re-open the investigation on her parents' deaths," Remy ordered quietly.

"What?"

"Kennedy said the fire wasn't an accident. She told me her father killed himself and her mother."

A stark pause. "Wasn't Kyle Clarke on the boat the day it burned?"

Joshua would be familiar with all the details of the Clarke family. Just as Remy was. Or at least, they'd thought they were familiar. *But the whole family was lying about so much.* "Yes, Kyle was there." And Remy knew exactly what Joshua was suspecting...

Because I suspect the same thing.

"Did he do it?" Joshua asked bluntly.

"Kennedy says no."

"Is she covering for him again? You believe her?"

"She's a better liar than I thought." Those words were so cold, and Remy felt like shit just saying them. Her scent was still on him. He could still *feel* her touch, and he was selling her out. Selling out the secrets she'd told him as tears filled her eyes. "But..." He blew out a hard breath as he spun his chair to face the door. The last thing he wanted was to have her sneak up on him. He kept his gaze on the door and said, "I believe her about this. Kennedy doesn't think her brother killed her parents."

"Yeah, well, I never heard so much as a whisper about some freaking murder suicide. You don't just wake up one day and kill your wife. That shit doesn't happen. There would have been signs, there would have been—"

"The dad was abusive. Controlling. Kennedy said he especially liked to hurt her brother."

Silence.

"It fits the profile, doesn't it?" Remy prompted. The profile that Joshua had created. Long before they'd focused on Kyle Clarke as a suspect.

Because this case wasn't just about the two victims in New Orleans. There were more women out there who were possibly linked to the Broken Doll Killer. Women who'd been taken from Alabama. Florida. Mississippi. They hadn't been linked publicly to the Broken Doll Killer because the FBI was trying to keep its full investigation contained.

The FBI believed the killer had been slowly evolving. He'd been experimenting, perfecting his craft. The first victim, taken from Mobile, Alabama, had been held for two months before she was killed. She'd been found with a blindfold over her eyes.

The next victim had eventually been found…with a blindfold, too. The third—she'd been discovered with her body posed to resemble a broken doll, and, of course, the fucking blindfold had been on her, too. The perp had slowly developed his signature, advancing until he left his kills all the same way…

Blindfolded. Posed to resemble a broken doll. Necks slit from ear to ear. A pool of blood beneath them.

If they were right with their suspicions, there were at least six victims. Six, not two. And that was part of the reason why Remy was undercover. Why so many rules were getting bent as they hunted this killer.

"It fits the profile," Joshua replied slowly.

"Kennedy said their grandfather covered things up." Wouldn't be the first time a rich and powerful figure had used his influence and cash to hide trouble. Not the first time, not the last. "And she told me that her brother got sent off to a psychiatric facility somewhere in Europe for some treatment after their parents' deaths." It was his job to pass along this information. So why did he feel like a traitor?

Oh, right, because he was.

"Guess you got her trust, huh? That was fast," Joshua muttered. "She must think you're her white knight to share so much."

Like Remy needed to feel more like shit.

"Why'd the brother get shipped away?"

Remy's temples throbbed. "Because one night, she woke up to find the asshole standing at the foot of her bed with a knife in his hand."

"Fucking hell."

"Exactly." The throbbing got worse.

"There haven't been any other murders since Kyle Clarke's car was pulled out of the Mississippi. Maybe the guy *is* dead. Maybe—"

"I'm supposed to find solid proof, one way or another, that shows his guilt or innocence." With the other unsolved cases in the other states, the FBI Brass wasn't going to take any chances. As far as the guy being dead or alive... "Kennedy thinks he's still out there."

"Does she think or does she *know*?"

"She just said she felt it. Some kind of twin thing."

"Yeah, um, I'm calling BS on that," Joshua immediately declared.

Remy didn't speak.

"Did you get the name of the facility in Europe?"

"No. But I figure we're the mother fucking FBI, so we can figure it out."

"Yeah, yeah, we can. I know of about four places off the top of my head that could be contenders. The problem is these places aren't going to share confidential information with us, at least not on the record."

"Then we go off the record. We find an ex-employee who won't mind spilling, and we go from there."

"Uh, that's not the kind of evidence that could be used in a court case," his partner chided him.

Joshua was so by-the-freaking-book. Always. After the way things had gone down on his last big case, Remy couldn't say that he actually minded that particular personality trait. "This isn't about building a court case, and you know it. This is about Brass wanting us to be sure we're focused on the right man." Other agents were out there looking at other leads, boots were on the ground in Florida and Mississippi, but so far…all signs pointed to Kyle Clarke.

He'd been *in* Florida and Mississippi at the time of the other abductions. There was more circumstantial evidence, more links, but—

"I'll find someone to talk." Joshua cleared his throat. "What about her, though? I mean, that painting today, man, that was bad."

Yes, it was.

"If he's still out there, if Kyle's alive and he's our killer, his focus is on her. Kennedy could be the next target. The guy has a taste for killing now. There is no way that he stops. He can't quit cold turkey. If he's out there, if he survived, Kyle is going to kill again."

Yes. Monsters didn't just wake up and decide to be the good guys.

A scream cut through the night, echoing through his house. "Shit, Kennedy!" He hung up the phone and rushed from the room. His feet flew over the stairs.

Another scream echoed, but this one broke off.

He threw open the bedroom door and flipped on the lights.

Kennedy sat in the middle of the bed, the sheets clutched to her chest. She blinked against the light, looking dazed and frightened and too freaking sexy in his bed.

His gaze swept the room, looking for a threat, but there wasn't one. No one else was in the bedroom.

"I'm sorry." Her shoulders hunched. "I had a bad dream."

And she'd nearly given him a heart attack. When he'd heard her scream, his only thought had been to get to her. He'd been absolutely, freaking desperate.

"Kyle was lost in the dark," she whispered. "He was hurting, and he was desperate, and there was nothing I could do to help him."

Remy stalked toward the bed. Stood there, helpless, as he wished he could make her feel better.

"I was always afraid he'd get lost in the dark." Now she looked up at him, and there were tears on her lashes.

She knows. Or at least, she fears the truth. Because she wasn't talking about some kid getting lost in the dark woods or some shit like that. She was talking about the darkness that could live inside of a person.

"We're going to find out," Remy promised her, and on this, there was only truth. "We'll find out if he's the killer or another victim. One way or another, we'll know for certain."

Her fingers tightened on the sheet. "Do you think he's alive?"

"If he was alive, he would have contacted you by now." Every piece of intel he possessed told him that Kyle would not stay away from his sister. "*Has* he contacted you?"

"No." She stared straight at him.

"Where would he go, Kennedy? If he wanted to hide, is there *any* place he'd be that you haven't told the cops?"

Her gaze cut from his.

There is.

"I've checked every place," she said quietly. "He wasn't there."

The FBI had suspected her family had holdings they couldn't track. When you had more money than God, it was easy to hide sins.

That's why I'm here. To find every single sin.

"Let's check again," he told her flatly. "Because maybe I'll see something you missed. And we'll start with your family's cabin." The one that had been in the picture back at Stacey's condo.

She gave a slow nod.

She'd taken his bait. And once more, he felt the stab of guilt that went straight to his heart. *If she's hiding a killer, I have to track him.*

In the end, what would Kennedy do? When she learned the truth, how would she look at him?

He'd turned on drug lords. He'd taken down men who ran sex rings. He'd infiltrated a cult. He'd been right beside some of the worst criminals in the world, and he'd never hesitated to do the job.

Was it different this time because he was lying to someone who *wasn't* a criminal? Because while her brother might be twisted as fuck, Kennedy was innocent?

"I'm sorry I screamed."

His chest ached. And the phone he gripped in his hand — the phone he'd forgotten about as he rushed down to her — vibrated. Remy glanced down at the screen.

Joshua.

Hell. His fingers slid across the screen. "Hello?"

"Is everything all right?" Joshua blasted. "Or do I need to have the cavalry come and kick down your door?"

"No, there's no need for that," he replied briskly. "I'll give you a call tomorrow, and we'll wrap up the case."

"Okay, so that means everything is totally under control?"

He stared at Kennedy. "I've got this." He ended the call and tossed the phone onto the nightstand. Remy made a mental note to request a second phone from the Bureau, ASAP. A phone that he'd keep upstairs for his check-in calls with Joshua. The last thing he wanted was for Kennedy to catch a call or text she shouldn't receive. He eased out a slow breath and said, "You don't need to apologize to me."

She bit her lower lip. She'd done that when he'd been inside of her, trying to hold back her cries, her needs, and he hadn't wanted that. He wanted Kennedy to talk to him. To speak freely.

Why? So I could use everything she says against her?

He stalked toward the bed. Her head turned toward him, and his hand rose to cup her chin. "I am a fucking bastard."

Her lashes fluttered. "What? No, you—"

"I don't deserve you. You'll realize that, eventually."

"Remy—"

"I should keep my hands off you. I should back the hell away."

"But I like it when your hands are on me."

Holy fuck. He couldn't handle her honesty. *I like having my hands all over you, baby.*

"I can't stop. I want you, Kennedy." More than he'd expected. More than he could remember wanting anyone. He climbed onto the bed, and his lips brushed over hers. "I want you now."

"I want you, too."

One day, she wouldn't want him. She wouldn't let him touch her. She'd stare at him with hate instead of desire. If he was a gentleman, he'd back out of the room.

If he was a gentleman, he wouldn't be there with her at all.

Her hand rose to press against his chest, settling right above his heart. "I'm sorry you were hurt, Remy."

Her gaze was so bright on him. A man could probably get lost in eyes like hers.

"Promise me one thing?" Kennedy asked, voice husky.

He waited and wondered what she'd ask him. If she was going to try and get a promise that if they found her brother, he'd let the guy go, or if Remy found evidence proving Kyle's guilt that they'd discard it or —

"Don't get hurt. Don't get another scar, not because of me. I don't want you hurt because of me." She kissed him. Soft. Careful. Tender.

A lover's kiss.

And Remy kissed her back the same way. The first time they'd been together, raw need had taken over. A savage desire that had caught him completely off-guard. This time, he was determined to go slow. This time, he was determined to savor her. To kiss and caress every single inch of her body.

He pushed her back so that she was lying on the bed. Quickly, Remy stripped. He eased on top of her, bracing his weight on his arms because he didn't want to crush her. His head lowered, and Remy pressed his lips to her neck, right over her racing pulse. The scent of strawberries teased him, and his cock shoved against her.

But his control held.

He feathered kisses over her collar bone. Over her shoulders. Down, down he went, and he caressed her tight, pink nipples. He laved her nipples, making her gasp and moan, and his fingers slid between her thighs.

He could probably get drunk on her taste. She went straight to his head. His fingers stroked her clit, then he eased two fingers into her. "So tight," he muttered. "Fucking fantastic." Remy remembered how she'd tensed when he'd taken her body for the first time. His head lifted. "Kennedy, how long had it been?"

"You're...ah, asking that *now?*" Her hips arched into his hand.

"I don't want to hurt you." He kept his touch easy as he worked her soft sex. "Tell me."

"A year? Maybe more?"

What?

Her lashes had been closed, but now they flew open as she fixed her stare on him. "It doesn't matter. You aren't hurting me. You *won't* hurt me."

Yes, I will.

"I want you. You want me." And she surged up. Her hands flattened on his chest, and Remy let her push him back. Regretfully, his fingers slid from her sex. She straddled his hips and stared down at him as her hair tumbled over her shoulders.

Gorgeous. Hot.

His.

His cock pressed against the entrance to her body. He didn't have a rubber on. He should reach into the nightstand. He should *not* stroke her again. He should not —

She was kissing his scars. The delicate movements of her lips were tender and sensual, and his hands rose to curl around her shoulders.

She kept kissing the old wounds, moving down his body, sliding and repositioning herself until—

His teeth clenched.

She licked his cock. Licked the head and then took it into her mouth. She sucked him. Kissed. Caressed. He'd thought this time would be different. That they'd go slow. He hadn't even got to fully explore her body. He hadn't gotten—

He pulled her up. "Baby, I will fucking *come*." His voice was gravel-rough. "Condoms. Nightstand." Okay, now he wasn't even making full sentences. His dick bobbed eagerly toward her, and he wanted her mouth back on him. Or he wanted to be *in* her tight, wet sex.

She stretched and reached the nightstand drawer. Fumbling, Kennedy pulled out the condom. Rolled it on him a few moments later. His hands locked around her hips. He lifted her up and then, inch by slow inch, he lowered her onto the length of his cock.

Her lips parted. Her moans were the best music he'd ever heard. Up and down, she rode him, and his hold on her just tightened. Her body was a warm, wet heaven. Tight enough to make him go insane.

Remy saw the pleasure hit her. Her lips parted as her head tipped back and she called out his name.

He drove into her, faster, harder, making her climax last and last, feeling the contractions of her inner muscles clamping around his cock, and she pushed him over the edge. Fired him into sweet oblivion as his climax rammed into him.

His heart thundered in his chest. Kennedy collapsed on top of him, all silken limbs and sweet strawberries. Carefully, he withdrew from her body and ditched the condom. He went to the bathroom and came back to her with a warm cloth. She smiled at him as he gently cleaned her — then he went right back into the bed with her.

And it was only as he pulled her into his arms that Remy wondered...

What in the hell am I doing?

He didn't spend the night with lovers. Didn't get close enough to form any sort of connection.

This doesn't count. Kennedy asked to stay here because she was scared. This isn't the same thing —

Only...it was. He could walk out of the room. He could sleep on the couch. He could leave her alone. Instead, Remy found himself pulling her even closer and asking, "Why a year?"

"Because I got tired of men wanting my family's money or my family's name or —"

He laughed as his fingers trailed over the curve of her hip. "Men want you. Period."

"No." Sadness. "I've seen it before. They pretend to be interested, but it's just the money. It's not me."

He wasn't buying it. "Then they must be fools."

A soft laugh. "They were." Her hand pressed over his heart. Felt right there. "After a while, I realized it was better to be alone than to share yourself with someone who told you the sweet lies you wanted to hear."

His heart jerked. Shit. *Shit.* She must have felt the telling—

"Remy? Is everything all right?"

No, it wasn't. "What was different? Why did you approach me in the ballroom?"

"Because you looked at me, and I saw desire. I looked at you, and I felt the same thing. I've never been the type for instant attraction, but, you were different."

He swallowed and reached out to turn off the light. All of the lights in the house were connected to his phone. So, a quick swipe had them plunging into darkness.

She cuddled against him. And he liked it. Liked the way she felt and smelled. Liked the soft sound of her breathing.

"Have you ever been in love, Kennedy?" The question slipped from him.

"I thought I was. A long time ago. A guy I grew up with. He seemed perfect, but then...then he just left one day. He had a choice to make, and he didn't choose me." A pause. "What about you?"

He stared up at the darkness. "I've never been in love." Because he'd never let anyone get close enough to really know him. Maybe because he was afraid of what a lover would think, if she truly saw the real man beneath the lies.

"Tell me a secret," she urged softly when the silence stretched between them. "I told you all of mine. Tell me something. Give me something."

His head turned. Her hand was still over his heart, and the soft touch felt almost like a brand, marking him. A mark that went far beneath the skin.

What is she doing to me?

"What kind of secret do you want?" Remy wasn't sure what to say. Was she looking for an angle? Something to use against him?

"Something you haven't told anyone else."

Fine. "I hate Christmas."

He felt her start of surprise. "Hate it? Why?"

"Because my parents were murdered two weeks before Christmas. And I had to stare at the fucking tree in my house after I buried them. I had to find the fucking presents they'd left behind. And I had to be alone." Shit. As soon as he said the words, Remy wished he could bring them back. He hadn't meant to tell her that. Hadn't meant to say —

She shifted her body. Pressed a gentle kiss to his lips. "I'm sorry."

His heart raced and his muscles tensed. "You didn't do it. You don't need to be sor —"

"Sometimes, we're just sorry because we don't like the pain that someone else has to carry. I'm sorry that you hurt. I wish I could make it better." Another soft kiss. Then she just eased back beside him. Kept her hand over his heart. "I won't ask you for more secrets." Her words were husky. "If there's anything you want to tell me, then you tell me. I don't want to ever bring you more pain."

But his chest was aching again. And his body was tight. She was messing with his head. With his heart? He didn't want to bring her pain. He'd like to make her laugh. Like to see her smile and to have her just feel free. Happy. To not be scared. To not worry about her brother or —

"Is it okay if I sleep with you?" Her question was halting.

It was his out. The moment to reply that no, he didn't *sleep* with lovers. A cold-as-ice statement that he'd said to others because he was a cold bastard. But when Kennedy asked the hesitant question, his hold on her tightened. "I want you to stay with me." *That* was what he said. It was what he meant. He didn't want to let her go. Screw his rules about never staying close with a lover. Maybe those rules were shit.

Maybe it was time for the rules to change.

Maybe…maybe it was time for *him* to change.

Her breathing slowly evened out, and Remy felt his own eyelids grow heavy. Kennedy was warm and soft against him, and for some reason, she just felt right.

Dawn would come soon enough. He'd have to go back to wearing his mask and playing his game, but for that night, he'd sleep with his lover in his arms. And he'd pretend he wasn't a bastard.

CHAPTER TEN

The phone rang, the distant sound pulling Kennedy from sleep. She was warm and comfortable—and sprawled across a man's chest.

As soon as that realization sank in, she jerked her head upright and met Remy's dark stare.

"Good morning to you," he murmured. For the first time, she heard the hint of the south slipping into his voice.

The phone rang again.

"Someone's calling you," Remy told her helpfully, a slight grin pulling at his lips.

She'd slept with him all night. Or maybe she'd slept *on* him all night. Kennedy swallowed and pushed off his chest. She climbed from the bed and when she felt a distinct draft, she realized she was still buck naked.

Remy gave a whistle.

The phone stopped ringing. Kennedy just stood by the side of the bed, confused as all hell because she was always groggy when she woke up and—

Her phone started to ring again.

She hurried forward. Found her phone on the dresser. *Unknown number.* Probably the wrong number. Probably nothing. She should just put the phone down. Get back into the bed.

But her finger swiped across the screen. She lifted the phone to her ear. "Hello?"

"Kennedy."

Just that one word—her name. Her name and her legs nearly gave way because that particular voice haunted her dreams. That voice was burned into her mind.

Her brother's voice.

"Kyle?" she gasped out.

Remy leapt from the bed. He was at her side in two seconds.

"Kyle, talk to me!" She was begging and demanding at the same time. But this was her brother. *His* voice.

"Help me."

Her heart stopped. "Kyle, where are—"

Remy took the phone from her. His hand swiped over the screen, turning on the speaker. "Who the hell is this?" Remy barked.

No answer. The call ended.

He immediately grabbed his own phone. His eyes were flat and hard as he dialed someone. As she watched, dazed and stunned, he said, "You're tracking her phone? Right. Yeah, yeah, she just got a fucking call. I want to know who made the call. Where the hell it originated. Get me that information *yesterday*."

"The call was blocked," Kennedy whispered as she grabbed for a sheet and wrapped it around her body. "Unknown number."

"Nothing stays unknown. I've got friends monitoring your line. I had them start the minute you hired me. They'll find the guy."

They'd find her brother.

Kyle is alive.

Her heart was racing now, pounding hard in her chest. A smile tried to curve her lips as relief left her dizzy. She'd been right, all along. Kyle had survived. He'd made it, he'd —

"Are you *sure* that was your brother?" Remy growled.

"I know Kyle's voice." She licked her lips. Nodded. "That was him."

The chill didn't leave Remy's stare. "You know what that means."

And her smile vanished.

"If he's been out there the whole time, baby, then your brother has been hiding. Hiding from the cops. He *killed* those women."

"No, no, it—"

"I want you to take me to every holding that your family has. Every single place, including locations that are off the books. If he's hiding, we're finding him. And if he's innocent, then he can prove it."

The innocent don't hide.

She swallowed. "He asked me to help him."

"Isn't that what you're doing? Isn't that why you came to me?"

"Y-yes."

Remy nodded. He hauled on some pants, and she took her phone back. She stared at the screen, willing the phone to ring again.

It didn't. But Remy's did.

She turned toward him when he took the call.

"What? Are you shitting me? That can't be possible." A furrow appeared between his brows. "Yeah, yeah, get Detective Amanda Jackson on the line. *Now.* We're on our way."

He was already contacting the detective? "No!" Her protest was instinctive. "You can't go to the cops!" Not yet. Not—

A muscle jerked in his jaw. He lowered his phone and told her, "They triangulated the signal. Tracked the call. It came from *her* apartment."

Now Kennedy took a step back. "That's not possible."

"Yeah, I said the same shit." He raked a hand through his tousled hair. "But my team swears they aren't wrong. And we need to get the hell over there, now, and figure out what's happening."

***

Remy knew they were going to find trouble long before they arrived at Detective Amanda Jackson's place. The clench in his gut told him that this shit couldn't be good. The phone call *coming* from the detective's home? No, no way. And the fact that his team had told him they couldn't get the detective to pick up when they tried to reach her...

He had suspicions about what was happening, and Remy prayed that he was wrong.

But when he and Kennedy turned the corner, and he saw the flash of blue lights in the street... "Fuck."

"It looks like a crime scene." Kennedy's voice was shaking.

"Because it is." He parked the car and jumped out as fast as he could. He ran for the front of the building, with Kennedy right behind him.

Joshua came out, a crime scene tech behind him. The tech was holding a plastic bag in her hand—an evidence bag. A phone was in the bag.

Joshua saw him, and the guy's eyes widened. "Stop!" Joshua held up his hand. His gaze darted between Remy and Kennedy. "You're not going in there, neither one of you."

Amanda's partner, Brock Mayo, strode from the building. He immediately stalked to Remy and Kennedy. "Where the hell is she?" Brock Mayo demanded. *"Where is my partner?"*

Remy ignored him. "Agent Morgan," he said as he addressed Joshua, "what's happening here? I know my team notified you of the call and—"

"There are signs of a struggle in the residence." Joshua's voice was flat. "And Detective Amanda Jackson is missing."

"Missing?" Kennedy repeated, her voice sharp.

Joshua's narrowed gaze focused on her. "We found a discarded burner phone inside her home, right near the bed. I've been informed that the phone was recently used to call *you*. Want to tell me who made that call?"

Her frantic gaze jumped to Remy.

"Her brother," he said flatly.

"You *heard* the guy?" Mayo burst out. The detective sounded as if he were strangling. "Kyle Clarke is alive?"

No, he hadn't actually heard the fellow's voice and that bothered Remy. "Kennedy heard him. She positively identified the caller as her brother, but, no, I didn't speak to him."

Mayo wrapped his beefy fingers around Kennedy's arm. "Where the hell did your freak of a brother take my partner?" Spittle flew from his mouth.

Oh, the hell, no. "Get your hand off her," Remy ordered, his voice lethally soft.

Mayo didn't listen to his order.

Remy gave him one more warning. "Get your hand off her, or I'll be moving it for you."

Mayo let her go and threw Remy a glare of pure rage. "She's helping him! Hiding that asshole! He *took* Amanda. The phone is proof of that! You know what he does to his victims. He's out there torturing her. *Hurting* her. Over and over. And we're just gonna sit here and coddle this little bitch!"

"*Stop,*" Remy snarled.

Kennedy had gone pale. A tremble shook her body.

"Your brother made the call," Mayo fired at her. "He left the phone here for us to find. He *wanted* you to know what he'd done. He *wanted* you to figure it out. The proof is plain to see for us all, but, hell, I knew it from the start! Your brother is a killer. He's a fucking monster, and if you don't help us, if you don't help us to *find* Amanda before that prick kills her — then you are just as much of a killer as he is!"

"Back the hell up," Remy ordered quietly. But he didn't wait for the detective to move. Remy put his body between Mayo's and Kennedy's. He reached for her hand and found it to be cold as ice. "She didn't do this."

"Yeah? How the hell do you know? How do you know she didn't help her brother to — "

"She was with me last night. All night, okay? I was there when she got the call. She didn't know a damn thing about what was happening."

As Joshua looked on, Mayo stepped toe-to-toe with Remy. "You don't see it, do you? That woman is *playing* you. Amanda knew it, and I know it, too." His voice was a disgusted growl. "While Kennedy was screwing you, her brother was abducting Amanda. They do this twisted shit together."

Remy's body locked down as rage poured through him. "Kennedy isn't her brother. She didn't do *anything* with him."

"She's got you by the balls!" Mayo thundered. "You don't even see—"

"*I didn't help Kyle!*" Kennedy's desperate voice rang out.

Remy and Mayo both swung their heads toward her.

Still too pale and with eyes that were too big and stark, Kennedy repeated, "I didn't help him. I *wouldn't* do something like this." She shook her head. Swallowed. "But, God, he did." Her lips trembled. *"He did.* It was Kyle on the phone. I know his voice. And the phone was here. It was *here.* He took her. Oh, God, I'm so sorry. I'm so sorry for everything. I didn't…" Her lips pressed together.

Silence.

"I wanted him to be innocent," Kennedy mumbled. "I needed him to be."

She hadn't wanted to see the killer right beside her.

"Where would he take her?" Joshua asked, and there was no emotion in his voice.

Her chin rose. She focused on him, seemed to blink in confusion.

Uniformed cops and crime scene techs buzzed around them.

"No one knows him better than you," Joshua added.

But Kennedy shook her head. "Actually, I don't think that I know my brother at all."

***

"Kennedy, think about it, is there *any* other place your brother could have gone?"

She rubbed eyes that felt as if they burned. They'd been searching her family's holdings all day long. The family cabin. Old rental property. Abandoned warehouses that her grandfather had kept under the aliases of other corporations. Every single place that she knew about — she'd searched.

And they'd turned up nothing.

"I gave the cops access to all of the company's files." She sat hunched in the front seat of Remy's car. A chill had settled into her bones. *Amanda is out there. He's hurting her.* "There isn't any other place that I know about."

He turned toward her, his left hand still gripping the steering wheel. They were in the parking lot of an abandoned rental house, one on the outskirts of New Orleans. Cops were still searching inside, even using their dogs, but it seemed to be another spot that was going to turn up nothing.

How could you do this, Kyle? I trusted you.

"Think, baby," Remy urged her. "It would be some place remote. A place where he could work and not be disturbed."

Work. She flinched. If she'd eaten anything that day, she might have vomited it up. But she hadn't eaten. She couldn't. "He's going to kill her."

"Not if we find her. Not if we get to them first. There has to be a place. You know it, just — *think.*"

There was a rap on the passenger side window. Kennedy jumped and turned to find the FBI Agent — Joshua Morgan — frowning at her. Kennedy hit the button to lower the window.

"Nothing," he snapped. Impatience had deepened the faint lines on his face. "There has to be another spot."

Different cops were checking different places. Teams had been sent out to hunt all over the town. Detective Amanda Jackson's face had been plastered across the news.

But time was ticking away, and they hadn't found her.

"Kennedy, I need you to think like your brother," Agent Morgan instructed as he leaned closer to her. "The guy would have gone back to a place where he felt as if he were in control. A place where he was safe. A place where he felt—"

She had a sudden flash in her mind. *Safe.* Kennedy sucked in a sharp breath. "No."

"Kennedy?" Remy's voice rumbled. "What are you holding back?"

She wasn't holding back. She was telling them *everything*. She wanted to find the detective. She was desperate to find her. "There was another place that we used to visit when we were kids." She licked her lips. "A lake house. But it wasn't our property. It belonged to family friends."

The agent's head cocked. "You think your brother felt safe there?"

She knew he'd felt safe there. She'd felt safe there, too. Their father had always been on his best behavior at the lake house. *Because others had been there to watch.* "He was always safe there. It was the one place where Kyle knew he wouldn't be hurt."

"Hurt?" Joshua jumped on that word.

Don't tell him about your father. Don't tell anyone. Keep those secrets. Her grandfather's voice whispered through her head. He still haunted her. "It was a happier time," Kennedy said carefully. "But it wasn't our land."

"Who did it belong to?" Remy wanted to know.

"Connor's family. Connor Wise. I don't know, um, I think it still might belong to him, but Connor moved away years ago, and Kyle would know that. Kyle would know that no one would be there. He'd know—"

"It's isolated?" Remy demanded.

"Yes. It's the only house on Lake Bevens. No one else is around for miles." *No one would hear the screams.*

The agent's hand hit the side of the vehicle. "Could be the place. I'll mobilize the search team." He whirled away. "Let's go! Let's—"

"Why is this lake house so special?" Remy's voice was low.

She looked into his dark eyes. "Our father was good at the lake house. Always on his best behavior." The place had just clicked for her when Joshua talked about a *safe* location. "Kyle told me once that he always felt safe at the Wise's lake house. It was because our father didn't show anyone outside of the family what he was really like. When we were with the Wise family, we knew our father would keep up the appearance of being…" Her voice trailed away. *Good.* "You don't let the outside world see your darkness." Not if you were a Clarke, you didn't.

Remy cranked the car. "Tell me how to get there."

***

Search lights flashed in the distance. She wasn't in the car, not this time. Kennedy stood near the vehicle's hood, her arms wrapped around her stomach as she waited for the cops to come out of the house. They'd gotten permission to search the property—they'd called Connor and he'd immediately given the authorities full access. The moon hung heavily in the sky, its image reflecting in the dark surface of the lake. Lights blazed inside of the lake house, and voices rose and fell.

"We spent Fourth of July here each summer when we were growing up," she said, her gaze sliding over the familiar structure of the house.

A lifetime ago. She'd been a different person back then.

Her gaze sharpened as she stared at the dock.

She'd gotten her first kiss on that dock. Connor had kissed her. Told her that he'd love her forever.

Forever hadn't lasted very long.

"I want to help search," Kennedy said as she squared her shoulders. "Do you think—"

"I think they're not going to let you step so much as a foot closer to that place." He took off his coat and put it around her shoulders. "We have to give them time to do their job."

She pulled the coat closer. The lake house was huge. Not some tiny little vacation spot. From her youth, she remembered the place having at least ten bedrooms. In the top of the house, there was an attic that stretched forever. Below the main level, the lake house even had an old basement—a walk-out basement because the land slanted as it slid away from the cabin. They were an hour away from New Orleans and on much higher ground. The first time she'd visited the lake house, she'd remembered being scared of the basement. They didn't have basements in New Orleans, not like that. And she'd thought the basement was so spooky and dark.

She'd played hide and seek in the lake house. So many times. Kyle had once hid from her so well that she'd been sure she'd never find him.

Actually, she *hadn't* found him. She'd looked for over three hours, and she'd never discovered his hiding place. He'd finally just appeared, laughing and telling her that he had a secret.

He had so many secrets that she'd never suspected.

Too many.

Joshua Morgan strode down the curving porch steps. He turned on his flashlight, shooting it toward the woods in a quick sweep. Dogs barked in the distance.

The dogs were searching the woods.

"He didn't find Kyle," she murmured.

Remy eased closer to her side.

The FBI agent headed toward them. "Connor Wise said he hasn't used this place in over three years." He stopped right near Remy. "But I found food in the fridge. Someone has sure as hell been here."

Remy swore.

"The team searched the place from top to bottom. If Kyle was in there, he's gone now. Hiding someplace else or —"

"I'd like to go inside," Kennedy blurted.

Agent Morgan shared a long look with Remy. Why was he looking at Remy? She'd been the one to speak.

"Uh, excuse me?" Kennedy cleared her throat. "I want to go in. I know that house. Most of the nooks and crannies. Maybe I can find something Kyle left behind."

The flashlight was aimed at the ground. "You think you can find something my team missed?" Agent Morgan seemed doubting.

"Agent Morgan —"

"Joshua," he growled. "At this point, call me Joshua."

Kennedy cleared her throat. "Contact Connor Wise. He can give you permission to take me inside if this is some sort of — of legal issue." She had no idea how that worked.

Joshua let out a sigh. "I don't see how you going in—"

"Let her go." Remy's voice held the edge of authority. "She won't touch anything. I'll make sure of it. But let her walk through the house. Maybe she'll see something that her brother left behind. If he was there, he could have left some sort of message for her."

Wind blew against Kennedy, raising goosebumps on her skin.

"I'm guessing *you'll* want to be at her side?" Joshua asked.

"Damn straight. That's exactly where I intend to stay."

Joshua nodded. "Fine, but neither of you touch anything, got me? And I stay with you both at all times." He pointed at her with his left hand. "You see something that sticks out at you, you tell me, got it?"

She nodded. "Got it." When he turned away, her breath left her in a fast rush. She reached for Remy's hand and curled her fingers with his. "Thank you," she murmured.

Remy leaned toward her. For a moment, she thought he might kiss her, but he stopped. His gaze searched hers. "Anything that sticks out at you, anything that reminds you of your brother, say something. No holding back."

Did he really think she would? "A woman is missing. I want to find her." She had to find the detective.

Didn't he trust her?

Joshua called out to them, and they hurried forward. The porch steps creaked beneath her feet. A wide, sprawling porch. She and Kyle and Connor had often sat on that porch, staring at the lake for so long.

A cop approached Joshua. "Should we search the lake? See if there are any bodies in there?"

Oh, my God.

Her head jerked as she looked over at the black, still water.

For a moment, the past pulled at her.

"Want to go skinny dipping, Kennedy?" Connor flashed her a wide smile. At fourteen, he'd already been muscled and strong and so charming with his dimples. *"I'll lose my clothes if you do."*

Kyle had shoved him back. *"Jesus, man! I'm right here! Stop trying to get my sister naked before I have to deck your ass."*

"I was just kidding." A wink to Kennedy. *"Mostly."*

Joshua cleared his throat. "Are you coming in?"

She nodded. "Yes. Yes, I'm coming."

He held the door open for her. She hurried inside, with Remy right at her heels. As soon as she crossed the threshold...

So many memories. I was a different person here.

"Don't touch anything," Joshua blasted. "Just look around. If you see something that belongs to your brother, tell me."

The furniture was different. The pictures on the walls were different. She edged closer to one picture, surprised to see that it was...her. Sitting on the dock, smiling in her bathing suit as Kyle wrapped an arm around her shoulder. His smile was just as wide as hers.

Why had Connor kept that picture?

They moved through the house slowly. Checking the bedrooms. One by one. The covers in one of the bedrooms had been shoved back.

It was the bedroom she'd used when they'd visited the cabin.

Who's been sleeping in my bed? She cleared her throat. "This was my room. I mean, the guest room that I always used."

A crime scene tech was snapping photos of the bed.

A shiver slid over Kennedy.

Remy guided her down the hallway. He started to take her up the stairs.

"No." Something nagged at her. This place...so long ago...*Hide and seek.* "I want to see the basement." Her head turned toward him.

"When we were kids, Kyle always hid in the basement."

Because he'd liked the dark.

Her hand rose and pressed to her heart.

She'd liked the dark, too. It was easier to hide in the dark.

Joshua led them down the narrow staircase that led to the basement. Remy was a dark, strong presence behind her. "You okay?" The low rumble of his words reached her ears.

She gave a quick nod. She was fine. Better than Amanda Jackson. *Where are you? Where would he take you?*

The lights were on in the basement. All of the old boxes and toys and furniture that had been stored down there when she was a kid — they were all gone. Everything had been cleared out. *Everything.*

"He's not hiding down here." Joshua tilted his head. "There's not a damn thing down here —"

Actually, there was still *one* thing down there that had been in the house when she'd been a kid. "The bookshelf." A large, towering shelf that covered the far wall. From floor to ceiling, the shelf used to be packed with old books that had belonged to Connor's father. Dusty, faded books.

The books were gone.

She hurried to the shelf. Almost touched it, but Remy caught her hand.

"No touching, remember?" he muttered. His fingers curled around hers.

Her head turned so that she was staring into his dark eyes. "There is something we're missing," she said, sure of it. Absolutely sure. "When we were kids, Kyle could hide in this basement for hours. I never found him. I always thought that maybe—maybe there was some hidden space down here. Some place I missed."

Remy lifted a brow. "You think there's a secret room down here?"

When he said it out loud, it seemed crazy. But… "Why is the bookshelf still here? Can we…can we move it? Just to check?"

Remy glanced at Joshua. Remy's head inclined.

"Get back," Joshua ordered. He called for assistance from the techs. A few moments later, they were carefully moving the shelf. She held her breath as they backed away and she saw—

A wall. Just a wall.

With his gloved hand, Joshua rapped on the wall. He checked the surface, looking for any sort of break or give but—

"It's just a wall," she said, as her shoulders sagged. Jesus, had she really thought this was some Scooby-Doo shit? That there was a secret passage in the basement? Was that how crazy and desperate she'd become? Kennedy shook her head.

"We'll get the house plans from Connor," Joshua announced as he backed away from the wall. "If there are any hidden spaces, we'll find them."

But they weren't finding any hidden space then. They weren't — *"Kyle!"* His name just broke from her. Maybe something inside of her broke. Past and present collided as the pain inside of her exploded. *Her brother — a killer? Lies. So many lies.* The detective was missing. The world was a river of blood. The murders wouldn't stop.

Her brother was missing. He was lost. He was hiding?

For a moment, she was a kid again. Standing in the dark, dusty area, spinning round and round, frustration boiling inside of her. *"Kyle, come out!"* She'd been seven. She'd been nine. She'd been thirteen. *"Where are you? This isn't funny any longer!"*

The past and present merged.

Kennedy found herself whirling around. Staring at the walls. Staring at *nothing.* "Come out, Kyle!" Kennedy cried out, her heart absolutely breaking. *"This isn't funny!* Come out, come out —"

"Wherever you are," Remy finished roughly. His arms closed around her. "Baby, stop."

She didn't want to stop. If she screamed loud enough, long enough, then maybe —

Tap.

Kennedy stilled.

Tap.

"What in the fuck?" Remy jerked her back. He shoved her behind him and stared down at the floor.

Tap.

That sound was coming from beneath them. Impossible. There…there wasn't anything beneath them. They were on the bottom level of the house.

Weren't they?

Joshua crouched near the slats in the floor. "Where's that sound coming from?"

"Maybe plumbing?" one of the uniforms said.

Tap.

It wasn't plumbing. Her heart was about to surge out of her chest. "He always hid somewhere when we were kids. I-I couldn't find him. He laughed. Said it was a secret."

"We need to rip up this floor!" Remy snapped.

Joshua's head whipped up. "We don't have authority to—"

The taps stopped.

"Look for a groove in the floor," Joshua directed the cops. "Some sort of switch. Something. If anything is beneath this level, I want to know about it."

Footsteps rushed on the stairs. "Agent Morgan!" An out-of-breath cop heaved. "The owner of the house is here. He wants to speak to you!"

"Send him down here," Remy barked. The guy was giving orders to the FBI and the cops, and Kennedy blinked, caught a bit off-guard. But then Remy added, "If anything is beneath this level, he'll know."

Joshua gave a nod toward the young cop. "Bring him."

Her hands twisted in front of her. Why had the tapping stopped?

Two uniforms were going over every inch of the floor.

"Could be nothing," Joshua announced, his brows pulled low. "Houses make noises, they settle."

Remy took Kennedy's hands in his. "Call him again," he urged her.

Her lashes fluttered as she stared at him. "What?"

"Scream for your brother again."

She licked her lips. "Kyle?"

"Say it louder," Remy ordered, a muscle jerking in his jaw. "*Scream* it like you did before."

She stared at him, her heart aching.

Footsteps pounded on the stairs. Her head turned, and she locked eyes with Connor Wise.

Handsome, charming Connor. He hadn't changed much since she'd last seen him a few years ago. His face was a little harder, but his eyes were still the deep green she remembered. His brown hair was shorter, his body more muscled. He wore a suit coat and dress pants. He looked rich and successful, and he stared at her as if she were a ghost from his past.

She was.

"*Kennedy.*" Connor immediately surged toward her as he left the stairs.

Remy turned to face him, but he kept his grip on Kennedy's hands. "What's beneath this level?"

Connor drew up short. His gaze darted to Remy and Kennedy's joined hands. "What? Uh, nothing. This is the basement level."

Joshua paced closer to Connor. Flashed his badge. "I'm Special Agent Joshua Morgan. We spoke on the phone."

A bit dazed, Connor nodded.

Joshua's lips thinned. "There's not a single thing beneath the floor? You're sure?"

"I-I—"

Remy's hold tightened on Kennedy. "Call for your brother. *Now.*"

She took a breath. "*Kyle!*"

Connor flinched.

Silence.

"Uh," Connor began, looking and sounding uncertain, "I'm not sure—"

Tap.

A tap that had come from *below* them.

"Give us permission to rip up the floor," Joshua barked.

"What? Why—"

Tap.

Connor's eyes widened. "A wine cellar. Shit. My dad told me...when the house was first built, he tried to put in a wine cellar but the ground was too damp and he had to seal the area up before the—"

"*Give us permission!*" Joshua's voice snapped like a whip.

Connor nodded. "Go. You have permission!"

Remy pulled Kennedy closer to him.

"Take her back upstairs." Joshua waved his hand toward Kennedy. "Secure her outside."

She didn't need to be secured. "Kyle hid here when he was a child." Now her gaze flew to Connor. "There has to be a way to access the area." An easier way than ripping up the boards. Some kind of mechanism that opened things. Her gaze darted around the room. Taking in the blank walls, looking for some sign. *Anything.* "Connor, help me!"

But he just gaped at her, as if he didn't understand.

"Take her upstairs," Joshua ordered again.

"She's staying right the hell here," Remy snapped. "The only reason you know to search down there is because of her."

The FBI agent didn't argue with Remy. He also didn't look happy. "Then keep her back, understand? Or you're both out."

Everything happened so fast after that. The cops couldn't find any openings in the floor so they brought in crow bars. They yanked up the slats, they tore into the floor, and she couldn't take her eyes off them as—

"*Stop!*" Joshua's voice rang out.

Tap.

Now that the slats were gone, Kennedy could see the opening of some kind of metal, trap door. Long, narrow. Joshua shoved the cops out of his way. He drew his gun and flipped open the door.

The scent of stale air and human waste drifted to them. She tensed and suddenly, Remy wasn't holding her hand any longer. She was desperately gripping *him*.

"Stairs," Joshua bit out. "I see stairs leading below. Dark as fuck down there." He yanked out his flashlight. Joshua glanced over at Remy. His eyes narrowed. "Keep her there." And then he disappeared into the dark, yawning opening.

***

Joshua crept down the too-thin stairs. His nostrils burned from the acrid smell, and he was so damn afraid of what he'd find down there.

The place was small. So tight that he felt claustrophobic. But when he hit the last step —

"H-help…"

The voice was weak, hoarse. His light hit the figure huddled on the floor. A man in dirty, blood-stained clothes. A man who had a long, thick length of chain around his right ankle. As Joshua watched, the man weakly lifted what looked like a huge rock, and he hit it against the chain, making a hollow, metallic —

Tap.

Joshua lifted his light, shining it on the man's face. "Fuck."

The guy flinched away. *"K-Kennedy…"*

They'd just found Kyle Clarke. A man who'd been chained up and held captive in a hole. He looked like hell, his body shuddering, and Joshua knew there was no damn way this poor bastard could have abducted Amanda Jackson.

So, if he didn't take her…who did?

CHAPTER ELEVEN

Joshua's head appeared once more. Immediately, his gaze went to Kennedy. Kennedy, then Remy — and Remy clearly read the message in his partner's eyes even before the other guy ordered, "Get all civilians out, *now*. I need bolt cutters, and I need a medic team."

Kennedy tried to surge forward, but Remy hauled her back. "No, baby. *No*."

"Kyle's alive," Joshua said flatly. "But you have to get out of here. *Now*. Take her upstairs, Remy. Get her out of here."

She fought him, but Remy just tightened his hold on her. He knew those two, powerful words — *Kyle's alive* — would be ripping through her. But the FBI had a job to do. He had a job to do. And Remy had to follow orders. When she fought him, he just lifted her into his arms.

"Remy, no! That's my brother! That's my — "

He carried her up the stairs. Kept a tight hold on her. He wasn't letting her go. He didn't quite understand what was happening. Wasn't sure that anyone did. But priority one was getting her out of there so the others could do their work.

Connor hurried out with them. He was right behind Remy the whole time. They cleared the first floor. Remy climbed down the porch steps. He took Kennedy back toward his car —

"You bastard! Let me go, now!" she screamed.

He put her on her feet. He didn't let go. "They have a job to do, Kennedy."

Blue lights swirled around them. They lit up her face, showing Kennedy's clear rage. "He's my brother!"

"And you heard Agent Morgan. Your brother is alive, but you have to let the authorities do their job. Let them get him out." He had no idea what condition Kyle Clarke might be in. Joshua's expression had been too closed for him to get any clue.

But this case — shit, it had just taken a turn he hadn't expected.

Bolt cutters?

All signs had pointed to Kyle Clarke being the killer. So how the hell had he gotten locked beneath the freaking floor? How long had he been down there?

"Kennedy, I'm so sorry." That was the other guy's voice — Connor Wise. He surged forward and lifted a hand toward Kennedy, as if he'd touch her, comfort her. But he stopped. Connor stared at her with torment on his face. "I had no idea that Kyle was here, I *swear*."

Remy didn't like the way the guy was looking at her. With torment, yeah, but there was more. It was in the way he said her name. Too much longing. Too much emotion.

Remy put his body between them. "Your freaking house — and a man was just found sealed away beneath your floor. What in the hell?"

Connor scrubbed a hand over his face. "I haven't been here in *years*. The place holds too many painful memories for me. I stayed away. I-I didn't know." His head craned so he could see Kennedy. *"I didn't know."*

"You didn't know about the secret pit in the basement?" Remy fired at him. "Or you didn't know that a man was being held captive down there? Didn't know what, exactly? Explain this shit to me."

"I didn't know *anything*," Connor threw back. His hand dropped and clenched into a fist. "Kennedy, I'm sorry. God, I should have gone to you when I first heard about Kyle. I thought you'd hate me, thought you'd never want me close, but I should have come anyway."

Now why in the hell would she hate him?

"I wanted to come to you," Connor added. "I was even going to that damn gala a few nights back…"

Voices rose behind him. Remy turned and saw a stretcher being rushed into the house.

Kennedy tried to surge toward the house. Hating it, hating what he had to do, Remy grabbed tight to her. "No, baby, no."

She stared up at him with tears in her eyes.

No one spoke. Didn't say a word, and the silence ticked by far too painfully before the EMTs were back. They came running out of the house, carrying the stretcher, carrying the man on it, and as soon as Remy got a look at the battered figure on it—

Kyle Clarke.

A thin, bleeding, wreck of a man.

A chain hung from his ankle. *Chained?* Hell, no wonder Joshua had requested bolt cutters.

A sob broke from Kennedy. *"Kyle!"*

Her brother's head jerked toward her. His hand lifted, as if he could reach his sister.

The EMTs loaded him in the back of the ambulance.

Remy wrapped his arms around Kennedy's stomach, holding her back and trapping her against him as she struggled with all of her might. She wanted her brother more than anything, and he could feel the pain splintering through her.

The case had just changed. *Everything* had changed, and her pain was tearing his heart apart.

Joshua hurried from the house. He pointed to some uniforms, and then they were all closing in on Remy, Connor, and Kennedy.

"We have questions." Joshua's hands went to his hips. "You're all going back to New Orleans. Going to be held for questioning right now."

"What?" Connor's voice was sharp. "I'm cooperating! I didn't *know* – "

"A man was just found captive in *your* house, Mr. Wise. A man who—judging from the conditions down there—has been held for weeks. You can bet your ass the FBI has questions for you. A whole lot of them."

Connor stepped back. "I'm getting a lawyer."

Yeah, not at all surprising.

Remy's arms still curled around Kennedy's stomach.

Joshua's gaze darted to her. "You're going to interrogation."

"Again?" Her hoarse whisper. "No. No, I'm going after that ambulance. I'm going to the hospital. I have to see my brother – "

Joshua's face was grim. "You're not talking to him. You're not saying a word to him, not until the FBI has a chance to speak with Kyle Clarke first. A detective is still missing. Women are *dead*. And you are right in the middle of everything."

"You can't still think my brother is involved! That I'm involved?" Frantically, Kennedy shook her head. "Kyle is the victim! If he was held captive this whole time—"

Joshua motioned to the cops near him. "Take her into custody."

Remy tightened his hold on her.

"You can't do this!" Kennedy cried out. "You can't—"

"Damn right they can't." The hard words burst from Connor, and then he was there. Moving too close to Kennedy even as Remy still held her. "I'll take care of this." His eyes were on her. "I'll fix it, Kennedy, I promise. I'll get my lawyers to have us both out of their custody in no time. You'll see your brother. *I will fix this.*"

***

Dawn had come and gone. The night had been one hell ride after another. Remy stood in the FBI's field office, his gaze directed through the one-way mirror that showed Kennedy. Dark shadows lined her eyes, and her shoulders slumped. An empty coffee cup sat in front of her.

She'd been kept there overnight. Questioned again and again.

And he'd just watched.

Watched as a hard fury had knifed through him. Watched as rage and guilt ate away at him.

The door squeaked open behind him. He glanced back and saw Joshua. Hell, the guy looked exhausted, too. They all did. Cops and agents had kept searching for Amanda Jackson all night. They'd turned up nothing.

Was she even still alive?

"We have a very big problem," Joshua announced.

Shit. "Her brother—" Remy began as his stomach clenched. *Don't be dead!* Joshua had been at the hospital, waiting for Kyle Clarke to be conscious enough to speak and tell them what the hell had happened to him. If Kyle had died, then Kennedy—

"Yeah, he's the problem." Joshua paced toward the one-way mirror. He stared through the glass at Kennedy. "Still no lawyer for her? I thought that Connor guy was getting her one."

She didn't need Connor. "Kennedy can afford her own lawyer. She just doesn't want one. She wanted to answer our questions." He blew out a hard breath. *Not our.* Because he hadn't been in the room with her. He'd just watched while other agents went at her, again and again. Detective Brock Mayo had wanted a chance in the room with her, but Remy had refused the guy. Mayo was too on edge. Remy didn't want the guy near her. "She wants her brother," he gritted out. "She needs to see him."

"And I need to ask you a question." Joshua's voice was off—too stilted.

Remy narrowed his eyes.

"When Kennedy got the call from her brother, did you *hear* any word spoken to her?"

"No, I told you this already, man. When I put it on speaker, the caller just hung up."

Joshua's mouth became a thin line.

"What the hell is it?" Remy demanded. If he didn't get to Kennedy soon, Remy felt like he might go insane. He needed to touch her. Hold her. The woman looked far too fragile, and his self-control was going straight to hell.

Joshua started to answer, but stopped. He seemed to gather his thoughts and finally muttered, "I need to talk with Kennedy."

The guy turned away, starting to head out.

Remy grabbed his arm. "I'm going in, too."

Joshua stiffened. "Look, I'm not so sure that's a good—"

"I got off the phone with FBI Brass five minutes ago. I was just waiting to brief you." As per protocol with a partner. "My original goal was to find her brother. To see if she had intel to lead us to him. We found the guy. *That* part of my job is over. Now all of our resources are to be directed to finding Detective Jackson." He blew out a hard breath. "I've been told that an undercover persona is no longer needed. I'm free to drop the ruse."

And face Kennedy's fury.

"We don't know who the killer is." Joshua's eyes glinted behind his glasses. "And right now, I don't trust your lady."

"She's *not* mine." When Kennedy found out the truth, she never would be. "And as far as going into the interrogation room is concerned, it's not your call. I'm the senior agent here."

"Fine. Do it. Come in the interrogation room. But *listen* to what I have to say in there, okay? Hell, let's both listen to what she has to say. Because I think there is more going on here. More she could know." A moment later, Joshua yanked open the door, and they stalked to the interrogation room.

As soon as Remy entered, Kennedy rose to her feet. Some of the worry seemed to leave her face as her eyes latched onto him. "Remy, please, have you heard…Kyle—is he—"

"Sit back down, Ms. Clarke," Joshua instructed curtly.

Her lower lip trembled. "Please tell me that my brother is okay. I-I just need to know—"

Her pain knifed right through Remy. "*Tell her.*" He crossed to her side, drawn to her, helpless. He wanted to pull her into his arms, but he didn't dare touch her.

What in the hell was happening to him? He never reacted like this on a case. Sure as hell not with anyone he'd worked with while undercover.

I should have kept my hands off her. I'm compromised. She's gotten beneath my skin.

Joshua exhaled on a long sigh. "Your brother is in stable condition at Our Lady of Grace. He was malnourished and severely dehydrated. When I left, he was hooked to IVs. He'd suffered broken ribs and multiple contusions, but the doctors believe he will make a full recovery."

Her shoulders sagged. "I have to talk to him. I have to—"

"Talking *is* the tricky part." Joshua advanced toward the small table that sat in the middle of the room. "I need you to explain something to me. You got a phone call from your brother, correct? When you were staying at Remy's place?"

She cast a quick, nervous glance Remy's way. "Yes."

"What did your brother say?"

"He said he needed help."

Joshua nodded. "And did he identify himself? Did he say, 'This is Kyle and—'"

"No, he didn't! I recognized his voice! I know my own brother's voice. He must have gotten access to a phone and was able to call me. I'm so glad he did. If he hadn't, then we wouldn't have—"

"His voice was totally normal on the phone?" Joshua interrupted.

Where was Joshua going with these questions?

"Y-yes." She slanted another confused look at Remy, then darted her stare to Joshua.

His gaze was ice-cold. "That's impossible. Your brother can barely speak above a whisper. The doctors said it's probably because he screamed so long that he damaged his vocal cords. I just left the hospital. I *heard* him myself. His voice is gone. It will come back, in time, but for now, Kyle Clarke can barely get a word out. That's why he was banging a rock against the chain in order to get our attention. He couldn't call out, not loud enough for us to hear him."

She backed up a step. Put a hand to her head. "I heard his voice. It was him on the phone."

Suspicion filled Joshua's eyes. "You're the only one who heard him."

Dammit. Now he knew exactly where Joshua was going with these questions. "Kennedy..." Remy reached for her. His hand closed around her shoulder.

A shudder shook her body. "It was his voice. I *know* I heard his voice."

"It's just not possible," Joshua stated flatly.

Her breath heaved in and out. "Then who did I hear?"

"According to your brother, Kyle discovered his fiancée's body. He was hit from behind, and he woke up, chained in that hole. He wasn't even aware of how much time had passed. Kyle said he hadn't left his prison. Hadn't seen anyone. Food was tossed down to him every few days. Water came in from some sort of pipe. He was there, the whole time, and he swore he didn't call you."

Kennedy's bright gaze shot to Remy. "He did." But she didn't sound as certain now.

"Perhaps it was a recording," Remy gritted out. "Someone had a recording of her brother's voice—"

"The man who took him." Her eyes had gone huge at his words. "That's who you think called me?" Her gaze flew from Remy to Joshua, then back to Remy. "But why? As soon as we got that call, I knew Kyle was alive. That's when the pieces all fell into place. That's when we found him."

"Yes," Joshua agreed. "Because I think that's what the killer wanted. I think the killer wanted Kyle to be found. He was battered and bloody. He'd tried his damn hardest to get out of that pit. Broken his own ribs. He was barely conscious when we got to him. The killer didn't want him to die. Not Kyle. Which makes me think the killer had a connection to your brother. To you."

Her hands clenched and unclenched. "Stop it." She stepped closer to Remy. "Let's get out of here, right now."

The case had changed. He was supposed to
drop his undercover persona. Supposed to tell
her the truth now that the objective had been met
and her brother found.

"He thinks it's me." Anger vibrated in her
voice as she pointed at Joshua. "That I faked the
phone call? That I had my own brother
imprisoned? This is so ridiculous. I've been
cooperating, but I'm sick of the accusations. I'm
sick of—"

"You have an alibi for Amanda Jackson's
abduction. The FBI does not think that you are
responsible for her disappearance." Remy kept
his voice careful. The Bureau wasn't looking at
her for this crime. She'd misunderstood what
Joshua was saying.

Baby, you aren't the threat.

The Bureau thought that she was being
targeted. They thought she was in danger. And
he wasn't going to let her wind up like her
brother, held captive in some godforsaken pit.

Her long lashes flickered.

"I think you're a target," Joshua told her. "I
believe you've been the end game all along."

She licked her lips. "I'm ready to leave." Her
gaze searched his. "Remy, will you please take
me out of here?"

"Yes." God, yes, he would. "But first…"

He needed to spit the words out. Just damn
well *tell her.*

First, baby, you need to know that I'm not a PI. I'm a Fed. I arranged our first meeting. I manipulated you from the word go because the Bureau thought your brother was a killer. Then we found him chained like an animal, and everything has changed. Now, I really am here to protect you.

"I want to see my brother. I *have* to see him." She turned her head. Shifted all of her attention on Joshua. "Is the FBI going to stop me?"

"No." He shook his head.

Remy could hear the thunder of his heartbeat in his ears. He knew what came next. "They won't stop you, but they are going to insist you have a guard with you. Someone to watch you."

"Because they think I'm a threat!"

"No, baby, because you are in danger." He took her hands in his. "We need to talk. Alone. Now."

A furrow appeared between her brows. Her lips parted, but in the next moment, before she could utter a word, the door flew open. A man in a suit—a perfectly pressed suit and tie—stormed inside. His hair was slicked back from his forehead, and he gripped a leather briefcase. "My client is done here. You've held her captive far too long."

"Who the hell are you?" Joshua snarled as he swung toward the guy.

"Dudley Richardson, Esquire." He pulled out a card with a casual flick of his wrist. "I'm Ms.

Clarke's attorney, and this unwarranted questioning is at an end."

Connor Wise appeared behind him, a dark growth of shadow on his jaw. "Come on, Kennedy, it's time to go."

Oh, hell, no. "She's not going anywhere with you."

Dudley looked him up and down. "And who are you?"

"He's my PI," Kennedy said quickly. Then she turned toward the attorney. "And you are *not* representing me. I didn't hire you."

"I hired him." Connor hurried toward her, worry clear to see on his face. "You've been here for hours, and they aren't letting you leave. Don't you see what they're doing? The Press crucified you for weeks. *Because the Feds let them.* This has been a set-up from the beginning. You have—"

"I've answered their questions because I don't have anything to hide." Her voice was clear.

"She *has* been forthcoming," Joshua allowed as his brows rose. "Unlike you, Mr. Wise. Kyle Clarke was found on *your* property—"

Connor's face flushed. "Property I haven't used in years! I told you that. I told you—"

Dudley put his hand on Connor's chest. "Not another word."

Connor's lips clamped together.

Dudley gave a Cheshire cat smile as he rounded on Joshua. "Now, who are you, exactly? You're the only one in here that I see wearing a badge so…"

Joshua bit out, "Special Agent Joshua Morgan."

"Agent Morgan, my client gave you full access to his property. He had no idea Mr. Clarke was being held at the lake house. He's horrified and wants the man who hurt his friend to be brought to justice."

Connor pulled away from Dudley and moved to stand in front of Kennedy. "I should have come back to you sooner." His gaze burned with emotion. "I thought you didn't want me anywhere near you. After what happened, shit, *I'm sorry.* But I'm here now, and I'm going to help you. You can count on me. I *won't* let you down again."

She reached for Remy's hand. "Thank you, but I don't need you to get me an attorney, Connor. I can afford one on my own."

Remy's fingers tightened on hers.

Her voice remained flat as Kennedy continued, "I'm going to see my brother now. I-I had Henry go to the hospital while I was being questioned. He's been in the waiting room the whole time and—"

Surprise flashed on Connor's face. "Henry is still with you?"

"He's family. He's always stayed with us. When I got to the station, I called him. I wanted someone who cared about Kyle to be at the hospital. I didn't want him to be alone again." She swallowed. "But I've done my part. I want my brother. *Now.*"

There was pain in her voice, and it was knifing through Remy. Screw this. The FBI had asked their questions, and she deserved to see Kyle. She'd done nothing but cooperate.

"Get out of the lady's way," he ordered, voice turning lethal.

Connor frowned at him.

Joshua backed up.

So did the lawyer. "Are my services not needed?"

Remy didn't answer him. Neither did Kennedy. Remy guided Kennedy out of that room. He kept her at his side. The lies would come to an end, but he'd tell her the truth when they were alone. Not when there was an audience watching their every move. And the thing that mattered most now — it was getting Kennedy to her brother.

She needed him.

And Remy — hell, he just needed to make some of the pain in her beautiful eyes vanish. He didn't like her pain. He wanted it gone.

Remy was starting to think he might do just about anything to take away her pain.

CHAPTER TWELVE

Her brother was pale and still. Tubes ran to his body—an IV. Monitors were lined up near his bed. The machines gave a steady *beep, beep* beside him. She crept toward the bed, her body icy as chill bumps skated over her. Remy was right behind her. A quiet, steady force.

Kennedy glanced back over her shoulder, and her gaze darted to the cop who waited by the door. Her brother was being guarded constantly, and she was glad.

He was gone for weeks. I left him in that place for weeks.

As she drew closer, she saw that Kyle's lips were cracked. His hands were bandaged. He looked so broken as he lay there, far too thin. Her tough brother. The fighter.

She wanted to reach out to him, but she was afraid to touch him. Afraid that if she did, he might vanish.

But his lashes fluttered, as if he sensed her, and his eyes opened. Eyes exactly like her own locked on Kennedy. His cracked lips parted.

"Kennedy…" A bare whisper. So hoarse and rough.

She tried to smile for him. She would *not* let her tears fall. The last thing she wanted to do was add to her brother's pain. "You're going to be okay."

His bandaged hand lifted toward her. Careful now, she reached out to him. Her fingers curled around his wrist because she just needed to touch him. To make sure he was real. Alive.

"You're…safe?" Each word seemed to be a struggle for him. Agent Morgan had been right. Kyle's voice was so weak and shattered.

Then how did I hear him on the phone?

She cleared her throat. "I'm fine. Got my very own bodyguard to keep me safe." Her gaze flickered toward a silent Remy.

A muscle flexed in Remy's jaw. His hard stare was directed straight at her brother.

"Knew…f-find…m-me…"

Kyle couldn't know that she'd doubted him. That she'd let the fear win, and she'd thought her brother was a killer. That would rip him apart. "Do you know who took you?"

Kyle gave a slow shake of his head. *"N-never…s-s-saw…"* His eyes squeezed shut. "S-Stacey?"

Pain twisted inside of her. "I buried her, Kyle. I'm so sorry."

The machines beeped louder.

"You're going to be okay," she assured him quickly. "You're going to get stronger, and you're going to get out of here. You're going to—"

His eyes were sagging closed.

A nurse bustled inside. She had a Santa cap on her head, but a fierce frown on her face. "My patient can't handle a high stress level right now. With the medication that he's on, he needs to sleep." She stared pointedly at Kennedy. "You'll have to come back and see him later."

But I just got in here! I just got him back. The last thing she wanted to do was leave. She wanted to stay right there. Not move at all.

"His welfare has to come first," the nurse added. "I'm sure you understand."

Dammit. *Dammit!* Yes, she did. But she also just wanted to cling tightly to her brother. Kennedy bent and her lips brushed over Kyle's cheek. He'd been in hell. She'd left him there. "I'm sorry."

His eyes flashed open. He stared straight at her. *"Don't tell..."*

"Kyle?"

He blinked. His head turned, and he looked at Remy. Frowned. *"Who...?"*

"That's my friend, Remy St. Clair." So much more than a friend. Right then, he felt like her life-line.

"Protect..." The word broke. Kyle sagged back against the mattress.

"Don't worry," Remy's voice was strong and clear. "I won't let anything happen to your sister, I promise you that."

Kyle's eyelids were sagging once more, but he managed a nod.

"Baby, we need to go." Remy wrapped an arm around her shoulders.

She didn't want to go, though. She wanted to stay and protect her brother. To make sure he was alive and safe. She couldn't just walk away now.

"You're dead on your feet," Remy continued as the nurse glowered. "You've been up all night. Let's get you home. Get you some rest. Some fresh clothes. Some food."

She couldn't remember when she'd eaten last. And her eyes were bleary from lack of sleep. But it was Kyle in that bed. She couldn't just leave him alone.

I left him alone for weeks in that pit.

Her shoulders straightened. "I'm going to sleep in the chair." Home could wait. She needed to be there. She needed —

"FBI orders," the cop at the door said as he crossed his arms over his chest. "No one stays in the room with the patient."

They were forcing her to leave her brother? When he'd just been found? She felt like screaming. He was all that she had left. Her only family, and for weeks, he'd been trapped.

Guilt ate at her. She should have found him sooner. Dammit, *why* hadn't she?

"Come on, Kennedy. You're exhausted. You can't help your brother if you collapse." Remy took her from the room. They started down the corridor, and she caught sight of Henry's familiar figure. He hurried to her, rushing down the tiled hallway.

"You did it!" A wide grin split his face as Henry pulled Kennedy into his arms. "You brought our boy back!"

She held him as tightly as he held her. Henry had always been a fixture in her life. He'd taught her to throw her first softball. He'd listened when her first boyfriend had broken her heart.

He'd stood by her side when she'd buried Stacey and the whole world had said Kyle was a monster.

"He's hurt so badly, Henry," she whispered as she clung to him. "Why would someone hurt Kyle this way?" She eased back and stared up at him.

The lines on his face appeared deeper. Far more grim. "I don't know."

"I'm taking her home," Remy announced. "The guard will be staying."

"Yeah, yeah, I know he will." Henry glared at the cop. "Guy gave me some song and dance about no one being able to stay inside the hospital room. I told them I was family, but he still only gave me five minutes with Kyle."

The nurse had just exited the hospital room. She sniffed. "It's because the patient's health comes *first*. He should be in ICU, but the Feds insisted on giving him this private room. So, per doctor's orders, his visitors are to be limited until he's recovered more." When her eyes moved to Kennedy, her expression softened — a bit. "Come back and see your brother later. Give him some time to rest. We won't let anything happen to him."

That was her fear — that he'd just disappear again. Vanish on her.

"He's not going anywhere, Kennedy," Remy promised her.

"Damn right." Henry's chin notched up. "I'll be in the waiting room. I'll make sure of it." He pointed to her. "Sweet girl, you need rest. You're swaying. Get some sleep, then come back here. I won't leave."

"But —"

"You were up all night searching for him, weren't you?" Henry pushed.

Yes.

"Sleep. Before you collapse."

She squeezed his hand. "I'll be back in a few hours."

He pressed a kiss to her temple.

Then Remy led her down the hallway. The place smelled of antiseptic. Everything was so white and sterile, and she passed the myriad of rooms in a blur.

When they got in the elevator, Kennedy closed her eyes. She could see the lake house. See the torn slats that had been the wooden floor.

Trapped in there.

If they hadn't found him, would Kyle have died in that hole?

"Baby?"

Holiday music drifted through the speaker in the elevator. Her lashes lifted.

Remy stared tenderly at her. "We're in the parking garage."

She hadn't even realized the elevator had stopped. Dragging up a last bit of energy, she lurched forward. They made it to his car. He buckled her in when she just wanted to sag limply in the seat. A few moments later, Remy was in the driver's seat, and he was taking them away from the hospital.

Things seemed foggy to her. Exhaustion? Shock? She had no clue. She did need to say…

"Thank you."

His fingers tightened on the wheel. "I don't deserve any thanks."

"You do." She'd never be able to repay him.

"You found him, Kennedy. You don't owe me a damn thing."

Her head turned as she stared out the passenger window. "Do you leave now?" She hadn't meant to ask that question, but her gas tank was absolutely empty. She was running on pure fumes, and there was no filter that she could apply to herself. "The case is over. Are we over?"

"The case isn't over. I want to know who the hell put your brother in that hole."

She flinched. "I do, too." Her eyes sagged closed. She just couldn't stay awake any longer. The adrenaline had fled her system. She'd seen her brother. Seen with her own eyes that he was safe, and she was *done.* "I want to find that bastard," Kennedy added, voice slurring. "And I want to kill him."

***

"Baby, wake up."

She forced her eyelids to lift.

"You're home."

She could see the house behind him. But it wasn't home. It never had been. Sometimes, you just stayed in a prison that looked so nice, you never realized it was hell until too late.

Kyle was in prison. He was trapped, and I didn't know.

"Loop your arms around my neck. That's it. Up we go." Remy lifted her into his arms.

He didn't need to do that. She could walk. Maybe. But if he wanted to carry her, well, he could just go for it.

Remy hurried toward the house. Unlocked the entrance with her key. "Tell me the code."

She did. Mumbled it.

Then they were inside. He secured the door even as he kept holding her, and, a moment later, he was taking her up the stairs.

The guy might throw his back out with the Rhett Butler routine. "You don't…"

"I can carry you, baby. I've got this. Let me take care of you."

It was nice to pretend that he would be there to take care of her. To always be there. To share all of her pain and secrets.

"Which room is yours?"

"First…right."

And in moments, they were in her bedroom. He lowered her onto the bed. Frowned down at her. "Sleep or food?"

Both sounded like heaven, but she couldn't keep her eyes open.

"Sleep." He stroked her hair back from her face. "Relax, baby. I'll be here when you open your eyes."

"Promise?"

His fingers slid over her cheek. "I'm not leaving you."

***

Kennedy was out cold. Remy sat on the edge of her bed, his hand still on her cheek. She needed sleep and she needed food, and when she woke up—he'd make sure to feed her the biggest freaking meal she'd ever had.

And after that meal, hell, he'd have to come clean.

She'd try to kick him out of her life. He didn't doubt it for a moment, but it wasn't safe for her to be alone. Her brother was in danger. She was in danger. And Detective Amanda Jackson—she was still out there. Somewhere.

Was Amanda alive? He hoped so. But right then, the only hope the FBI had of finding the detective—Kennedy and her brother were that lead. The killer had reached out to Kennedy. He'd wanted her to know that her brother was alive.

Would he want her to know that Amanda was alive, too?

Kennedy had fallen asleep with her clothes on. He removed her shoes, pulled the covers over her, and then stared down at her as she slept. Exhaustion pulled at him as he watched her. It had been one hell of a night. He needed sleep, but he wasn't going to leave her.

He took off his shoes. Climbed into the bed beside her. Immediately, Kennedy rolled toward him. Her hand rose to press right above his heart.

His eyes closed. He'd rest. Only for a little while. Then he'd check in with Joshua. He'd just get a little bit of sleep first…

***

His eyes flew open, and Remy coughed. His lungs burned, and the acrid scent of smoke—

The scent of smoke?

He jerked upright in the bed. He could see smoke coming from beneath the closed bedroom door. Sonofabitch! He grabbed for Kennedy.

But she wasn't there.

Her side of the bed was empty. What? *"Kennedy!"* No answer.

He ran for the door, almost reached for the knob, but then remembered his training. Panic had been driving him. He pressed a hand to the door, feeling the heat. He grabbed a sheet and covered the doorknob before he twisted it. The door flew open. The top of the stairs was filled with smoke. Black and thick. Remy could hear the crackle of the flames.

He rushed to the banister and looked down. Below him, red and gold flames raged as they stretched their way up the stairs.

Holy shit. *"Kennedy!"*

Why the hell hadn't an alarm gone off? And where was Kennedy? She couldn't be downstairs. She couldn't be—not in those flames. Not her. He covered his mouth and started to—

He saw a shadow from the corner of his eye. He whipped around, and there she was. Standing near an open bedroom. One of the four in that hallway. He ran to her. She didn't move. Didn't cough. Didn't do anything.

Her eyes were wide open, but she stared at him without a single drop of recognition on her face. He grabbed her. *"Kennedy!"*

Her body jolted. She screamed and blinked quickly, her gaze turning desperate in an instant.

"Baby! Baby, it's me!" For a moment there, she'd stared at him with zero recognition.

Her hands rose. Hands stained with black soot. She grabbed him. "What's happening? Why—"

"The house is on fire, and we're getting the hell out of here." But they weren't going downstairs. They had to find another way out. The smoke was rising too fast, thickening around them. Once more, Remy wondered why he didn't hear any alarms going off. The woman had a security system that should have detected smoke and flames, but there was no blaring warning.

Just the hiss and crackle of flames.

He pulled her back toward her bedroom. Remy shoved the door shut and then got some covers to put near the bottom of the door.

"We can go out the balcony," Kennedy told him quickly. "There's a big oak tree nearby, and the branches almost reach the house." She rushed toward her balcony and threw open the doors.

He grabbed their phones and the keys and hurried out behind her, sucking in deep gulps of air, but the smoke was everywhere, dammit. A glance below also showed him that the fire was even worse than he'd suspected. He heard glass shatter as the first-floor windows erupted. "We need to go, *now*."

Unfortunately, the oak tree's massive branches weren't as close as he would have liked. They were going to have to jump.

She climbed onto the wooden balcony railing, and without so much as a moment's hesitation — as if she'd done it a hundred times before — Kennedy leapt onto the outstretched limb of the oak tree. The hanging moss on the tree swayed as the branch slid a bit beneath her weight. She hurried toward the tree's thick trunk, pausing only long enough to glance back. "Come on, Remy! Hurry!"

Well, damn. He jumped after her, his moves one hell of a lot less graceful as he took shelter in the massive tree's branches. They both rushed down the tree as fast as they could, and the heavy bark cut into his arms, but he didn't mind at all. The bite of the bark was a whole lot better than the burn of flames.

When they hit the ground, he pulled her away from the house. The flames were devouring the place, moving so incredibly fast. Glass was all over the ground. And Kennedy didn't have on shoes. Shit. Neither did he. He scooped her into his arms.

"Remy!"

"You're not getting cut! There's too much glass!" He rushed her toward his car. The vehicle was far enough away from the blaze that it would be safe. Remy opened the passenger-side door and settled her inside. When she was safe, he pulled out his phone, dialing nine-one-one and rushing out the address as he told the dispatcher to get the fire trucks out there, as fast as possible.

"It won't be fast enough," Kennedy said softly. Her head tilted as she watched the flames through the windshield. "We're too far away from the city, and that fire is too hot."

She was right. He knew it, but… "God, sweetheart, I'm sorry."

Her home was going down in flames.

"What happened? What were you doing?" Why had she just been standing there?

Kennedy looked down at her hands. "I don't know."

"How did the fire start? How—"

"*I don't know.*" She lifted her head, but Kennedy stared at him, not the fire. "I sleepwalk sometimes, okay? Haven't done it for a very long time. I don't know how I got out of my bedroom."

Glass erupted from a second story window.

The fire was spreading far too fast. And the alarms still hadn't sounded.

Shit. His extra gun was in the glove box. He unlocked the box and pulled it out. "Lock the doors." He pushed the car keys and her phone into her hand. Grabbing her phone had been pure impulse. He'd taken his and snatched hers at the same time.

"What?"

"It's not an accident." He didn't believe that for even one moment. Not with everything that had happened. "Lock the doors. Stay here until I get back."

"Remy?"

"I have to check the perimeter." There were no other cars there. But he was scared as hell, and every instinct he had was screaming at him.

Someone just tried to kill us both. If he hadn't woken up, if she'd been sleepwalking and she'd gone straight into the fire...

He slammed the door, checked his weapon, and Remy made sure she locked the vehicle. He looked at the driveway, the long, winding drive, but he saw nothing. The sun was overhead, but all of the heat came from the fire as it crackled and roared. He rushed around the house, checking the place, looking for any sign of the arsonist who'd set the blaze. *Can't be coincidence.* No alarm? Impossible.

He rushed around the house, made two loops, but didn't see anyone. His gaze narrowed when he caught sight of the nearby guest house. Henry's place. The fire hadn't touched that house, and a cold chill slid through him.

Henry was at the hospital, but as Remy advanced toward the guest house, he realized that the front door hung open.

He slipped inside. "I'm armed!" Remy yelled. "So, come out with your hands up!"

No one came out.

When he took a few more steps, he realized why.

The woman's body was on the floor, her arms at her sides, her legs sprawled around her. Her neck was turned to the side, posed so that she looked just like a broken doll...even as blood pooled beneath her. Blood that poured from the gaping wound at her throat.

Her eyes were covered by a black blindfold, but Remy knew exactly who he was staring at. He'd known as soon as he saw her dark red hair.

Detective Amanda Jackson.

Sonofabitch.

CHAPTER THIRTEEN

They weren't going to be able to save the house. Kennedy knew that even before the first fire truck rushed onto the scene. She huddled in the front seat of Remy's car, her gaze on the blaze as it destroyed her home.

There was soot on her hands. Black ash. And she didn't remember how she'd gotten it on her skin. Had she been downstairs? She didn't remember getting out of bed, much less going down and back up the stairs.

She hadn't walked in her sleep — not for years.

The first fire truck came toward the house with a roar of its sirens. Police cars followed it. Another fire truck zoomed up to the scene. The firefighters leapt into action, running toward the blaze.

Remy still wasn't back. And she was scared. Kennedy shoved open the car door. He'd told her to stay secured, but she had to make certain he was all right. The cops were there now, they could help her. She saw two uniformed officers —

a man and a woman. "I need help!" Kennedy
called to them. "My friend is missing, he's — "

Remy was running toward them. He still
gripped his gun as he rushed forward, and one of
the officers called out, "Freeze!" as she
immediately drew her own weapon and aimed it
at Remy.

"There's a body in the guest house." He
lowered the gun to the ground. He let it go, then
rose, showing he was unarmed with his open
hands. "Call FBI Agent Joshua Morgan. Get him
out here *now*. Tell him that we found Detective
Amanda Jackson."

Oh, God. Kennedy shook her head.

"We need a crime scene team out here. The
Broken Doll Killer left her body for us to find. I
think he fucking set the fire." Rage trembled in
every word that Remy spoke. *"Get FBI Agent
Joshua Morgan here."*

Kennedy's knees nearly buckled. The
detective was in the guest house? *The Broken Doll
Killer left her body for us to find.* "She's dead?"

"Don't let anyone in that guest house," Remy
blasted. "Don't let anyone touch *anything*."

Her gaze whipped toward the guest house.
Henry's home.

The heat from the fire lanced her skin.

The killer had come to her. He'd had the
detective right there. Had Amanda been in the
guest house when they'd arrived? They hadn't

even checked it. What if Amanda had still been alive? When Kennedy had arrived with Remy, she'd just gone inside. Collapsed. *Slept.*

And the other woman had died?

Kennedy's arms wrapped around her stomach.

One of the cops was calling in the murder.

Remy stood there, with his hands in the air, and his face carved from granite.

Behind him, her house burned.

She didn't even feel the tear that slid down her cheek. *I'm in a nightmare, and I just can't wake up.*

***

Water slid down her cheeks. The water from the shower pounded over Kennedy's body as she stood beneath the spray. The firefighters had still been battling the blaze when she'd been driven away. The FBI had arrived. More cops. Crime scene techs.

Detective Amanda Jackson was dead. Her body had been staged in the guest house. As far as the blaze that had consumed Kennedy's home, the authorities suspected arson—she'd heard them talking about different accelerants. Her family's home had burned, and Amanda had died.

And Kennedy had *slept* through that shit.

The shower's rushing water muffled the sob that broke from her. She didn't care about the house. That bitch could burn. It held so many painful memories. And it had always been more like a prison than a home. Cold and clinical. Not warm like the homes of her friends. There'd been no laughter or joy in her house. Just suffocating secrets.

So many. Too many.

What hurt Kennedy was that Amanda Jackson had been murdered. That the detective's life had been taken away by this bastard...*I'm so sorry.* She and the detective had argued, yes, but the other woman had been trying to stop the killer. Amanda hadn't deserved to be tortured and killed. To be thrown away.

No one deserved that.

Sorry. So sorry.

She'd called Henry and told him about the fire. The cops had turned his guest house into a crime scene, so he wouldn't have a place to stay. She'd gotten him a room at a local hotel, but he'd told her he wouldn't be leaving the hospital anytime soon. He'd camped out in the waiting room, and that was where he intended to stay.

The water poured over her. Kennedy turned, letting the water hit her back, and, through the glass door of the shower, she saw the bathroom door open. Remy stepped inside. He stood there a moment, his dark, hot stare on her.

He wouldn't see the tears on her cheeks. Or if he did see them, he'd just think it was water from the shower. He wouldn't understand how gutted she felt. She'd gotten too good at hiding her feelings. At hiding everything.

She didn't want to feel more pain. He could give her pleasure. They could give each other pleasure. So much that it would wipe away everything else.

His face was hard. Savage. He yanked off his shirt. Tossed it to the tiled floor. Discarded his shoes and socks. Shoved down his pants and underwear. His gaze was on her every second. Hot and consuming.

She opened the shower door. Tendrils of steam floated away as he stalked toward her.

Then his hands were on her. His fingers curled over her shoulders as he pushed her back, and his mouth took hers in a hungry, desperate, greedy kiss. She rose onto her toes, trying to get closer to him. Needing him so badly.

He was an escape.

No, no, he was *more.*

His hands slid down her body, stroking and caressing, and she loved his touch. Her body was slick, and the water pounding down just made her feel more sensitive. He backed her up until her body hit the cold, tiled wall of the shower. Remy lifted her, holding her easily as he took one nipple into his mouth.

She moaned at the sensual pull of his lips and tongue. Her hands rose and sank in his hair. The shower was hitting him more than it was her. Remy was blocking the spray with his body. His mouth laved her breast. Licked. Sucked. When she felt the edge of his teeth in a light, sensual bite, her whole body tensed.

He kissed his way to her other breast even as he held her there. Kissed and licked and the desire just beat even hotter in her blood. She wanted him in her. Wanted him driving them both straight to oblivion. *"Remy!"*

His head lifted. His eyes glittered at her. She'd never seen such dark lust in a man's eyes before. Never stared and seen that much focus, that much total need. It only came from Remy.

"I need to fuck you, baby. Right now."

She nodded, more than ready. Right there. Yes. *Yes.*

The head of his cock pushed between her legs, and she wanted him *in* –

"No condom. Shit."

Kennedy almost cried out in frustration as he backed away. *No, no, no –*

He scooped her into his arms. Carried her out even though they were both dripping wet. He paused only long enough to turn off the spray of water, and then they were back in the bedroom. They fell onto the bed, soaking it, and he grabbed a condom from the nightstand drawer. In record time, he had that condom on, and he was back at the entrance to her body. His hands braced on either side of her head. Her legs locked around his hips, and he drove into her.

Remy sank deep with one hard, long thrust.

For a moment, she froze. Time froze. She couldn't look away from him as his cock filled her completely. He withdrew. Thrust.

And she arched up against him. Her nails raked down his back, and it was as if her control had snapped. There was no holding back. Nothing but a clawing, desperate need.

They rolled across the bed, and she rose on top of him. Her hands splayed over his chest. She lifted her hips up, then slammed down, moving faster, wilder, needing this release—no, needing *him* so badly.

His hand slid between their bodies. His fingers strummed over her clit, and the orgasm hit. A tidal wave of pleasure that crashed over her. "Remy!" Her sex gripped him as the contractions of her climax sent her inner muscles clenching around his cock.

He kept thrusting, nearly lifting her whole body off the bed. She saw the pleasure hit him. It blazed in his eyes, and he roared her name. He pulled her toward him. Kissed her deep and hard.

No pain. No fear. Just for a little while, it was all gone.

It was just the two of them. Pleasure. Safety. He'd given her everything she needed.

***

"Baby, open your eyes."

Kennedy cracked open one eye.

Remy sat on the side of the bed, his hair tousled, his chest bare. And he had a plate in his hands. "Scrambled eggs, bacon, and pancakes." He slanted a fast glance toward the clock. "We're long past breakfast, but you've got to eat."

She sat up, pulling the sheet with her. "You...cooked me breakfast?"

"Absolutely." He leaned forward and kissed her. This kiss was softer, far gentler than any other they'd shared. When he pulled back, his expression was tender. "You need to keep up your strength. Things are going to get dark, and you know it."

"They already are dark." And she was starving. She took the plate and tried not to shove her whole face into it immediately.

Bacon was her kryptonite. Always had been.

"You sleepwalk often?" The question was casual.

She swallowed a bite of egg. "No. I stopped...or I thought I'd stopped when I went to college. I have to be really, really tired in order for it to happen." Like she'd been. So exhausted nothing would have kept her awake. "I first started doing it after my parents died. Sometimes, Kyle would find me outside. Staring at the—" She stopped.

He waited.

"At the guest house." She rolled back her shoulders. "My feet would be covered in dirt. And I'd have no memory of how I got out there."

"You could have walked right into the fire."

"Yet another reason I'm glad you were close." And she was. She finished her eggs. He offered her a glass filled with orange juice, and she drank it quickly. "I mean it, you know." Her hand tightened around the glass. "I'm glad you're with me. You've been saving me pretty much from the moment we met."

He glanced away. His jaw hardened.

"This whole thing...I know it's way more than you signed on for." She was struggling to find the right words, but he needed to know how she felt. She put down the glass, and her fingers curled around his wrist. "I'm grateful to you."

He stared down at her hand. "I don't want your gratitude."

"What do you want?" The question slipped from her.

His lips thinned. "Finish breakfast. We'll talk after you're done." He rose, swallowed, and his hands clenched and unclenched at his sides. "Think I'd better finish that shower I started."

She knew the smile he gave her was fake. It never reached his eyes.

The bathroom door closed behind him, and she heard the thunder of the shower turning on. She finished the food — because she was absolutely starving and bacon should never, ever go to waste — and then Kennedy slipped from the bed. She grabbed a discarded shirt — one of his shirts — and pulled it on before she made her way toward the bathroom door. At the door, she paused. Maybe he'd like company.

Or maybe she just wanted to be with him again.

But as she reached for the doorknob, Kennedy heard a faint peal of sound. Her shoulders stiffened as she glanced back. That was a phone ringing. She was sure of it.

Only the ringing wasn't coming from the bedroom.

Following the sound, she hurried from the bedroom and darted down the hallway. When she got into the den, the phone was still ringing. She glanced around —

The sound stopped.

Okay. That was weird. Because she could see Remy's phone. It was tossed on the couch. And her phone had been in the bedroom, but Kennedy had been sure that she'd heard the sound of a distant phone — with one of those standard ring tones that everyone seemed to have and —

The ringing started again.

Her gaze darted upward. The sound was coming from upstairs. She hurried up there, wondering if Remy had accidentally left another phone in that space. Before, he'd told her the house was under renovation on the second floor. At the top of the stairs, she went to the right. A door had been left open a bit, and she slipped into the room there.

The phone kept ringing.

But Kennedy wasn't focused on the ringing any longer. She was staring at a large cork board. One that took up most of the far wall and contained pinned images of—

The Broken Doll Murders.

She saw the crime scene photos, all tacked up carefully on the board. And as she inched forward, drawn helplessly, Kennedy realized there were reports from the coroner there, with sections highlighted. There were pictures of her and her brother scattered across the board.

The phone stopped its ringing. A chill skated over her spine. A desk waited near the board, and there was a laptop on the desk. One that was shut down. A phone rested beside it, and when she glanced at the phone's screen, she saw the two missed calls.

Joshua Morgan.

Her fingers slid over the desk, then moved down to the top desk drawer. No lock barred her from opening the drawer, and it pulled open with a faint groan. A gun waited inside, tucked in a holster. And beside that gun—

"Kennedy?"

She jerked at his voice, and her head whipped up.

Remy stood in the doorway. His hair was wet, slicked back from his forehead. He'd donned a pair of jeans. His eyes narrowed on her, and, yes, that was suspicion in his gaze.

Suspicion.

"What are you doing up here?" Remy asked her.

Her spine straightened. "Your phone was ringing. I heard it and followed the sound."

"You shouldn't come up here. There's a lot of reconstruction work—"

"I don't see any reconstruction work in this room." Her voice was so calm. So normal. Strange, because normal and calm weren't even close to the way she felt. Her hand lifted and pointed to the wall. What did cops call that? A murder board? She'd seen stuff like it in TV shows. "What's up with the artwork?"

He took a step toward her. "It's to help me with the case. As soon as we started working together, I pulled up all the evidence I could find." His gaze roved over the desk. He bent and scooped up his phone.

"It's Joshua Morgan. Calling you on…a separate, second line?" Kennedy let the question linger in the air.

"I have an office number and a private number. I gave him both. My office calls are automatically forwarded to this cell."

"You have an answer for everything," she murmured.

If possible, his face hardened even more. "Kennedy, let's go back downstairs. We need to —"

She reached into the drawer. Pulled out the item that had caught her eye. "Got an answer for this?" She lifted the ID. The badge. The freaking FBI badge.

And she saw it on his face. *Fuck me.* He might as well have mouthed the words because he'd just realized that she had him.

To be extra certain, she studied the ID that was with the badge. Oh, yes, that was his picture, all right. But the name beneath the picture —

The chill she felt got worse. It seemed to sink beneath her skin, going straight into her bones. "You're not a PI."

"Kennedy —"

"Who in the hell are you, really?"

CHAPTER FOURTEEN

This was bad. One of those worse-case scenario kind of deals. Every muscle in Remy's body stiffened as he stared at Kennedy. She was dressed in his shirt, her breasts thrust against the thin cotton, her hair was tousled as it hung over her shoulders. She looked so beautiful she made him ache. Sexy. Delicate but —

Her bright eyes stared at him with a barely contained fury. "Let me ask that question again. I mean, it's obvious *what* you are, right? You're an FBI agent. You're — "

"I was working undercover."

She shoved his badge and his ID back into the drawer. Slammed it shut.

Oh, shit. "I was going to tell you. I was going to tell you right after I got out of the shower." That part was true. It *had* been the plan.

"Right. You just had to fuck me again first, huh?"

Worse-case scenario. "The fucking was separate from the case."

Okay, in his head, those words sounded a whole lot better, but when they actually came out of his mouth, Remy knew he'd screwed up. A major clusterfuck.

Kennedy skirted around the desk and marched for the door.

He moved into her path, his hands lifting. "Kennedy, let me explain —"

"Touch me, and I'll kick your balls into your throat."

Well, that was, um, a new threat from her.

He dropped his hands. "Let me explain. *Please.*"

"Get out of my way."

"Kennedy."

"Get out of my way. I'm leaving this house, and I'm going to the hospital to see my brother."

His eyelashes flickered. The faintest of movements.

But her lips parted. "OhmyGod…it was about him, wasn't it?"

Remy wanted to touch her. Wanted it so badly that he knotted his hands into fists. "My job was to find him. The Bureau believed you might have been aiding and abetting your brother —"

"He's another victim! Not the killer!" The words tore from her with the fury of a hurricane.

"Kennedy —"

Her hand slammed into his chest and she shoved him back. She rushed past him, going right for the stairs, and he followed behind her. "Kennedy, listen to me!"

At the bottom of the stairs, she didn't even slow down. Just turned for the bedroom—

He caught her hand.

"I warned you," she gritted out.

He moved fast, making sure she couldn't reach his balls. "Baby, calm *down*."

She wrenched free. *"Don't."* A whip of fury and pain. "Don't act like you care about me. Don't act like you were doing anything but using me."

"Isn't that what you were doing to me? Using me to escape?"

And...fucking hell, another thing he should *not* have said out loud. What was *wrong* with him?

Pain flashed on her beautiful face, and Remy felt like the worst kind of asshole in the world. Oh, wait, he felt that way, because he was. "I am sorry." Truer words he'd probably never spoken.

Kennedy wrapped her arms around her stomach. She'd schooled her expression. The pain wasn't on her face, but it was in her eyes. Those gorgeous eyes that were going to haunt him for the rest of his life.

Fix this. Could he fix this? Maybe if he could just explain... "I was given a job. That job was—"

"Me." Brittle.

But he nodded. "I was told to approach you at the gala."

She laughed, yet the sound held no humor. "Only you didn't even have to do that, did you? I went up to you. I was the desperate one who ran to you because you looked at me as if I wasn't some freak." She licked her lips. "A lie. You thought I was guilty all along."

"Kennedy…" His chest ached.

"You used me."

"I did my job!" Dammit. "It's a job I'm very good at, okay? I go in, I assume an identity, and I get close to the target. No matter what it takes, I do the job." Why did the words sound so hollow? Why did he feel so hollow?

Her head tilted. "How many jobs have you done? Jobs like this?"

Remy didn't answer.

"Do you not remember? Or are there just so many you're afraid to tell me?"

There'd been too many. He'd been a CEO. A criminal. He'd posed as a drug dealer. As a sex trafficker. He'd brought down the worst of the worst, starting first as an undercover PD officer, and then working his way to the FBI. Being a chameleon was his talent, and it was a talent that his bosses had always used to their maximum advantage.

She exhaled on a long sigh. "Was sleeping with me part of the job?"

"Kennedy, *no*."

"Then why did you do it?"

"You wanted me, you—"

"*Stop*."

His back teeth ground together.

"Let's be very clear here. I wanted a man named Remy St. Clair. I wanted the PI that I hired. I wanted the man who was there to help me when no one else was." She gave a sad shake of her head. "You aren't that man."

"I *am* Remy—"

"Is that your real name? Because St. Clair wasn't on the ID upstairs."

Shit.

"You're not a PI. You weren't with me because you wanted to help me." Her eyes narrowed. "What was your objective?"

"To find Kyle Clarke."

She backed up a step. "We found my brother yesterday."

Yesterday, last night—shit, time was a mess for him right then.

"But you just had sex with me. You kept up the lie when the job was over." Kennedy took another step back. His shirt slid against her thighs. "*Why?*"

"I just got clearance to tell you the truth. I was going to do it at the station, but then—"

Remy raked a hand through his hair. "You were dead on your feet! You wanted to see your brother, then you needed to rest, and then the fire had us both running for our lives! There wasn't time to tell you."

"Liar."

He flinched. Her voice was so cold and...final.

"You could have told me before you stepped into the shower with me. You could have told me before you carried me to the bed. You could have told me before you fucked me." A tear slid down her cheek.

He lurched toward her. "Kennedy, *listen*."

"I am listening. Are you?"

He was listening as every single word she uttered seemed to be like a nail driving into what was left of his heart.

"You used me," she said, her lips curling down. "Tricked me. Made me believe you were someone else. I took a lover to my bed, but he was a stranger. You wanted me to trust you, and I think you were willing to do *anything* so that I'd tell you all of my secrets."

At that one word...secrets...he couldn't help but tense.

"Oh, my God." Her eyes squeezed shut. "You used it all, didn't you?"

"Kennedy, the Broken Doll Killer is out there. I have to find him. I have to—"

"You thought he was my brother, and you used what I told you." Her eyes opened. The blue was so bright it almost hurt to look into her stare. "How long did it take you to report back to the FBI when I told you that my father killed my mother?"

"Baby—"

"Don't!" She swiped at the tear on her cheek.

He wanted to pull her into his arms. To hold her tight. To tell her that he hadn't been using her.

But then...wouldn't he just be...

A liar.

"How long before you told them?" Kennedy demanded.

He had to unclench his back teeth. "As soon as you went to sleep that night. It was important intel. Joshua needed to know about that development. I had to get agents researching the facility in Europe that your brother was sent to, don't you understand?"

Her shoulders straightened. "I understand that you're a cold-hearted bastard."

Yes, he was.

"I cooperated with the police. Time and time again—"

"You held secrets back." The words were wrenched from him. "Like the truth about your parents, about Kyle's time at the psychiatric facility—"

"Stay the hell away from me and my brother." She turned on her heel. Stalked down the hallway that led to his bedroom.

He couldn't stay away. She was in pain, and he wanted to help her. He wanted to take the terrible, stark look from her eyes. He wanted her…dammit, he wanted her to look at him the way she had before.

When she'd trusted him.

When she'd wanted him.

When she'd thought he was the guy who was there to help her.

I want to be that fucking man.

When Remy went into his bedroom, she was naked. His shirt was on the floor.

"Nothing you haven't seen before." She yanked on her clothes. "But you will *never* be seeing this show again."

He stood in the doorway and tried to figure out how in the hell he could fix this. "It was my job."

Her lips curled into a sneer. "Destroying my family?"

"We *found* your brother."

"Yes, yes, we did, and I'm so grateful that he's alive. But we could have found him without you sleeping with me. Without you —"

"I slept with you because I have never wanted a woman more in my life!"

Her lips parted. Her gaze searched his. "I can't tell." She slid on her shoes. Walked toward him. Brought the delectable scent of strawberries and woman to him. She gazed into his eyes. "I don't think I'll ever be able to tell. You're far too good."

"Good at what?"

"Lying."

His heart wrenched in his chest.

"Never wanted anyone more? Isn't that what you said?" A sad smile curled her lips. "I don't think I can believe you. But…here's a truth from me." Her hand rose and pressed to his cheek. "I did want you. I gave myself to you with no reservations. I thought you were someone I could trust. I've been burned before, but that particular story is a secret I didn't share with you. I needed you to be different." Her lips trembled. "I needed you."

And he had the feeling — the terrible, twisting, sinking feeling — that something important was being taken from him. Inside, Remy could feel pain growing. Surging too fast and too hard. This wasn't supposed to happen. He'd had a plan in place. He was going to explain. She was going to understand. She was —

"When I leave you, I'm going to make sure that I talk with my lawyers. I played nicely with the PD and the FBI, and you all just screwed me over. My lawyers will never let you near me again." Her chin notched up. "I won't be nice again." Her hand fell away from him. "Now get the hell out of my way."

He didn't move.

"Get. Out. Of. The. Way."

"I'm sorry I lied to you." He meant it.

"You lie very, very well."

Yes, dammit, he did. But there had been a reason for his lies. There was *still* a reason. "Women are dead—more than just the ones you know about. This killer has been hunting for a while, leaving a trail of bodies. At least six victims."

Kennedy shook her head. "That's not possible."

"The victims cross state lines. Mississippi. Alabama. Florida. Louisiana. It's the same man." His words tumbled out because she had to believe him. "When the FBI thought it was your brother, yeah, we fucking bent the rules to try and get to him. They believed you were hiding him—"

"*You* believed it." Kennedy's whisper cut through his words.

Hell. "Yes," he gritted out. "I thought you were sheltering him. At first, I thought—"

Her eyes widened. Her lips parted. "Oh, my God. I'm a fool."

"No, no, you—"

"The near hit and run? The one you saved me from? Was that a setup?"

"It *wasn't*." But the Feds had planned to stage a scene to convince her that she needed him. Only the hit and run had come first.

"The doll. The damn doll at my house! Did *you* put it there?"

"No. Look, I get that you think I'm a piece of shit, but I wouldn't do that to you. I wouldn't —"

"Lie, deceive? Make me believe you were helping me when all along you wanted to destroy the one person I love in this world?"

Her loyalty to her brother — he'd known it would be a problem. "Are you angry because I lied to you or because I tried to take him down?"

"He's innocent."

No one in this world was completely innocent.

"Get out of my way."

Her eyes glittered with tears and fury. And against her tears, he could do nothing. Nothing but back away. Nothing but follow her — in silence — as she grabbed her phone and headed for his front door. "Let me call you a cab," Remy said, hating the wooden tone of his voice.

"It's the city. Cabs are everywhere."

He had to touch her. When she reached for the doorknob, his fingers curled around her shoulder. "But you don't have any money on you. No purse. Nothing. Let me give you some money. Let me—"

"I just want to be away from you."

Right. He let her go. A small table was positioned near the foyer wall. He opened the table's top drawer and yanked out some cash. "Take this. Please. You need money for the cab."

She made no move for the money.

"Baby…"

Kennedy immediately tensed.

He tried again. "You don't have to use a cab. I can take you wherever you want to go."

She stared at the cash in his hand. Snatched it even though she obviously hated to take it from him. "I can tell you exactly where I want you to go. But I bet you can guess the location, too."

"I already feel like I'm in hell." And it was true. The way she was looking at him, the pain Kennedy was obviously in…*I did this. I hurt her.* He hadn't realized… "You have to care in order to be hurt."

Her laugh was brittle. "Who told you that lie?"

His mother had, a lifetime ago.

Had…had Kennedy actually cared about him?

She looked up, her gaze directed at the ceiling before she rolled her eyes. "What did you think? Really? That it was just sex for me? How clueless could you be? I'd gone a year without sex. I like pleasure, yes, who doesn't? But it was always more. At least for me, it was."

Fucking hell. "Kennedy—"

"Now it will be less." A hoarse whisper. "So much less."

No, no, *no*. He was hurting, too. Feeling as if his very heart had been ripped from his chest.

You have to care in order to be hurt.

And hadn't he sworn, when he stood over his parents' graves, that he wouldn't care again? That he'd stay separate and keep up walls to protect himself? That he wouldn't let anyone close? He'd always intended to be the ghost, drifting in and out of other people's lives. Doing his job, taking down the enemy, never letting anyone know the real man behind the mask.

You have to care—

Fuck, he was hurting.

"You shouldn't go out on your own, Kennedy. The killer is still out there. He's targeting you. You need protection. You need—"

"A new PI? Don't worry, I'll get one ASAP. I'll get a bodyguard. I'll get anything I need."

I need you, baby. Why hadn't he realized that sooner? "I can help you."

She turned away from him. Opened the door. "Help me by finding the killer. Stop him. Lock him away." Sunlight poured inside.

"It's *not* safe for you to be out there alone."

She gave a mocking laugh. "I can see a cab from here. I'll walk to the vehicle, he'll take me to my brother, and I'll have guards before you can blink. You don't need to worry about me, not anymore."

"Kennedy…" Remy had the feeling he would always worry about her. Something had happened between them. Something he'd never expected. "I'm sorry."

"No, you're not. If you had to do it all over again, you would."

He…shit…For a man who usually felt as if he had ice water flowing through his veins, each word she spoke sent a spike of fire through him. Rage—directed at himself.

What have I become?

"Stay away from me," she told him. She didn't look back as she made her way to the cab.

He didn't look away from her. Remy watched as she slipped inside the vehicle. As she slammed the door shut behind her. A moment later, the cab was rushing away.

Why did he feel like something important to him had just left in that vehicle?

No, no, she needs me. The case wasn't over. It had changed, that was all. He wasn't undercover any longer. Since he wasn't undercover, Kennedy could get to know the real man that he was.

And who the hell is that? Remy wasn't even certain he understood himself.

He shut his door. Hurried and grabbed his phone. The phone. *Sonofabitch*. It had seemed smart to get a second line. A private line to use while he was undercover. The damn phone had *just* been delivered, too. With Kennedy being so close to him now, he'd made the request for it. If Kennedy had ever grabbed his personal phone, he hadn't wanted her to see any calls or texts from Joshua.

Screwed the pooch on that one.

His finger swiped over the screen, and his partner answered on the second ring. "Yo."

"Where are you?"

"Our Lady of Grace. Gonna take another stab at Kyle soon."

He wouldn't have long. Not before Kennedy had her lawyers closing in. "Kennedy knows."

"Good news. Then we can work to —"

No, not good. "She found out on her own before I had the chance to break the news to her."

"What? How the hell did she do that?"

"She heard the phone ring when you called."

Silence. Then… "Fuck. Sorry."

"The phone was upstairs. She found my badge and ID." He stalked in a circle as he talked. "She's on her way to the hospital. When she gets there, make sure you keep eyes on her. Kennedy and her brother both need a protective detail until we can find the perp. He's fixated on them. If he took the brother…"

"Then you think he could go after her next."

It was what he feared. What terrified him. He had a flash of Amanda's body. The black blindfold wrapped around her eyes, the bloody pool beneath her body.

I can't let that happen to Kennedy. "She hates me right now. That can't matter. The FBI is going to put her into protective custody — "

"Uh, whoa, slow down, buddy. I didn't get that order from the Brass above us."

"You will." Because FBI Brass owed him. "She's in danger. Her home was torched, her brother abducted." *If the killer took her...*no. Remy wouldn't let that happen. "They're both going into protective custody. She won't like it, but too damn bad. Keep her with you until I get to the hospital." He'd be calling the higher ups at the FBI on his way over.

Remy hung up the phone and rushed to get dressed. Kennedy might never want to see his face again, but he wasn't going to let her life be put in danger. He was going to protect her, no matter what.

And maybe, if he was really lucky, she might stop looking at him like he was the worst piece of shit she'd ever seen.

Kennedy, I'm sorry.

He needed another chance with her. And in order to get that chance, she had to stay alive.

CHAPTER FIFTEEN

Kennedy rushed through the automatic hospital doors. Her heart pounded even as fury still had her shaking.

He'd lied. Every step of the way, Remy had betrayed her. And she'd just fallen for his lines, been so *eager* to have someone finally on her side that she hadn't questioned him.

Such. A. Fool.

She hurried toward the elevator. When she slipped through the elevator doors, she was the only one inside, and Kennedy spun around to jab at the control panel.

"Kennedy, wait!"

Connor appeared just as the doors were sliding shut. He put up his arm, halting the doors, and then he slipped into the elevator with her. "Thought that was you." He seemed a little out of breath. "We need to talk."

The doors slid closed.

He stepped closer to her. "Kennedy, God, it's been too long."

"Connor." She wasn't exactly in the mood to handle him right then. One lying bastard at a time was normally her rule.

His gaze drifted over her face. "You are even more beautiful now than you were years ago."

The elevator needed to move faster. Like, a lot faster. Her brother was only on the ninth floor and—

He pressed the stop button.

The elevator stilled.

No. Absolutely not. She reached around him, about to stab her finger into the button—

He caught her wrist, locking his fingers around her. "Give me just a few minutes, please. I need this time."

Once, his touch would have thrilled her. Her heart used to race, and nervous, excited energy would seem to heat her blood. A girl's first lover was special, wasn't he?

Or, at least, he was supposed to be. He wasn't supposed to turn out to be a traitorous asshole.

Oh, Jesus. Do I have a type?

"I'm sorry, Kennedy. I'm sorrier than I can ever say. I should never have—"

"Accepted five hundred grand from my grandfather as payment for walking away from me?" There. Bam. Why sugar coat and dance around that crap? Maybe she just didn't have any other fucks to give because it had been *that* kind of year, but she just threw the words at him.

He didn't deny her words. How could he? They were the truth. There was a reason he'd run far when Connor had once planned to run *away* with her. He'd been bought off.

"My family was broke, Kennedy. My father lost *everything*. The banks were coming after the property. I had one chance—just one—to save part of a legacy that had been built over four generations. I-I made a choice, and…" He trailed off.

"The choice wasn't me." It had been money.

"I turned things around. I was able to save *everything* with the right investments. I went back to your grandfather. I tried to pay him the money back." Connor shook his head. "He wouldn't take a dime. He just—"

"You didn't even tell me. You just left. One day, we were talking about running off and getting married, and the next, you were gone."

His gaze never left hers. "I was trying to help my mother and father. Trying to save the family business. Trying to salvage something of my life."

"Were you asking me to marry you for the same reason?" Because she'd figured that part out long ago. She'd fallen for him. He'd used her. "Did you think that if you married me, you'd get access to the money my grandfather controlled?"

He swallowed, his Adam's apple bobbing. He didn't lie to her. She supposed that was something.

No, really, it wasn't.

Connor wet his lips. "Your grandfather said he'd cut you off without a dime if I went through with the wedding. I couldn't ask you to live that way for me. I couldn't—"

Oh, for shit's sake. Kennedy rolled her eyes and yanked her hand from his. "I don't have a problem living without the money. Apparently, you did." And he'd taken that five hundred grand and vanished in a blink. "You stayed away from me for years. Even though my grandfather died, you stayed away." She punched the button to get the elevator moving. She'd wasted more than enough time with him already.

"I stayed away because I thought you hated me."

You aren't wrong.

"But then when I heard about everything happening with your brother..."

The elevator was moving. Finally.

"I wanted to come to you. I wanted to help. I had planned to talk with you at the charity gala— I knew it was *your* gala. You won't believe this, but, I swear, Kennedy, I never stopped loving you."

The doors opened. She slipped through them and glanced back. "You're right. I don't believe it.

Because I don't think you ever did love me."
Now, she needed to get to her brother. She had to
check in with him and make certain he was doing
okay. She took two quick steps forward.

Connor's hand closed around her shoulder.
"I did love you. And *do* love you."

"Let me go."

The nurses were close by, bustling behind
their work station. They'd put a small Christmas
tree in the middle of the station, and the tree was
circled by tiny Christmas stockings.

"He was in my lake house, Kennedy. Do you
know how that makes me feel? If I'd just gone
there, if I hadn't been staying away because your
ghost haunted the place, haunted me, then I
could have found Kyle. He was my best friend. I
could have helped him. I could have —"

FBI agent Joshua Morgan stormed down the
corridor, heading straight for her. His gaze
darted from Connor's hand on her to Connor's
face, and Joshua's expression hardened. "There a
problem here?" he asked.

Connor's hand fell away.

"No problem," Kennedy said clearly. "Just
closing the door on old business." She
straightened her shoulders and focused on the
agent. "I want to see my brother."

"Absolutely. And he wants to see you." He
motioned her forward.

She heard Connor's footsteps follow them, actually *felt* him behind her —

"Family only at this point," Joshua said crisply. "The FBI certainly appreciates your cooperation, but I'm sure you understand that, given Mr. Clarke's condition, we are restricting his visitors."

"But —"

"Though we definitely have more questions for you, Mr. Wise."

She slanted a glance back at Connor. His eyes glittered.

"My attorney will be present for all additional questioning. I had nothing to do with Kyle's abduction." Connor's gaze locked on Kennedy. "Nothing," he emphasized. "And I truly wish that I had gone to the lake house sooner. I wish I could have found Kyle."

"Obviously, someone knew you kept the property vacant," Joshua drawled as he cocked his head to study the other man. "Someone, I believe, who knew both you and Kyle Clarke. That's why I want you talking with my team. I want to know every single person who had access to your lake house. Every single individual who knew the place was empty. My crime scene team is going over that location with a fine-tooth comb right now. And when they're done…" He exhaled.

But Kennedy felt a chill sweep over her. "You think the killer took other victims there?"

His head turned toward her. "It's the perfect killing ground. And we will be searching the lake, too."

Because…oh, God, because Remy had told her there were other victims. Victims from other states. *Six victims?* Her gut clenched. But those victims—he'd said their bodies had been discovered. If the FBI was searching the lake, didn't that mean they suspected there might be even *more* victims out there?

"How many victims do you think this guy has killed?" The question came from Connor—and he looked a bit sick.

Joshua's eyes went dark. Hard. He motioned with his hand, and a woman in a black suit stepped forward. She'd been standing near the nurse's station. "Agent Kinley, will you make sure that Connor gets downstairs?"

She nodded.

"But—but—"

Joshua pulled Kennedy away even as Connor sputtered. They turned the corner, and she stopped. "Do you think Connor could be the killer?" His house had been used, his lake, his—

"According to his alibis, no."

Alibis?

"And he's got an alibi for the time of Amanda's abduction. For Stacey's abduction, he wasn't even in the country. Yeah, I checked. His lawyer was ready to provide me with all the corroborating material, tied up with a nice, red bow." Joshua shrugged. "Doesn't mean I'm still not digging on my own. Doesn't mean that witnesses can't be bribed or travel logs faked. But for now, I have to say he's clear. Just believe me, the FBI is digging beneath the surface of *everyone* tied to this case."

Her shoulders stiffened. "I do believe you. After all, I'm perfect proof of that. You had an FBI agent in my bed. I know just how hard you're all digging."

Joshua's face flushed. "Uh, that wasn't—"

"Part of the plan? I think it was part of Remy's plan." Her eyes raked him. "Tell me, does he do that a lot? Seduce women when he's undercover? Is that part of his technique?" Because it had sure worked like a charm.

The agent was starting to sweat. "Remy is the best undercover operative that we have. His skills have proven incredibly useful."

"You didn't answer my question." Though his avoidance *was* an answer, but she still pushed, driven by the terrible pain that stretched inside of her. "Has Remy slept with others while he's been working undercover?"

Joshua's spine straightened. "You'd need to talk with him about that."

"That's just not going to happen. I don't plan to talk with him about *anything*." She turned on her heel and marched down the hallway. She saw a uniformed cop in front of her brother's room.

"Don't be too sure about that." Joshua's voice followed her.

Kennedy stilled. Suspicious, she glanced back at him. "Want to say that again?"

He winced.

Uh, oh. "Do I need to call my lawyers?" Yes, she totally did, she'd just wanted to talk with her brother *first.*

He stared at her. "The FBI wants to keep you safe."

"I want to be safe, too. That's wonderful. Looks like we have the same goal." Her voice was clipped and she was angry and she wanted this nightmare over. "It would be great if you could find the killer out there. Before, you know, he comes after my brother again." She reached for the door.

The uniformed cop tensed.

"It's okay, Gus," Joshua announced. "She's his sister. She has clearance to go in, just like Henry Marshall, but no other civilians, unless you get the official approval from me or another FBI agent on my team."

The cop eased to the side.

"And, for the record," Joshua added as he moved to stand directly beside her, "I don't believe the perp would go after your brother again."

Okay, now his words had her glancing at him with a slant of her eyes.

"Your brother isn't his preferred victim type. That's why the perp let him go."

"He didn't *let* him go. We *found* Remy—"

He nodded toward the door. "Visit with your brother, then I'd like to talk to you about a few things."

"What things?" Her stomach knotted.

"My profile. The killer. Who I think he really wants."

A tremble slid over her.

Joshua nodded. "Right. I can see you already suspect the same thing. But we'll talk in a bit. I understand the importance of family. Your brother is more alert now, and I know he wants you with him. Go talk with him while we wait for my partner to arrive."

Oh, no. *No, no, no.* "Your partner?"

The agent lifted a brow.

Shit.

She rushed into the hospital room. Immediately, her gaze went straight to the bed. To Kyle. Kyle who looked a bit less like death warmed over, but was still too haggard and pale. He was propped up on a pile of pillows, and an IV fed into his arm. He looked bruised and battered, and—

"Kennedy." His voice was a weak rasp.

She had to blink away tears as she rushed toward him. She threw her arms around him and held him as tightly as she could. "I was afraid you were dead." She had to swallow twice before she could speak. "The cops found your car — they pulled it out of the river. Stacey was dead. Everyone said you were dead or you were the —" She stopped, unwilling to say that final word to him.

His hand rose and lightly stroked over her hair. "Kil...ler." His voice was so terrible to hear. Rough. Breaking.

She eased back, just enough to stare into his eyes. "Yes. That's what the newspapers said. What the cops thought. I couldn't find you, and I got so desperate." So desperate that she'd trusted the wrong man.

He tried to smile for her. A long, white bandage covered his cheek. The bandage pulled at his skin when he smiled. "F-found...m-me..."

She was right in front of him, and she still had to strain in order to clearly make out his words.

Her gaze darted to the right, and she saw that a write-on, wipe-off board had been placed beside the bed. A black marker lay next to the board.

"S-sorry..."

Her stare immediately jumped back to Kyle.

"Y-you…hurt…"

She bit her lower lip as the pain wrapped round her heart. "I hurt because I was afraid for you. You're my family. My blood. There is no one closer to me."

The machines around him beeped faster, harder.

And the door opened behind her. "Got some coffee," Henry's voice grumbled. "That shit down in the cafeteria is like tar, so I ran out to get—" He broke off when she turned back to look at him.

She knew he'd see her pain and grief. Henry—he'd been her rock in many ways. Usually standing in the shadows, but always there when she or Kyle had needed him.

Just as he was there, right then.

He could have left them long ago. He hadn't. She didn't need a driver or a ground's keeper. But she'd asked him to stay.

He'd been her one tie to the past when Kyle had vanished.

Sometimes, she even thought of him as a father. He'd been there when she'd graduated high school. When she'd gone to college. When she'd cried over Connor. He'd mourned with her when she'd buried her parents. He'd sat at her grandfather's death bed.

He'd always been there.

She'd always needed him.

"What happened?" Henry immediately demanded. His stare whipped back to Kyle. "Boy, you all right? You didn't tear out those stitches?"

"*N-no.*"

"Then why does your sister look like someone punched her in the gut?"

Because someone had. "He wasn't a PI."

Henry's thick brows beetled. He headed for the hospital bed. Offered her the coffee. She shook her head.

And she kept one hand locked with Kyle's. *He's alive. He's safe.* No matter what else happened, she had her brother back.

"Who…" Kyle's weak gasp.

She'd never kept secrets from him before, and she wasn't going to start now. "I hired a PI to help me find you. Remy St. Clair. Only it turns out, he wasn't just some PI." A long, slow exhale. She needed something way stronger than coffee. Kennedy wondered if the cafeteria served vodka. "Remy was FBI. He was working undercover all along."

Henry's face didn't flush red. It mottled purple with his fury. "That bastard!"

Yes, absolutely.

Kyle's fingers tightened on hers.

Her head turned toward him.

"He…hurt you?" So rough. She knew it pained him to speak.

She forced a smile. "I'll be fine. Really."

His stare didn't leave her face. He'd always known when she lied.

But she'd never been able to really tell when he lied.

"He did save my ass," she said, speaking quickly. And that was true. No matter what else had happened… "Remy got me out of the fire." *Crap. She'd have to tell Kyle about their family home –*

"Still can't believe the manor house went up in flames!" Henry set the coffee cup down with a hard jostle. "Some bastard just came right up and torched the place! With you inside! What in the hell is happening?"

"Remy got me out. I owe him for that."

But Kyle shook his head. "Owe…nothing." She could see anger simmering in the bright stare that was so like her own. Kyle had always been protective of her. Only fair, she'd kill for him.

"Tell me what happened to you," Kennedy whispered. "How did you get in that pit? How did your car get in the Mississippi? Did you see who took you? Did you—"

His lips twisted. His lashes lowered and covered his eyes. "Don't…know."

"Kyle?"

"I…remember Stacey. She…bleeding. I-I heard…" His voice died away. His mouth opened and he tried to speak, but nothing came out. Frustration flashed on his face.

"Here." She handed him the write-on, wipe-off board.

His fingers trembled as he took the marker. Then he scrawled.

Stacey. Bleeding. He paused, then wrote...*Moaning.*

Oh, my God. If he remembered Stacey moaning, then he'd been with her while she'd still been alive.

Someone hit me... He stopped. Stared down at the scrawl of his hand-writing. The clock on the wall tick, tick, ticked as the moments passed. Finally, he wrote, *From behind. Woke up – in pit. In the dark.*

"That poor boy has been through hell," Henry growled. "The cops and the FBI keep badgering him. That Agent Morgan was in here again. Kicked me out, said he had to talk with Kyle privately."

"There will be no more private talks." She turned her head and glanced toward the door. Joshua had to be waiting outside. She was surprised he hadn't followed her in. "I'm done playing nicely with the FBI."

Just as the words had left her mouth, the door opened. She expected to see Joshua in the doorway. Instead, Remy stood there, his wide shoulders filling the space, his handsome face locked into grim lines.

Her whole body jolted. "No." Her chin notched up. "Get out. Get—"

"I need you to listen to me. Please, Kennedy. I know I've hurt you, but I can't leave you."

Her brother's marker flew over the board in his hand.

She glanced at the words he'd written.
This the bastard?
She nodded.
I will kick his ass.

A part sob, part laugh escaped from her. Kyle couldn't even walk, but he was still trying to defend her. Trying to protect her. That was what her grandfather had never understood. He'd mistakenly thought Kyle was a threat to her. He hadn't been. She knew that. Kyle had always wanted one thing...

To protect his little sister. The sister who was younger by all of two minutes.

"Let me talk to her."

A woman's voice. Soft. Calm. Cutting right through the thick tension in the room.

Remy stared hard at Kennedy for a moment longer, but then he stepped to the side, clearing the path for a woman in black dress pants and a crisp, white blouse. Her heels clicked over the floor and a badge gleamed on her hip.

"I'm Special Agent Bree Harlow, and I've recently been assigned to your case." She inclined her head toward Kennedy and Kyle. Joshua Morgan slipped into the room behind her. "I believe you know my associates, Agent Joshua Morgan and Remy—"

"We know them," Henry snapped. "And don't like them much. Especially that Remy asshole." He stalked toward Remy. Stopped when he was right in front of the other man. Remy stood several inches taller than Henry, but that fact didn't seem to bother Henry as he glowered at the man before him. "You were supposed to help her. I thought you were *protecting* her."

"I am. And I will. I will not let anything happen to Kennedy, you can count on that."

"Like we're supposed to believe you?" Henry stabbed his finger into Remy's chest. "You hurt her. I can see the hurt in her eyes. Haven't seen this kind of hurt caused by a guy since that asshole Connor came and—"

"Stop." Kennedy's voice was shaking. She wished that she could sound cool and in control like Bree Harlow, but that shit just wasn't happening.

Remy's head turned toward her. His jaw was clenched tightly shut. After a moment, he gritted, "I will not hurt you again. I will not lie to you again."

Right. "I'm supposed to believe that?" *Fool me once.*

"No!" Henry snapped. "You're not! FBI Agent or PI St. Clair or whoever the hell you are, get away from her. Get out of this room. Get —"

Agent Harlow cleared her throat. "Kyle and Kennedy, the FBI is placing you both under protective custody."

"What?"

Agent Harlow squared her shoulders. She was a beautiful woman, with blonde hair cut in a perfectly straight bob that skimmed her shoulders. Her eyes were set, fierce, but her face flickered with compassion when she glanced at Kyle. "You're both in danger. I've read the reports. And I've been working on the new profile with Joshua. The killer is fixated on you two. He *will* come for you again."

He couldn't get Kyle again. She felt the tremor that shook her brother.

"Kyle will keep having an around-the-clock guard while he recovers," Agent Harlow explained. "When he is finally discharged from the hospital, he will be taken to a secure safe house."

"For how long?" Henry barked. He'd stalked across the room to grab his coffee and take an angry sip. "Last I checked, you FBI agents have jackshit. The killer is still on the loose, and you aren't close to catching him."

Agent Harlow exhaled slowly. "For as long as necessary, I'm afraid."

"What does that mean?" Kennedy asked with a sinking heart. "Days? Weeks?"

The FBI agents remained stoic. Were they trained for that crap?

"Months?" Kennedy threw out. "My brother just got out of one prison. I'm not having him thrown in another!"

"The protective custody is for you *both*." Agent Harlow's lips curled down. "I'm sorry, but it is necessary. Your home was torched. Your brother was kidnapped. The killer left a victim's body on your property. You have to see the danger that surrounds you both."

Yes, dammit, she did see the danger. She wasn't blind. She was terrified. She wanted the bastard caught.

"Kennedy…" Remy's voice was a low, deep rumble. "Please, give us a chance to talk to you."

Joshua shoved his glasses a bit higher on his nose. "I want to talk about the profile with you. I think you both…I think you and your brother know the killer."

Kyle wasn't writing on the board. He'd gone statue-still.

Joshua glanced toward him. "You told me that you never saw your abductor's face or heard his voice. That he originally attacked you from behind."

Kyle gave a slow nod.

"It's because you knew him. If he'd talked, you would've recognized his voice. If you saw him, you'd realize you knew him. I think that's the reason he left you alive. The guy *knows* you. He has some kind of tie or bond to you. You told me the injuries you have — most of them came from your own attempts to break out of that pit."

She looked at Kyle's fingers. The tips were bandaged.

What had he done?

"Your abductor fed you. He kept you alive. That all goes back to him having a connection to you. It—"

"This is bullshit!" Henry huffed. "You're not locking these two away. I'm starting to think the FBI couldn't find its own ass if—"

Joshua's lips flattened. "I think you should wait outside, Mr. Marshall."

"Oh, you do? Because you don't like what I have to say?" Henry drained his coffee cup. "Screw that. These are *my* kids you're talking about. I won't have them locked away while the FBI twiddles its thumbs. I won't have it, do you hear me?"

Remy rolled back his shoulders. "I found Amanda Jackson's body. Her throat had been slit, from ear to ear. She was lying in a pool of her own blood. She was blindfolded and left in a pose that made her look like a broken doll. He was…kind to her, I guess you could say."

What? Was Remy crazy?

Remy winced when he caught Kennedy's expression. "I mean the perp didn't torture her the way he'd done the other victims. Maybe he didn't have time to do that. Maybe…" He rubbed his chin. "Maybe he couldn't use his usual torture spot because someone else was there."

Oh, God. She'd been sitting on the edge of her brother's hospital bed, but at those words, Kennedy leapt to her feet.

"Preliminary crime scene analysis indicates that other victims *were* held in the lake house." Agent Harlow's head cocked to the side as she studied first Kennedy and then Kyle. "There was a great deal of…blood and DNA recovered in that pit. It's going to take our team a while to sort through everything."

Kennedy's hand flew to her mouth. For a moment, she thought she might be sick. Her brother had been held in a room where women had been *murdered*?

"It's okay." Remy was right in front of her now. Staring at her with dark eyes that appeared concerned. Acting like she mattered. "Just take a breath. A slow breath." His hands rose.

"Don't." The gasp came from Kyle. "Don't…touch…"

"Don't touch me," Kennedy said.

Remy's hands fisted. "I'm sorry." The apology was stark and fell heavily in the room. "I didn't like lying to you. Sometimes, it's freaking second nature to me, but with you, it was different."

Everyone around them had gone silent. Probably because this was an awkward as hell conversation.

"I hated lying. You bared your soul to me, and I felt like shit." Remy shook his head. "It's not happening again. If you believe nothing else, believe that I can keep you safe. I will guard you and your brother. I will *not* let this bastard get close to you."

"I need air." Henry shuffled toward the door. "Screw that. I need a smoke."

She'd thought that he quit. She'd pushed and prodded and thought… "Henry…"

He turned toward her. "Just one, okay? I need it." Then he strode from the room.

Remy stayed close. The other two FBI agents were staring at her, waiting. She glanced at her brother. He was glaring at Remy. Hating him, because she did. Wasn't that the way they'd always worked?

It had been the two of them against the world…from the beginning.

But this wasn't their usual battle. And she didn't want Kyle ever to be taken by that bastard again. "Kyle gets protection."

The agents waited.

"And I want to hear this profile." *Was it possible? Do we know the killer?*

Joshua nodded quickly. "Okay, okay, this is what we're working with…" He started to pace.

A throbbing beat in her temple.

"Someone with an intimate connection to you. Someone—"

"Hold on." Her hand immediately flew up. "*Intimate* connection?" Kennedy repeated as shock sliced through her. "You're saying a former lover? No, no, I don't think—"

"We will need the names of your lovers," Agent Harlow told her firmly. "And your friends. Anyone who could have been in a position to be a confidant to you or your brother. The individual we are after—he's formed an attachment to both of you. He couldn't bring himself to kill your brother, and we believe the perp contacted you, Ms. Clarke, because he wanted you to find your brother. He wanted you to put the puzzle pieces together, and you did."

Joshua was in front of the window. "I suspect your brother caught the perp in the act of killing Stacey Warren."

"Jesus." Her stare whipped to Kyle.

He'd gone pale. His marker flew over the board. *Don't remember…*

"He said he was hit from behind. Memory loss can be common from a blow like that. He probably got a concussion. Or perhaps the memory loss is due to the stress of his abduction. I'd love to think he'll suddenly remember, but since he was hit from behind—" Joshua squared his shoulders. "Your brother just might not know who took him."

"And if he doesn't know..." Remy's voice was dark and dangerous. "Then the killer could walk straight up to your brother."

He wouldn't know.

"Safe house," she snapped. "Absolutely, you're going, Kyle."

He used his hand to wipe away a clear portion on the board, then Kyle wrote, *So are you.*

Her head turned as she stared at Remy once more.

"So are you," Remy assured her in that rough growl of his.

"What else?" Kennedy wanted to know. "What else is in this new profile?"

"The painting of you. The one we found at Stacey's place." Joshua's focus was on her and her brother. "Kyle told me that he had no knowledge of the painting."

The marker scribbled. *I don't.*

"I think the killer left the painting as a message for you, Kennedy. You're his ultimate target. Maybe he even fantasizes about you when he commits the crimes."

She was shaking her head. No, no, no.

"You're the end game." Remy stared down at her with banked fury in his eyes. "And the guy is ready for the end. That's why he set the fire at your home."

Agent Harlow edged closer. "He's trying to separate you from the safety nets in your life. He destroyed your home."

It didn't make sense! "But he gave me back my brother! If he was destroying things, then why would he do that?"

Agent Harlow and Joshua shared a long look. Then Agent Harlow said, "Because he didn't want your brother. He wanted you. I don't know if he was really giving Kyle back to you so much as he was…planning for an exchange."

For a moment, her heart just stopped. "Me for Kyle?"

Remy's gaze never left her.

"I would have made that exchange in a heartbeat!" Kennedy exclaimed. "If that is what he wanted, he should have told me from the beginning! I would never have let Kyle suffer. I would have agreed to any exchange. *Anytime.*"

"No," Remy rasped.

The marker slid over the board. *No.*

Her brother didn't get to make that call. Neither did Remy.

"He killed your fiancée." Joshua's gaze locked on Kyle. "But there is more to it than that.

Before he murdered Stacey, the perp must have forced Stacey to create the painting of Kennedy."

Kyle frowned down at the board. His fingers trembled. Then… "*Want to see it.*"

"I'll get photos brought in, but the painting itself is evidence. That won't leave holding."

Kennedy's temples were throbbing. Protective custody. *Months.* A killer who wanted her dead. "Why? Why is any of this happening?"

Remy reached for her, but seemed to catch himself. His hand hung in mid-air. "There's someone out there who is obsessed with you, Kennedy. Someone who is sick. Someone who has to be stopped."

"You said that he'd done this before. In other states. Not just here." Her breath heaved out.

Joshua's phone vibrated. He pulled it up, looking at the text.

Remy nodded grimly. "There are approximately six women we think we can tie to this killer."

"How? Why? You can't—"

"We've got bodies," Joshua said flatly. "They found them in the lake."

OhmyGod.

She took a step back. Her hand flew out and locked with her brother's. Squeezed tightly.

"I'm going back to the crime scene," Joshua continued briskly. "I need to see those bodies as they are recovered. These are *not* victims that we'd previously linked to this bastard. Dumping them in the water—that's not the MO of our guy. At least, not the MO he's honed. We could be looking at his first victims, and if we are, he could have been sloppy with them. Could have left clues that will help us."

"While you are at the crime scene, Remy and I will set up the safe house and security," Agent Harlow added. "Call us with updates."

Joshua left moments later, the door swinging shut behind him.

"We need to know everything you can tell us about Connor Wise." Agent Harlow blew out a slow breath.

"Look, Agent Harlow—" Kennedy began.

"Bree, please. We're going to be working very closely together, and there's no need to be formal."

Closely…for months? *No, the killer has to be stopped—now.*

Bree tucked a lock of hair behind her ear. "The killer used Connor Wise's place as a dumping ground. That shows us that the perp felt confident there. He was—"

"*No,*" a weak rasp from Kyle. "*Connor…killer.*"

Kennedy's blood iced. "What?"

He strained to speak again, but couldn't. Frustrated, he scrawled across the white-board. "*Connor…obsessed. Always…wanted you.*"

Her heart pounded in her chest. The hospital room had gone dead silent. She looked up and found both Remy and Bree staring at her. Kennedy shook her head. "He's not. We were over years ago. Trust me, Connor left me without a second thought." Running away with a pile of money could do that to a person.

"He was your lover?" Bree questioned her carefully.

Her face flamed as she saw Remy's jaw tighten. "Yes," she admitted.

"How long ago...specifically?" It was Remy who gritted out that question.

"My senior year in college, okay? So, it's been about four years."

Remy and Bree shared a long look. Then Remy growled, "I don't care how many lawyers he has, I want him in an interrogation room with me. Right the hell *now*."

Kennedy rushed forward. "Why does it matter how long ago it's been?"

It was Bree who answered. "We believe the killer we're after...the first vic we linked to him was abducted four years ago, just outside of Mobile, Alabama."

"Maybe if he couldn't have you," Remy said quietly, rage burning just beneath his surface, "Connor decided to take someone to fill your place."

CHAPTER SIXTEEN

"I want to watch the interrogation."

Remy glanced up at Kennedy's determined words. She was in his office at the FBI, a mug of some crap-ass coffee cradled in her hands. The station only had craptastic shit in the pot. Her hair had been pulled back from her face, she wore no makeup, and she looked absolutely, heart-breakingly beautiful.

"If you go in there with me, he'll clam up," Remy warned her. "I will already be fighting his lawyer every step of the way. I need to break through Connor's armor, and I can't do it with you in the room."

"He's *not* a killer," Kennedy fired back. She set the mug down on his desk. "He was an asshole, yes. He traded me for cash, but he's not a killer."

Traded her for cash? "Explain." What kind of dumbass would trade her for anything?

Red stained her cheeks but her gaze never wavered. "My grandfather bought him off, okay? Connor and I were planning on eloping after college graduation. But his family's business had taken a turn, they were going to lose everything, and my dear old, *loving* grandfather paid Connor five hundred grand to walk away from me." A shrug that was anything but careless. "And he did."

"He was a fool."

She surged toward him. "Don't act like you care. You're doing a job — fine. But don't say things like that to me. Don't act like you would have done anything differently. Don't act like — "

He had to touch her. He just couldn't control himself. But his hands were gentle, tender, as they closed around her shoulders. Because she deserved tenderness. She deserved every care in the world. "I would have done a million things differently, if I could." He wasn't talking about Connor. He was talking about them. About everything that had gone to hell between them.

Her chin lifted. "*Don't.*"

"Don't tell you I was a fucking ass? Don't tell you I hate the job that brought me to you — and then made me throw away something so important that I'm gutted right now?"

She shook her head. "You're not. You don't — "

"You got to me." Truth. "Beneath my skin. Into a heart that I thought was ice-cold."

Another shake of her head. "I'm done with lies. I'm done — "

"So am I. I only want to give you the truth from now on. I just hope you're ready for it." Because his truth wasn't pretty and sweet. It never would be. "After my parents died, I shut down. Decided I wouldn't care about anyone or anything but justice. I'd be a hunter. I'd do anything I had to do in order to stop the monsters out there." Some of the things that he'd done… "I was good at pretending. I could be a drug dealer, a crime boss, I could be a fucking billionaire. I could be anyone. My emotions didn't get involved because I didn't have any." He'd felt *nothing* for far too long. "On my last case, I had a one-night stand with one of the women at Kace Quick's club—"

Kennedy flinched and tried to pull away. "I don't want to hear about this! I don't want to hear about other women you've fucked—"

"I've fucked plenty of women. I only made love with you."

She yanked hard against him. Her hip banged against the desk, sending the coffee sloshing over the rim of the mug. "Don't you give me that bullshit! Don't you *dare*."

"Marie was murdered. I found her body, and when I saw her…God, she was a good woman. She had a great laugh. She had big dreams and hopes for the future. A killer took that all away from her. I saw her body, and I was ice-cold. I should have felt something. I couldn't. I haven't been able to feel a damn thing for years because I lost myself in the undercover work. I lost myself to the rage and the hate. When Marie died, I was determined to find her killer. I wanted him to pay. But I never grieved for her. I haven't grieved for any of the victims. I didn't even fucking cry when I buried my parents."

Her lips parted. "Remy—"

"Something broke inside of me. I didn't let myself feel. Feeling brought pain. So much damn pain." He could still remember what it had felt like to be ripped apart—to be torn open as he'd stood in front of a freaking glittering Christmas tree all alone. "I didn't want to hurt again. I thought I could help people by doing my job. When you're always pretending to be someone else, you don't have to feel anything. Marie didn't know who I really was. She died not knowing."

Kennedy just stared at him with her incredible eyes.

Remy sucked in a deep breath. "I want you to know who I am. I'm not going to lie to you again, Kennedy. I swear it. I want you safe. I want you happy. I want—God, I want a chance with you. A chance for you to know the man I can be." If he could just figure out who the hell he was. "You matter." They should be clear on this. "You were never just a case. I wanted you from the beginning. But...I loved you—"

Her eyes flared wide. "What?"

"I loved you soon fucking after. I know it's fast. I know we've been moving at a hundred freaking miles an hour, but you got to me. You clicked for me. And I hated the lies. I hated having to pretend. I hated not being a man you could love. After Marie, *I* changed. I swore I'd be different if I had a chance with someone special…and you, God, you're it. I want to be better for you. I want to be a man you could care about, too."

A knock sounded on his door. "They're in interrogation room one," Bree announced. "I'm ready when you are."

Kennedy licked her lips. "I-I don't know what to say."

"I know you don't love me. Hell, baby, you probably think you don't even know me." He took her hand in his and brought it to his heart. "You do."

Bree knocked again. "Remy?"

"Be right there," he called, not looking away from Kennedy. Then, lowering his voice, he told her, "This isn't a lie. It isn't a game. I'm not trying to use your emotions against you. I love you." The truth of that had settled within him the instant she'd walked out of his home. A heavy hollowness had descended on Remy, nearly suffocating him.

He'd realized—

I don't want this anymore. A void of nothing.

He wanted her. "I will do anything to prove myself to you. You matter. What was between us—it wasn't a lie. Yes, I'm a Fed. But I'm also the man who'd do *anything* for you. I'm going to catch the bastard who's been targeting you and your family. The man who has been hurting all of those women. It's not going to be pretty." She should know exactly what would happen. "I play hard and rough and dirty, but I get the job done. I'll end him, and you will be safe." It was a promise.

Remy pulled away from her and headed for the door.

"I'm supposed to just believe you...when you say you love me? How do I know that's not just another line you're feeding me?"

"I've never told another woman that I love her." He'd never even stayed the night with other lovers. With Kennedy, he wanted her in his bed. Wanted to go to sleep with her. Wanted to wake up with her. Remy glanced over his shoulder. "Even liars can tell the truth sometimes." Gazing into her eyes, he said, "I love you. I'm sorry I hurt you. It will *never* happen again, I swear it on my life."

"No."

No? His gut clenched.

"Don't swear on your life." She hurried to him. He turned to her, and Kennedy put her hands on his chest. "You trying to get more bad karma for me? Thanks, I already seem to have plenty." Her gaze searched his. "I don't want you hurt. Because lies or not, yes, I feel something for you. Something that scares me to death because I think it can overwhelm me. I don't want to be wrong about a lover again. I thought Connor loved me, but money was more important than I was. And you—you were working a case. You were—"

He kissed her. His mouth pressed to hers in a careful, soft kiss.

Her lips parted beneath his. Her hands rose and curled around his shoulders. The kiss turned deeper. The desire he felt for her flooded through his body. Did she understand? Did she realize? He always wanted her. Always needed her.

His tongue thrust into her mouth as he tasted her. Her taste was so delicious. Those strawberries that he craved. He could take her mouth forever. He would take *her* forever.

But the interrogation was waiting. The killer was out there. He had to keep her safe.

Remy pulled his mouth from hers. Put his forehead against Kennedy's. "Not everything was a lie."

"Remy…"

"You can't go in the interrogation room with me. And I can't let you watch from the observation room. I'm sorry, baby, but the FBI won't allow it. Stay here. I'll be back as soon as I can." Another kiss.

Then he made himself step back.

She stared up at him, her mouth red from his kiss. So perfect she made him ache.

I need another chance with her.

If he caught the killer, if he locked the bastard away, maybe she'd give him that chance. He had to prove himself to her. He would. He'd do anything for another shot with Kennedy.

Anything.

***

"This is ridiculous," the lawyer began as disgust curled his lip. "My client has done nothing but cooperate with you. He allowed you full access to his property. If he'd hidden bodies there, you can't really think he would have just said, 'Yes, please, FBI, go in and find them all!'" A bark of laughter came from the older, balding man who wore what had to be a thousand-dollar suit. Dudley Richardson, Esquire.

Remy didn't laugh. Neither did Bree.

As for Connor, he just sat in the interrogation room, his hands flat on the table before him, and his face locked tight with barely controlled fury.

Remy was going to use that fury to his advantage.

"Surely you understand," Bree began smoothly, "why we requested this sit-down? The number of bodies recently discovered in the lake..." She shook her head. "Our techs are estimating that, based on the decomposition, some of the dead have been there for years."

"I didn't do it," Connor rasped.

The lawyer touched his shoulder. "I'll do the talking."

Connor's jaw tightened.

That fury is about to explode.

"My client didn't do this." Dudley Richardson raised his hands in the air. "He, of course, wants the vile culprit caught, so we are here speaking with the FBI again as a gesture of *courtesy.*"

"Courtesy, my ass," Remy dismissed.

Connor's head turned toward him. "I...know you."

"Right. You do. I was at the lake house when we pulled Kyle Clarke out of the pit that was his prison."

Connor's brow furrowed. "I thought you were with Kennedy. You're... FBI?"

"Yes." *Push him. Get a reaction.* "And I'm very much with Kennedy."

Connor got the message. Remy could tell it had been received by the way the guy's eyes narrowed.

"I believe you were once, too, weren't you?" Remy kept his voice mild. "Years ago."

Dudley sniffed. "I do not see what this *personal* line of questioning has to do with anything."

Remy gave the lawyer a careful smile. "Then there's no harm in the guy answering, is there? I mean, Kennedy already told me that they were involved. Not like it's some big state secret. Why deny it?"

"We *were* involved," Connor admitted.

"But it didn't end well?" Bree murmured.

Connor's gaze cut to her. "No." Clipped. "It didn't."

"She broke up with you?" Bree pushed, nodding as if she understood.

Dudley's jaw tightened. "This line of questioning is—"

"I made a mistake." Connor's hands fisted on top of the table. "I let money be more important than she was. If I could do it all over again, I'd tell her grandfather to take his money and shove it up his fat ass."

The lawyer coughed, seemed to be choking.

But Connor wasn't done. "You don't realize what you have until it's gone. I signed a deal, promised to stay away from her, and I honored that deal."

"Uh, we should—" Dudley began.

Connor gave a short, negative shake of his head. "She went through hell, and I wasn't there. *Kyle* went through hell. He was my best friend. That bastard who took him—he kept Kyle in *my* house because he must have known that I had to stay away from them. I rarely come down to Louisiana because being close to something you can't have—it's a fucking nightmare."

"Why, yes," Bree tapped her fingers on the table top. "I bet that could drive a man crazy. Make him do all sorts of…unexpected things."

Dudley's eyes squeezed closed. The lawyer had obviously seen the trap coming.

"I'm *not* a killer," Connor barked back.

The lawyer's eyes opened. "I think we're done." A congenial smile curved his lips. "This talk has been very unhelpful. Connor, let's go." He rose.

Connor didn't rise. His stare jumped from Remy to Bree, then back to Remy. "You're fucking Kennedy?"

Remy's jaw clenched. For a moment, he thought about driving his fist into Connor's face.

"You're FBI and you're with her? Isn't that some super conflict of interest shit?"

"Yes," Dudley responded smoothly as his hand curved around Connor's shoulder. "It absolutely is. I'll be requesting your immediate removal from this case, agent."

And you can fuck off. "Kennedy's safety is my number one priority. I will be staying at her side until the killer is apprehended. So, request anything you want, it won't make a damn difference to me."

"Maybe she doesn't want you at her side." Connor stood. Glowered at him. "She loved me. Did you know that? She told me she loved me, and I still—"

"Threw her away?" Bree lifted one elegant brow. "Trust me, women don't like that. They don't forget or forgive easily."

Remy almost flinched then because he knew Kennedy wasn't anywhere near close to forgiving him. But this prick before him? He wasn't about to let Connor get a second chance with her.

"I've known Kennedy since she was a kid playing with dolls." Connor's lips twisted into a sneer as he glanced dismissively over at Remy. "You're just the agent who's with her this week. You won't last. The case will end. You'll go away—"

"Maybe I can get him gone *before* the case ends," Dudley threatened.

Bring it, asshole.

"You'll go away," Connor stated with the arrogant confidence only a total prick can have, "but I won't. I'll fight for her this time. I will get a second chance. I deserve that chance."

Dudley whispered to him.

Connor swallowed. "Fine. We're done."

Dudley's smile was as fake as could be. "Of course, we're happy to let the FBI continue searching the lake house property…"

Remy nearly rolled his eyes. "You don't have a choice. We've got warrants that let us search *every* place Connor owns."

"My client *is* cooperating. You need to stop wasting your time with him. Focus on the real threat. You've got a dead police detective. Her partner has been calling my office nearly non-stop, demanding answers. Don't you think you need to *find* those answers?"

Her partner had been doing what? Jesus. He'd have to bring the guy in, ASAP.

A few moments later, Dudley and Connor filed out of the office. Connor sent him one last, angry glance.

Remy waved bye with his middle finger.

When the door shut, Remy started to pace. "I don't like that asshole." And it wasn't just because the guy had once been involved with Kennedy. It was—

"He said something the lawyer didn't like." Bree's head tilted as she seemed to mull over the interrogation.

Connor said a lot of things the lawyer hadn't—

"Dolls." Her breath blew out.

Remy paused, his stare whipping to her.

"Connor said he'd known Kennedy since she'd played with *dolls*."

Fuck. He had said that shit.

"Connor Wise has got a romantic attraction to Kennedy. He's got a bond with her brother. He *is* the perfect suspect." Bree was on her feet. "His property —"

"*His* murders?" Remy finished because he was sure suspecting the same thing. "Let's nail this bastard's ass to the wall."

***

The door to the small office opened, and Kennedy immediately tensed. Remy filled the doorway, all broad shoulders and towering height. His eyes were so dark and intense.

I love you.

He'd said those words to her. Just dropped them easily.

She wanted to believe him.

But he'd lied before.

And she'd been burned before by a lover.

"It's time for us to go." He offered his hand to her.

"Go?" She rose from his chair, sending the wheels rolling back across the floor with a squeak. "Where are we going now?" To the safe house? To be locked away? For how long? She couldn't stay indefinitely. She had a life. Work.

She didn't just glide by on her family's money. Sure, since the media had linked her family to the murders, her party planning service had been sent straight to hell, but she had people who depended on her for salaries. She had to keep going.

"I want to talk with Kace Quick, and I want you with me."

Her eyes widened. "We're going back to see Kace?"

"Actually, Bree is the one organizing this trip. He always tells her more than he tells anyone else."

She hurried toward Remy. His hand took hers.

"It's because he's in love with her." Remy advanced toward the door. "You'll do just about anything for the woman you love."

"*Stop.*"

He stilled. Glanced back at her. "Problem?"

"About a million of them." She cleared her throat. "I want to know what happened during the interrogation."

"Connor slipped up. He said something he shouldn't have."

Her heart raced faster. "What?"

"He...shit, look, it was a small thing, but Bree is good at profiling, and it stood out to her. She's already called Joshua—he's still at the lake house—and talked with him. They both thought it was telling. I do the dirty work, but they—"

"Dirty work?"

His head cocked. "I go undercover. I become the monster, but they can pick a real monster apart from a thousand yards. Bree and Joshua can get in their heads."

"So can you," she whispered back. "You have to be able to do that, or else the undercover work wouldn't be successful. People would see right through you."

His lips thinned. "I'm just a damn good liar."

"Yes, you are." No argument there.

His hold tightened on her hand. "It's always been easy for me to fit in on the undercover jobs because I'm too much like the bad guys. Too much darkness and too much rage are inside of me. I like the danger and the adrenaline. I like the risk. Until you, there wasn't anything I liked better."

She was not ready to touch their relationship yet. "Don't you see, though? That's why you are good at understanding the perps. Because you can become them so easily. Because you can walk in their world." And never get caught. She tried to ease her too-fast breathing. "What did Connor say that was so telling?"

"He mentioned knowing you back when you were playing with dolls. It was a fucking taunt. We're after the Broken Doll Killer...and Connor just randomly throws that crap out? No way. There is nothing random in this world. He was taking a jab at us, but when he did, he exposed himself. It's possible the whole reason he's posing the bodies this way is because—"

"No." She snatched her hand from his. Snatched it back and took a few quick steps away from him.

Wrong. Wrong. Wrong.

Her breathing came even faster. So did her heartbeat. It was galloping out of control as the past surged toward her.

"Kennedy? Baby, what's wrong?"

"I stopped...shit, I stopped playing with dolls when I was eight years old." The memory burned through her mind. "I-I had this doll. My mom had gotten it made for me in Atlanta. The doll looked *just* like me."

Remy waited.

"I found it one day, in my bed." *Oh, God. Oh, God.* The memory had been shoved down so far, so deep, but now it was bursting to the surface. *Wrong. It's wrong. I'm wrong.* "The eyes were gone."

"What? Kennedy, you should have—"

"It was over fifteen years ago! I didn't think some old doll I'd had could be related...God, no, I didn't think it could be related to *this!* The reporters just gave the killer this stupid name. I didn't think..."

"The reporters didn't give him the name." A muscle flexed along his jaw. "The sonofabitch called the *New Orleans Herald*. Told them what to call him. But the FBI demanded they keep quiet about his involvement. The *Herald* used the moniker but never revealed the killer had actually contacted their reporters. He gave them details of the crimes that only the real perp could know. The FBI wanted all of that kept under wraps because we planned to use the call as evidence later when we caught the bastard."

Her chest burned because she was breathing so hard.

"Connor." Remy nodded. "He's the one who destroyed your doll so long ago, isn't he?"

She shook her head. "No. No, it was my brother. Kyle did it. He cut the eyes out of the doll." It had been...*Kyle.* "He said he didn't think it hurt her. And he...he told me later that it wouldn't ever happen again."

CHAPTER SEVENTEEN

"What the hell do you mean, you don't know where Kyle Clarke is?" Remy glared at the young cop—a guy who was currently being treated by a doctor at Our Lady of Grace—

Because Kyle hit the guy from behind. Kennedy and Remy had gone straight back to the hospital. Remy had been determined to question her brother again, but when they'd gotten there, they'd discovered that Kyle was gone.

Her brother had hit the young cop. Stolen some scrubs. And just walked right out of the hospital.

God, Kyle, what are you doing? She'd thought her brother was so weak he could barely move. But he'd done this?

"I-I'm sorry," the cop stuttered. "I was supposed to stop people from getting in." He flinched when the doctor probed his wound. "No one told me the guy would try to get out. Never even saw him coming. Hit me from behind…"

Kennedy wrapped her arms around her stomach and slipped into the hallway. Henry was there, talking to Bree. Henry's face had locked into lines of worry.

"He can't be in his right mind," Henry was saying. "Kyle isn't violent. He never was. He —"

"That's not entirely true, is it?" Bree asked. Her voice was careful, her expression very watchful. "We learned that Kyle was sent to a psychiatric facility when he was a teen. According to witnesses we've spoken with, Kyle was very violent when he was first brought to the psychiatric facility. He fought the orderlies and demanded to be released."

Remy told her. But she'd expected that. He'd told all of his FBI buddies her secrets. Kennedy squared her shoulders. "You'd be violent, too, if you were held somewhere against your will."

Bree glanced her way. "You know this doesn't look good."

Yes.

"He's not in his right mind," Henry said again. "He's confused. Hell, the guy was pinned like an animal for weeks! We just need to find him and get Kyle the help that he needs."

"We intend to find him." Bree inclined her head to them. "Excuse me. I need to check in with Officer Flint's doctor." Her heels clicked over the floor as she walked back in the exam room.

Remy was still inside, too. For just a moment, Kennedy stood alone with Henry. "I'm scared," she confessed.

He scraped a hand over his face. "Me, too." His voice was low, for her alone.

"Do you remember…when someone broke my doll?"

"You cried for a damn week, of course I remember." His hands fisted. "I bought you that teddy bear to replace her, but it wasn't good enough to make you feel better."

She touched his fisted left hand. "I love Kyle, but I'm scared. He attacked that cop. And if he'll hurt a cop…"

Kyle, no.

"We'll find him." Henry stared hard into her eyes. "You know we will."

"Someone put him in that pit. The FBI— they're probably back to thinking that Kyle is guilty, *but someone put him there.* And I think he's gone after that someone. I think…I think Kyle remembered something. That's why he ran away. He remembered something, and he's gone after the killer."

Henry's eyes widened. "What can I do?"

She heard the door creak open behind her. Kennedy looked back and saw Remy closing in. "If Kyle reaches out to you, call the FBI, right away."

"*Kennedy*…what if they go in with guns blazing? You really going to risk your brother?"

Remy stopped at her side. "We are going to make every effort to retrieve Kyle Clarke without any additional violence. He just assaulted a police officer, and an APB is already out for him. Kyle isn't going to vanish, and he *will* be answering our questions."

Henry's stare darted back to Kennedy. "Where are you going to be? Your house—it's all gone. Everything is *gone* now."

"She'll be with me," Remy said. "The FBI is putting her in a safe house. You don't need to worry about Kennedy. I won't let anything happen to her."

Henry kept his focus on Kennedy. "You really think you can trust this jerk? After he's lied to you so many times? This is *Kyle*. He's not the Broken Doll Killer. He's scared and he's running, and if the FBI doesn't handle this shit right, they will *kill* your brother."

Could she trust Remy? Kennedy pulled in a breath and angled her head toward Remy. She found his stare locked completely on her.

"Do you trust him?" Henry pressed.

Kennedy couldn't answer.

She saw a flash of pain in Remy's eyes. Dammit, what had he expected? He *had* lied to her. Was she just supposed to instantly forget? Move forward? Her feelings for him were so mixed up that she didn't understand them at all.

She wanted him.

Needed him.

Cared for him…

Loved him?

Could you love a man who'd lied to you? Who'd used you?

Who'd...

Protected you? Fought for you?

"We need to get going," Remy told her, voice rumbling, as a mask slid over his features. "I want to check in with Kace. See if he has any insight on your brother."

"What?" Henry's voice rose. "Kace who? You aren't talking about Kace Quick, are you? Because Kyle stopped seeing that bastard years ago. He didn't go for the wild partying any longer."

"Sir," Remy's tone was flat, "with respect, I don't think you know Kyle nearly as well as you think."

"Kennedy?" Henry's voice cracked a bit. "Did you know Kyle was going back to those clubs?"

She nodded.

"*Why?*" Henry appeared confused. Lost.

"That's what we're going to find out," Remy replied. His fingers twined with Kennedy's. "Are you ready?"

There was nothing for her there. Her brother had vanished, and they needed to get moving. But... "You're staying at the Ritz, right, Henry? You're still settled into the room I set up after the fire?" Wasn't like he could go back to the guest house.

Henry nodded. "Thank you, Kennedy." His expression softened. "You always take care of me."

She always would. "Because you're family."

He smiled at her. "I love you as if you were my own. You and Kyle." He sighed. "If he calls me, I'll contact *you*."

He was saying he wouldn't be going to the FBI. He didn't trust Remy.

And she…

I can't let anyone else be hurt.

A few moments later, she and Remy were in the elevator. He was dead silent. The elevator felt far too small. Just as it had when… "I was in this same elevator with Connor," she blurted out. "He stopped it between floors. Told me that he wanted me back."

"*What*?"

"The past is over. I don't want to go back there." A bitter laugh escaped her. "Even if it turns out that Connor's *not* the killer."

Though signs were looking grim on that one…

"You think you know someone," she whispered. "You think you understand a person, then you find out all the secrets and lies. So many secrets." Sadness pulled at her. "Do we ever really know anyone? Or do we just know what people *want* us to believe?"

The elevator dinged. The doors slid open. She started to walk out, but Remy pulled her back. Her body slid against his.

"I want you to know me," he told her gruffly. "Every single secret. Every dark part of me. I want you to know everything. And then I want you to tell me all of your secrets. There is nothing you can't share with me. No truth that is too painful. Because I will love you, Kennedy, no matter what."

She searched his eyes. "The doors...they're going to close." They were already closing.

He swore. He let her go, then waved his hand to stop the doors from shutting. Remy stepped into the cavernous parking garage, and she followed him, shivering in the air that was surprisingly cold. Immediately, he shrugged off his coat and wrapped it around her shoulders. With his dark, intense gaze, Remy stared down at her. "I meant everything I said. One day, you'll believe me. And I'm not going anywhere. I can wait for that day. You'll see."

"Why?" If this was just about the case, about him being undercover, surely, he wouldn't be saying—

"Because you make me want a real life. Not just this pretend bullshit that I've been living. I want something more. I want it with you."

She didn't know what to say. What to do. "What is it you want from me?"

"Whatever you'll give me." His hand stroked her cheek. "But for now, I just want you safe. I want you alive. So, we'll see Kace, and then I'll make sure you're settled for the rest of the night."

His touch seemed to burn through her skin. The connection they had — it had been white-hot from the beginning. She'd looked across the ballroom and wanted him.

The first time they'd been together, she'd gotten lost in the pleasure. She hadn't cared about the future. She'd only wanted the moment. Why plan for the future when you didn't know what could happen?

But he wanted a future. He wanted her.

And that terrified Kennedy.

***

"Back to slumming so soon?" Kace Quick asked as he lounged behind his desk at Fantasy. Kennedy and Remy had just entered his office. He gave them a slow smile.

One that made Kennedy tense.

Then the door opened behind them.

Kace's expression completely altered. The mocking smile vanished, and warmth filled his gaze. "Ah, my love, I was starting to get worried." Kace rose and hurried around his desk as Bree headed toward him. She'd been the one to enter the room last. He pulled her close, pressing a soft kiss to her lips.

Kennedy shifted a little bit. The tender display from one of the most infamous guys in the city was—

"Odd, right? The man is locked tight around her little finger," Remy muttered.

"Like you're one to talk." Kace lifted a brow as he looked over at Remy. "I heard—through the grapevine—that the FBI Brass wanted to reassign you. Your undercover work is *done* on this case, and they needed you elsewhere. But you threw your very considerable weight around, and now you're Kennedy's personal bodyguard. An interesting position for an agent like you."

"Wait, what?" Surprise rocked through Kennedy.

Bree lifted her hands. "I am *not* his grapevine, by the way."

"Of course not." Kace kept one hand on her waist. "I would hardly ask you for confidential info. It's much better when others bring it to me."

"Dammit." Bree huffed. "I hate leaks."

Kennedy grabbed Remy's hand and pulled him closer. "You're not supposed to be working with me?"

His lips parted.

"Um…something about a drug cartel in Miami, I believe," Kace supplied. "Turned the bosses down, didn't you, Remy? And did I hear that you've requested a transfer?"

"Not a transfer," he snapped. "I'm getting out. This is my last case. It's time for a change."

He was leaving the FBI? He'd insisted on staying with her?

She searched his gaze. Was it true? Did he really care about her? Really love her?

"You are my mission," Remy told her simply. "My goal is to keep you safe."

"Yes…" Kace drawled. "I believe he thinks the rest of the world can go screw off. Very hard when you're the one caught in a trap you never expected, isn't it, Remy?"

Remy's head whipped toward him. "Don't make me knock your ass out."

Kace didn't appear concerned. "I believe the last time we fought, I knocked *your* ass out."

"*Stop!*" Bree's sharp voice had both men tensing. "We're here for business. Not to rehash your drama."

"Drama?" Kace tasted the word. "I have no drama." Now he looked insulted.

Bree ignored his affront. "Kyle Clarke is missing."

Kace immediately put all of his attention on Kennedy. "Again? How do you keep losing your brother?"

She took an aggressive step toward him.

Remy caught her hand. "Easy. I get it, I understand the temptation, believe me, but neither of us can punch him…yet."

Her hand had already fisted in prep for that hit. "Why did my brother keep coming back to you, Kace?"

"You know…" A shrug. "He liked the dark side. The drinks. The women. The fun."

She waited.

"He was a watcher," Kace added. "Liked to see the…*drama* that others created. Liked to observe. See the worst of people, never the best."

"Did he ever see anything that maybe he shouldn't have?" Bree asked carefully.

Kace cocked his head to the side. "My clubs weren't the only ones he visited. From what I know, though, he wasn't a user. Didn't do drugs. Didn't hurt anyone. Just slipped into the shadows. I felt like he was always looking for something. When he hooked up with Stacey, I thought he'd found it."

And then she'd been taken from him. "Has my brother contacted you?"

Kace's gaze was innocent. "You mean, since you dug him out of that pit? I don't believe so, but then, we were never exactly speed dial buddies."

"*Kace.*" When Bree said his name that way, serious and hard, the guy immediately locked all of his attention on her.

Once more, his expression softened. "I haven't heard from her brother, love. If I do, I will let you know immediately. But the guy never struck me as the killing kind, I can tell you that much right now."

"Anyone can be the killing kind, under the right conditions," Bree responded. "And you know that."

He didn't argue, but — "She cheated on him."

Surprise rippled through Kennedy when Kace made that flat announcement. "What?"

"The fiancée. Stacey." He waved his hand vaguely in the air. "I knew her, too. She enjoyed dancing. Drinking. And some of the darker treats that I *don't* allow here. Your brother thought she'd change for him, though. He was wrong. Right before she vanished, he caught her — at another club, according to the intel I've recently picked up — with a lover."

"No, that can't be right," Kennedy denied hotly. Kyle had *never* said anything about Stacey cheating.

He appeared insulted. "I assure you, my intel is very good. Why else would the FBI agents be here? After our last little meet and greet, I put out my feelers. People who wanted to gain my favor were only too happy to come to me with their whispers and stories." His brows lifted. "I even have the lover's name, if that will help you out."

Bree elbowed him. "Of *course,* it will help. But if you tell me it's Connor Wise—"

Disappointment flashed on Kace's face. "You already knew. Dammit, I wanted to give you a lead."

Bree immediately glanced at Remy.

But Kace wasn't done talking. "Connor tried one of my clubs a few times. He doesn't come to town often, but the man does like to party." He swiped away a speck on his shirt. "The first time he got rough with a waitress, he lost his pass to *all* my places. That's why I didn't have the intel directly. I don't stay in the same circles he does."

Her skin had iced. *Connor got rough with a waitress?*

Bree yanked out her phone. Dialed quickly. When she spoke, her voice held the hard ring of authority. "I want Connor Wise brought back to the station. Right the hell now. *Now.*"

***

Connor stared out at the city. He stood on the balcony, listening to the faint strain of jazz music in the distance. He'd always loved this city. The sights and the sounds. The people.

The energy.

Anything could happen in this city. *Anything.*

He turned from the window, heading back inside. He hadn't been to this home in ages, but his staff had put up a Christmas tree. The lights on the tree sparkled. He paused a moment, staring at them.

Then he heard the creak of the floor behind him.

He started to turn around, but a knife was already at his throat.

"You sonofabitch…" A too familiar voice snarled in his ear, "*I remember.*"

Connor swallowed and felt the blade press to his Adam's apple. "Kyle, I can explain…"

Kyle whirled him around. The knife came right at Connor.

CHAPTER EIGHTEEN

"Joshua and Bree are going to take care of Connor." Tension poured through Remy's voice. "They'll check in as soon as they have more information for us."

They were at the safe house, a condo in the city. The place was cold, somewhat stark. More like a hotel room than anything else. No holiday decorations. No personal touches.

But she was supposed to be safe there. Safe…from Kyle? Or from Connor? "Who's the bad guy…Connor? Or my brother?"

Or both?

He finished lighting the fireplace and crouched there as the flames flared. "It's possible your brother remembered something…and that he went after Connor." Remy squared his shoulders and rose. "But there are things that don't add up for me. Your brother destroying your doll when you were a child. Him standing over your bed with a knife. Baby, those are bad signs. Warning signs. He went to stay in a psychiatric facility where his behavior was described as violent. Both Bree and Joshua think those things could have been early indicators that he was—" Remy stopped.

She didn't. "You think those were some kind of early signs that something was…wrong with him. That Kyle was going to grow up to be some sort of serial killer?"

Remy faced her. He'd removed his holster and weapon—putting them on a nearby table before he'd lit the fire. "It's certainly possible. Those could have been warning signs of a behavioral disorder. If we could get his doctors from the clinic to talk to us—if we could get more than just accounts from the check-in staff—it would help us."

"He was happy with Stacey."

"And if she cheated on him, maybe that caused him to…revert. Revert back to a more dangerous time in his life. Or maybe it broke him or maybe—fuck, I don't know. We *can't* know for sure, not until we get him and Connor Wise at the station."

She rocked onto the balls of her feet as nervous—scared—energy hummed through her. "You want to be there."

He stalked toward her. "I want to make certain you're safe."

"No one knows where I am. You could leave me here. I'll be safe."

CYNTHIA EDEN   312

Remy shook his head. "Not happening. I'm staying with you. Bree and Joshua can handle the rest. Your safety is what matters most to me."

She thought about what Kace Quick had revealed. "You...you really turned down another case? You insisted on staying with me?"

He brushed back a lock of her hair. "When this is all over, I'm getting out of the Bureau. I figure it's time to go freelance. I don't want any other undercover cases. I want to take some time and see what it's like to just be Remy." A wry smile curved his lips. "Who knows? Maybe you might decide that you like the guy."

Her heart ached. "I do like him. That's why it hurt so much when I found out you'd lied to me."

His smile vanished. "I *won't* lie again."

She...believed him. "I'm scared."

Remy's jaw hardened. "I will keep you safe."

He couldn't protect her from this. "Kyle didn't put himself in that pit. Connor—I think Connor did it. And now my brother has gone after him, and Kyle might kill Connor." If he could, Kyle would. "I want to be out there. I want to help."

"Bree and Joshua will find your brother. You have to stay safe. You staying here—out of range—is the best thing to do. I *can't* put you at risk." He shook his head. "Every cop in the city is looking for them both. Detective Brock Mayo is leading the charge. After what happened to his partner, Mayo was chomping at the bit to get back on the streets and find her killer."

Except…Connor seemed to have vanished. When the Feds had gone to his hotel to collect him, he'd been gone.

Because her brother had taken him?

Or because Connor was the Broken Doll Killer…and he was on the run?

Remy continued grimly, "Bree has already got Connor's lawyer at the station, and he *will* talk. A team is searching every holding that Connor has. We're gonna find the guy."

"If Kyle had been watching him, if he saw Connor with Stacey, then he would know where Connor might be hiding."

Remy nodded.

"He could be there now." Maybe the hotel room had just been a cover. Maybe there was another place in the city that was Connor's true base.

"Yes."

Remy wasn't pulling punches.

So, neither would she. "And Kyle could be killing him."

"*Yes.*"

God. God! And she was just supposed to stand there and do nothing? Let her mind spin over and over again as she waited to find out if her whole world had just imploded—again? No.

"I need a drink." Or twelve. She headed toward the bar that waited in the corner but stopped — no, drinks weren't the escape she needed.

He was her escape.

Hadn't Remy been from the moment they met?

Not an escape.

He was…

Like a safe harbor for her, in a world gone completely, horribly insane. The one steady light when she was so freaking sick of the darkness.

She stopped, then slowly spun to face him.

Remy was staring at her. His expression — it was so tender. So…

Filled with longing.

"Remy?"

"The FBI will find them," he said immediately. "But I can't let you leave, baby. I'm so sorry. I need you to stay here. After the fire at your place, there's no denying *you* are a target. Your protection has to come first. *You* come first."

One slow step after another, she made her way back to him. She stopped just inches from Remy, and her hands rose to press to his chest.

"I will do anything to keep you safe," he rasped.

Kennedy shook her head. "No."

His eyes widened.

"Not anything. We'll stay at this place. We'll stay hidden. But you *won't* get hurt. You won't put yourself at risk. You won't ever sacrifice yourself for me." She sucked in a breath. "Because I can't have *you* hurt. You matter too much."

"You don't have to lie. You don't need to—"

"I love you."

Now Remy was the one to shake his head. "You don't. God, I wish you did. I'd give my fucking soul if you did. You don't know me. Not yet. You don't—"

"I know you. And I know how I feel. I. Love. You. The man who danced with me at the gala. The man who saved my ass in the street. The man who told me why he hates Christmas." She had to blink away tears. "That was all Remy St. Clair."

"Yes."

"That's the man I love. The man who made love to me. Who gave me more pleasure than I've ever had because I could really let go. I could give all of myself to you. And after we were together, you held me. You stayed with me."

"I will always stay with you...if you'll let me."

In a few hours...she didn't know what would happen. Her brother. Connor...

She swallowed to ease the lump that had risen in her throat. "Make love to me again. Right now."

"Kennedy..."

She pushed onto her toes and put her mouth against his. She needed this. Needed him. Needed him to know that whatever happened, she would choose him.

He kept her sane when the world went mad. She needed some sanity right then.

Her tongue slid over his lower lip. Into his mouth. His hands flew up and locked around her as he growled. Growled and kissed her back. Kissed her back with the wild passion that she craved. She needed him. All of him. Every single bit.

She had to stop the fear and the panic and the worry. She wanted to feel.

He lifted her into his arms. "Be sure..."

"I'm sure of you." She was. Completely.

"I love you."

Those words chased the chill from her—so much better than the fire. The fear lessened, just for a little while. She knew it would come back. But for this moment—this one moment...

I need him.

He carried her into the bedroom. Put her on the bed. Didn't bother to turn on the lights. She didn't want them on. She needed the darkness just as much as she needed him.

Hiding.

Hiding from the world, but not from him. Never again from him. They took off their clothes, stripping quickly. There was an urgency riding them both, she could feel the energy in the air. His hands slid over her body, caressing, stroking, and igniting her need to a fever pitch.

She'd never craved a lover the way she craved him. She didn't think that she ever would again.

He took a condom from his wallet. Slid it on. Came back to her and threaded his fingers with hers. "You are the most beautiful thing I've ever seen."

Her legs parted for him. The tip of his cock pressed against her. He didn't enter, not yet, she knew he was holding back. Trying to stay in control. Giving her tenderness.

But really, all she wanted was the rage of passion. To let go and not look back. Her hands wrapped around his shoulders as she pulled him closer. Their mouths met. She tasted him, arching toward him and taking just a little more of his cock into her.

Not good enough. She wanted everything. Her nails raked down his back. "*Remy…*"

"Holding on… for you." His hand slid between them. Stroked her clit. Rubbed it again and again in a fast rhythm that had her gasping. "Want you…come…first."

She was going to come. But not until he was in her. "*Now.*" She pushed hard with her hips, and she took all of him inside her.

Kennedy felt her control shatter. Hers. His. For just a moment, everything seemed to go absolutely primal. There weren't any slow, gentle thrusts. There was a desperate drive to completion as they rolled across the bed. He lifted her legs up, pushing them over his shoulders so that he could drive inside of her deeper, harder. Every thrust sent him surging against her sensitive core. Every thrust made her want and want and want.

She was gasping. Moaning. Her nails were biting into him now and she met him thrust for powerful thrust. The bed banged against the wall. Guttural groans tore from him.

It wasn't quite enough. The pleasure was just out of reach. She needed more. Almost there. Almost…

"Tight…hot…*perfect.*" He withdrew, thrust deep, withdrew — drove into her.

She shattered. Her whole body seemed to splinter apart as the release hit, and Remy didn't slow down. He kept pounding into her, his strong thrusts drawing out her climax and making the pleasure last and last even as she felt him exploding within her. His hips jerked against her, and the roar of her name broke from him.

The pounding of her heartbeat filled Kennedy's ears. The drumming slowly faded as her legs dropped limply to the bed. He was still in her. Still over her, but Remy had pushed up on his elbows so that his weight wouldn't crush her.

Darkness surrounded them, and she liked it. They were hidden from the rest of the world. Safe, just for a moment.

She wished that moment could last forever.

"My father loved my mother…" The words whispered from her. "And he killed her."

Remy pressed a kiss to her temple.

"I've always been afraid of loving someone too much." It was easier to talk about her fears in the darkness. "If you love someone so completely, you can lose yourself."

"Kennedy…"

"Kyle was lost, when Stacey disappeared." A soft sigh fell from her lips. "I think he's still lost."

"Do *you* feel lost, when you're with me?" A low rumble.

She shook her head, then realized he might not be able to see the motion in the darkness. "I feel happy. Even when the rest of the world is hell around us, you make me feel safe and happy."

It was true.

The phone rang. The peal scared her, and she flinched beneath him.

"Easy," Remy whispered. He slid from her. Rose from the bed.

Kennedy pulled up the covers, yanking them to her chin, and she saw the light from the phone illuminate his hard features.

"It's your phone." He offered it to her.

Unknown caller.

The phone rang again.

Her fingers slid over the screen, then she put the phone to her ear. "Hello?"

"*I'm…going…*" Such a weak, painful rasp. "*K-kill…him.*"

All of the breath left her lungs. "Kyle?"

"*Know…was him.*"

She had to strain to hear each savage word. The words seemed torn from him—so rough and ragged. "*He…f-fucked her…he…k-killed…*"

She squeezed the phone so hard that Kennedy was afraid it would shatter. "You're with Connor, aren't you?"

"Put him on speaker," Remy urged her. "Now."

She fumbled with the phone. Her fingers finally got the call on speaker.

"*F-found him…*" Barely a breath of sound.

"Where? Where are you?"

"*His dad—he had a…m-mistress in town…Uses same place…*"

He said something else, but she couldn't make out the ragged words. "Kyle, *where* are you?"

"Prytania Street. C-columns. S-saw him…here…with her."

"Kyle," she fought to keep her voice calm. "Have you hurt him?"

Silence.

"Kyle, don't do this. Don't kill him. The cops can come. Remy is right here with me, he can—"

"Make…him…confess…" His voice broke.

"Kyle, *no.*"

The line went dead.

Remy's fingers brushed her arm. "I texted Joshua and Bree. Gave them the location details we had."

She jumped out of the bed. Grabbed her clothes and dressed as quickly as she could. "We're close to Prytania."

"Kennedy…"

"He's my brother! And we can be there within minutes. Minutes! We'll beat the cops and the other FBI agents to the scene, and you know it." She grabbed his arm. "He's going to torture Connor! He's going to kill him. And if the authorities come in with guns blazing, they will kill Kyle." *No, no, no!* "We can stop all of this, but we have to *go.*"

She expected him to argue. She was ready for a fight, but he told her, "You stay with me. Every single second, you understand? I go in first, and if you can't talk your brother down, we get the hell out of there."

"Okay, please, let's just go!"

He grabbed his clothes. Yanked them on. A moment later, they were back in the den, and he picked up the weapon he'd put down earlier. He slid on his shoulder holster and checked his gun. When he was satisfied, his gaze slid over her face. "This is *your* life. And you will not risk yourself for your brother." He kissed her. "You matter. More than anything."

"Remy…"

"Stay behind me. I go in every door first. I take the threat, *first*."

With her left hand, she grabbed his shirt-front. "You matter to me, you understand? You don't get hurt, either. You called for back-up, and we're going to use your team. Everyone is going to be okay. *Everyone*." They just had to move. They had to get to the house on Prytania before Kyle went too far…

If he hasn't already.

***

"You can't…do this…" Connor's voice was weak. Rough.

Kyle stared down at the phone in his hand. It had been Connor's phone. He'd found it inside the guy's desk drawer when he'd searched the place. A burner phone. He'd tied the guy to the chair, cutting strips of the curtains to make the binds.

He'd punched the bastard. Hit him over and over, and the thud of flesh had made him feel better. This was the bastard who'd ruined his life. Who'd taken everything away from him.

He'd called his sister just so that Kennedy would know — she didn't need to be afraid any longer. He was going to eliminate the danger. He was going to protect her. Wasn't that what a big brother was supposed to do?

"I saw you with Stacey," Kyle muttered. His voice was broken. Little more than a whisper. He'd acted like he couldn't talk much at all to that Fed — Agent Morgan. Kyle could talk some, though, if he strained hard enough he got this piss-weak rasp. "I was at the club the night you first…hooked up. Did you know…she was m-my fiancée?"

Connor licked his lips. Didn't answer.

Kyle put his knife to the guy's throat. "*Did you know?*"

"Yes! Shit! I just — I thought it'd be fun, taking your girl. You deserved some payback. I *knew* you were the one who kicked me out of Kennedy's life!" Spittle flew from his mouth as Connor tried to crane his neck away from the knife.

Kicked me out of Kennedy's life.

Yes, Kyle had done that. Kennedy believed their grandfather had been the one to come up with the plan to buy off Connor, but it had really been Kyle.

He'd known the truth about his so-called friend for years. Connor was twisted on the inside. Messed up.

He'd realized that the day he'd found Connor with Kennedy's doll. The jerk had cut the eyes out of her doll, and then he'd begged Kyle not to tell. Kennedy had cried and cried. *I promised her it would never happen again. I told her I was sorry…but I never told her he'd been the one to break her doll.*

Connor had only gotten worse as they aged. Kyle had seen the cracks in the guy's surface. Seen the obsession that the fellow had with Kennedy. So, he'd convinced his grandfather that the guy had to go. Kennedy had loved Connor, but she'd never seen the real man. Kyle had protected her.

The SOB wanted to pay me back for shoving him out of Kennedy's life?

"Payback," Kyle tasted the word. "Were you giving me payback when you killed Stacey?" He *hated* the weak rasp of his voice.

"*I didn't!*"

"Or when you locked me in the bottom of the lake house?" His throat burned as he forced out the gasping whisper. "Was that…payback? Because I stopped being your friend? Because I saw what a f-fucking *freak* you were? Always targeting those who were weaker. Getting off on pain."

"I didn't kill her!"

He didn't believe him. *Liar, liar.* "Your house, Connor. You...fucked her. You locked me up. And you thought you were going to be safe. I was the one who had to go to the psych ward all those...years ago...when *you* were the one who got off on pain."

Connor froze. Then...he laughed. "It's my kink. So the hell what? I'm not a murderer." And he stopped trying to get away from the knife. Instead, he leaned into the blade. "Are you?"

"Connor..."

"Can you do it? Because I don't think you can. I don't think you can actually take that knife and cut my throat. You can't slice me from ear to ear. You can't do it. Because deep down, you aren't a killer. You don't have that primal instinct that can push you into the darkness." A laugh. Rough and mean. "You don't have the balls to do it. You and that broken ass voice — you can't do a damn thing!"

Kyle saw the blood drip down Connor's throat. "I was kept as a prisoner...for weeks. Left in the darkness. My fiancée was murdered. I didn't know if I'd ever get out."

Connor glared up at him.

"And you know what I realized? I realized I would *kill* to get out. I realized that when I ever escaped, I would hunt down the piece of shit who'd tried to destroy me…and I would make him pay. I would *end* him."

Connor's glare wavered. His eyelashes flickered.

Kyle shoved the knife harder against his neck. "I heard the Feds. They say my sister is the killer's next target. *Your* next target." He ignored the burn in his throat. Maybe these would be his last words.

"I'm not—"

"I will not let you hurt her." His words were so faint, but he knew Connor heard his grim promise. "*I'll…carve you up, I'll fucking eviscerate you, before that ever happens.*"

Connor twisted his body, snarling and grunting and—

Connor's hands were free. The damn curtains had torn. He surged out of the chair and Kyle shoved down with his knife.

CHAPTER NINETEEN

Lights blazed inside the massive, regency-style home on Prytania Street. Remy shoved on the brakes and turned off the car, adrenaline pumping through him. "I don't know what we're going to find inside—"

She shoved open her door.

"Dammit!" He leapt from the vehicle and raced toward her. He grabbed Kennedy and pulled her back. "*Not* the way this is working. We don't know what's inside. I have to check the scene. I'm going in first. I'll get it under control and *then* you can talk to your brother."

"Remy—"

"Baby, I'm not going to shoot him. Trust me. This is my job. *Trust me.*"

She nodded. Her gaze was desperate, but she said, "I do."

He kissed her. Hard. Fast. He shoved the car keys into her hand. "Lock the doors. Stay here. As soon as it's clear, I'll be back. You see any sign of trouble, you haul ass away from the scene. Your life isn't worth risking."

Then he let her go. He rushed toward the heavy gate in front of the house — of course, a gate that was locked — and he climbed over the freaking thing. He touched down on the other side and ran up the sprawling steps. Large columns waited beside the front door. This had damn well better be the right place —

"Help me!" A man's scream echoed from inside.

He grabbed for the doorknob. Locked. "FBI!" Remy yelled. He kicked the door, aiming for that lock, hitting it once, twice —

Wood broke. The lock gave away. The door flew open.

He raced inside, with his gun up. And he saw the blood. Blood on the marble floor. Blood dripping from Connor Wise's throat. He was on his knees, and Kyle Clarke was behind him. Kyle's knife was right at Connor's jugular.

One jerk of his wrist —

Shit. "Drop the knife," Remy barked at him.

Kyle's gaze rose. He stared at Remy. Frowned. "Where is…my sister?" A bare whisper.

"Drop the knife, and I'll go get her for you," he promised. "She's right outside. If you just drop the knife —"

And he heard the rush of footsteps behind him. *Someone else was there?* He whirled because he hadn't anticipated this threat. But he moved too slowly and a gun exploded.

The bullet tore into him, sending Remy hurtling toward the floor. The bullet had blasted through his gut. He tried to lift up his hand, but a booted foot came down, kicking Remy's gun out of his grasp.

"What are you doing?" Kyle gasped in his broken voice. "Stop, stop!"

But another bullet had just exploded from the assailant's gun. The roar of that bullet echoed in Remy's ears. The bullet slammed into Kyle's shoulder, and he fell back, the knife dropping from his fingers and clattering against the floor.

Remy could see Connor Wise. His eyes were huge and shocked, and he was scrambling for the knife that Kyle had dropped.

Connor won't make it in time.

Remy knew he wouldn't make it. He grabbed for the assailant, trying to pull the bastard over even as the blood pumped from Remy's body. Pain burned through him, but he wasn't going to stop—

Bam!

A third shot. A hit directly to Connor's forehead. The guy slumped without a sound.

Fucking hell. Remy shoved a hand over his bleeding wound. He needed to get his gun. He crawled forward. He needed—

His attacker was in front of him. "I like that you're still trying to win, but I'm afraid that's just not going to happen."

Remy glared up at the man who'd been waiting in the shadows. A killer he hadn't seen coming.

The guy aimed his gun at Remy's face. "Hope you like hell."

CHAPTER TWENTY

She'd heard the thunder of gunshots. One. Two...a pause, a pause that chilled her. Then—
Three.

Kennedy stared at the front of the house on Prytania. *Come out, Remy. Come out.*

But no one came out. Not Remy. Not her brother. Not even Connor.

Oh, God.

She fumbled for the glove box. It was locked but Remy had left her with the keys. She got it open, searched inside, looking for some kind of weapon. *Something* that could help her. Maybe Remy's backup gun was inside. No, dammit, the gun wasn't there, but—

Her fingers touched a hard sheath. She pulled it out and saw a blade strapped inside the sheath. Her breath heaved faster as she yanked the knife out of the sheath and ran for the house. Help was already on the way. Joshua and Bree would arrive any minute, but what if Remy didn't have a minute to waste? What if she was already too late?

He needed her, and she wasn't just going to sit her ass in the car while two men she loved were possibly dying in that house.

She threw the knife through the gate and scrambled over the damn thing, falling on the other side. Pausing only long enough to scoop up her weapon, Kennedy hurried toward the house. The door was open, but she didn't run inside. Instead, she crept through the open doorway and tried not to make a sound. Her heart thundered in her chest, but her steps were dead silent. She kept the knife by her side, hiding it behind her leg and—

Blood.

There was blood on the floor.

Bodies on the floor.

"Oh, thank God!" A familiar voice had her jerking.

And shaking her head in disbelief.

Because…Henry was there. *Her* Henry. Henry was crouched next to Remy, a Remy who appeared unconscious. *Unconscious, not dead. He can't be dead. He can't be dead.*

Henry had a gun in one hand.

She kept her knife near her side.

"He came in, with guns blazing…" Henry appeared dazed. "I was here—Kyle had called me. I tried to get Remy to understand that your brother wasn't a threat. But he didn't listen.

Remy just started firing!" His shaking left hand pointed behind him.

Behind him…

To the other two bodies.

Connor.

Kyle?

Her body trembled.

"I told him to stop!" Henry cried out. Tears fell down his cheeks. "I told him that the situation was under control! I'd talked your brother down! I had him calm. But Remy…he just fired. *Bam, bam!* One hit to your brother. One hit to Connor. And then—then he turned on me." He glanced at his right hand and appeared shocked to see a gun in his grip. "I brought my weapon with me. Just in case. God, you know this city. It can get crazy at night, and I thought…" His words trailed off.

Kennedy took a few careful steps toward Henry and Remy.

"He was going to shoot me." Henry's words were hollow. "I could see it in Remy's eyes. He was going to shoot me just like he'd shot Kyle and Connor. Because I was a witness. I saw what he'd done. I saw that he shot those two men in cold blood. But I wasn't ready to die. I-I fired and hit him."

Was Remy's chest moving? Rising and falling? Or was it still?

"I need to check your brother!" Henry barked at her. "Please, God, let him still be alive." He lurched to his feet. Ran to her brother. Crouched beside him.

She sank to her knees at Remy's side.

"He was crazy!" Henry called out. "Never seen anything like it. The man was destroying everyone in his path. And I thought he was supposed to be the good guy."

Blood pumped from a wound in Remy's stomach. And there was a big, heavy cut near his temple. As if he'd been hit by something.

By...

The butt of a gun? Because when she'd come in the home, Henry had been crouched near Remy — and he'd been holding a gun.

Her left hand rose to press over the wound in Remy's stomach. The blood immediately poured through her fingers. He let out a low gasp, and it was the most beautiful sound she'd ever heard. That pain-filled gasp meant Remy was still alive. She needed to apply pressure on the wound. She could keep him alive. Help would come.

"Kennedy! Your brother's alive!" Henry yelled. "Come help me! Kyle needs you!"

She didn't move. "Remy is alive. I'm putting pressure on his wound. He needs me."

"That bastard shot your brother! He would have shot me! He's not who you think. He's not—"

Trust me. She stayed exactly where she was. "More Feds are coming. They'll be here soon."

Henry's footsteps rushed toward her. "Your brother is *dying,* and you're trying to save the piece of shit who shot him—"

She could feel him behind her. Right behind her. Within striking range. Exactly where she wanted him. Kennedy whirled and shoved her knife up, catching him in the stomach, in nearly the same spot where Remy had been shot.

Henry's mouth parted. Shock flashed on his face. Shock. Betrayal. Pain.

Then rage. A whole lot of rage.

He still had a gun in his hand. The gun she suspected he'd used to shoot Remy. To shoot Connor. To shoot Kyle. She suspected he'd done it all.

"I raised you," he snarled as spittle flew from his mouth.

Her right hand was still tight around the handle of the knife.

His right hand—it was still locked around the gun he was raising toward her.

"I raised you…and you picked *him?*"

She yanked hard on the knife, ripping it sideways, and Henry howled. He fired his gun, but she leapt back, and the bullet just blazed a fiery path down her arm, grazing her. She jumped over Remy's body. She'd seen his gun on the floor. The Glock was a few feet away, as if it had been kicked aside, and if she could just get to it fast enough—

"I will put a bullet…" Henry's breath heaved out. "In his brain…right now. You *stop*, you hear me?"

She froze. The gun was so close. Two more feet, and she would've had it. But right then, it might as well have been a million miles away.

"Look at me!"

She spun around. Saw Henry. He stood over Remy. Had his gun pressed to Remy's forehead.

"Don't!" Kennedy begged. "Please, *don't!*"

Blood soaked the front of Henry's shirt. He gave her a twisted smile. "How did you know…it was me?"

Simple. Because…"I trust him."

Rough laughter. "But you don't trust me? I *raised* you. I protected you. Over and over again. From every threat out there."

"You were the threat." She had to keep him talking. Had to keep him from firing on Remy. Joshua and Bree would be there soon. They had to be. She just had to keep Henry's focus on her until they arrived. "I didn't see it. I should have seen it."

His smile was chilling. He didn't even seem to notice all of the blood pouring from his stomach. The knife still protruded from this gut. "What changed?"

"Remy promised me that he wouldn't hurt Kyle. He came in here to help Kyle, not to hurt him. I *trust* him."

Disgust tightened his features. "Because you think you love him."

"I *know* I do."

His cold smile stretched. "Your mother once thought she loved me."

Her breath caught in her lungs.

"She fucked me. Promised me that we'd be together. But I knew the truth. She wasn't going to leave all that damn money. Not willingly. I mean, she wouldn't leave the fucker when he put his fists on Kyle. If she wouldn't leave then, no way would she leave for me."

Kyle…

"When I told her that I was going to take her, that I was going to *make* her leave with me, she told your dick of a father about us. Well, I had to take care of them both then, didn't I?"

Her breath heaved in and out. "The fire?"

Henry — the man who'd *been* like a father to her — nodded. "I wasn't just going to watch while she lived the rest of her life with him." The gun never moved from Remy's forehead. But…

When her gaze darted to Remy, she saw his lashes flicker.

He's conscious. And she knew he was looking for a chance to attack. So, she kept talking. Kept

Henry's attention on her. "Why didn't you run after you killed them?"

Henry blinked. "Your grandfather asked me to stay. Said you kids needed me." A shrug. "Where was I going to go?"

Sweet hell.

"But Kyle...he was always a bit of trouble. Always a little suspicious. I wondered sometimes...did he see me on the boat? He never said, but sending him away, telling everyone that he'd gone a little crazy..." Laughter. "That worked for me. After all, who'd believe the boy who had the breakdown?"

"Kyle *didn't* have a breakdown."

"Thought he would," Henry muttered. "When I kept him in that pit. Saw it years ago, you know. Back when you kids used to go to the lake house. I went to the lake house, too. Got to say, Connor's mother was pretty...accommodating back then."

Connor's mother. She'd—oh, God, she'd died in a one-car accident when Connor had been a teen. "You killed her?"

A shrug. "I realized I liked to kill women. Only the bitches who deserved it, though."

No one deserved what he'd done. And they weren't *bitches*.

"Rich women like to fuck over their husbands. I gave them what they wanted, and in the end, they gave me what I needed."

What had he needed? Death? Power? "You're sick." Had she just heard a car door outside? "I thought you loved us."

His eyes widened. The gun lifted a little farther away from Remy's head. "I did! I do! I always loved you! You're my family. You became *mine!* That's why I—"

Remy threw his whole body against Henry's. Henry staggered back. Started to topple. As he fell, he fired his gun again.

"No!" Kennedy screamed. But the bullet had already fired. The blast had her ears ringing. Henry was trying to get back up. She wasn't going to let that happen. She grabbed Remy's discarded gun, and she bounded to her target. "Get away from him! No!"

Henry sat up, aiming his gun right at her.

Just as she aimed hers at him.

"I raised you," he growled. "You and your brother. You were *mine*. So I thought...they have to get my killer instinct, right? I let your brother catch his whore with Connor. I told him where to find them. But weak Kyle didn't do a damn thing. Maybe your dad was right about him. Maybe Kyle always has been broken."

No, he wasn't.

"So, I killed that bitch Stacey. Just like I'd killed the others. Then I put Kyle in that pit. I thought it would bring out his monster. The monster had to be there." Spittle flew from his mouth. "I'm the one who helped him get out of the hospital. I knocked out that cop, and I got Kyle out of there. No one suspected a fucking thing. Hell, I stood outside of the hospital exam room while that dumb cop got poked and prodded, and it was all I could do not to smile."

No, no!

"I made Kyle hide while I made that little appearance with you all, and then I went back to him. I'm the one who brought him *here*. I was waiting, I was going to watch him make his first kill, but he wouldn't fucking do it!"

Did she hear footsteps? Or was that just the thunder of her own heartbeat?

"I could see it as I watched from the shadows. He was backing down. Remy came running in, and your brother was going to be a pussy. I had to shoot. I had to kill again!"

"Drop your gun," Kennedy told him. "Or I will shoot you."

But Henry shook his head. "You don't have it in you, little girl. You're too much like your twin."

"I'm not a little girl."

"Why do you think I had Stacey paint you with a blindfold on? I put the blindfold on them all…because they couldn't see what was right in front of them. Walking through the world, weak and useless, not seeing any threat there."

The gun was shaking. She was shaking. "I see you."

"But you'll never pull the trigger. I will. I'll kill you. I'll finish off your lover. I'll end your weak brother—"

Bam.

Her finger squeezed the trigger. A fast, hard pull, and the bullet exploded from the gun. It hurtled, so fast, and then there was a giant hole in Henry's chest. His eyes widened. First with shock. Then with—

Pride.

"*My...girl...*"

She shot him again. Again and again and—

He fell.

"Kennedy!"

A man's voice, thundering at her. She whirled, weapon up, and found Joshua behind her. Bree was there, too. They were both armed and staring at her with hard eyes.

Probably because they'd just seen her kill a man. And they'd walked into a blood bath.

She dropped the weapon. Put her hands up. "Please...help Remy and my brother." She was pretty sure that Connor was far beyond any help.

"What in the hell happened here?" Bree asked as she shook her head.

"Henry." Goosebumps covered her arms. "It was Henry." Always Henry.

The man who'd raised her and Kyle. The man who'd lied to them. Tricked them. Hurt them.

The man who'd promised he'd always love them.

***

He fucking *hurt*. Remy let out a ragged groan and punched at the bastard who'd just come at him with one long-ass needle. "Kennedy!" He meant to yell her name, but his cry came out more like a hoarse growl. "Need...*Kennedy!*"

"Look, buddy, you need a hospital, you need stitches, and you need some blood. Settle down for me, will you?"

No. He surged up. "Kennedy!"

"Jesus," the EMT muttered. "Let's sedate this big bastard. Or — hell, is the woman he's asking for here? Bring her — "

In the next moment, Kennedy was there. He felt her hand curl around his. He turned his head. Focused on her even as he felt the EMT jab a needle into his arm. "You're...okay..." A rough rasp. Things around her were blurry and dark. Getting darker by the moment.

"I'm okay," she said. It sounded as if Kennedy was crying. He didn't like that. Kennedy couldn't cry. Kennedy needed to be happy. Safe.

"Baby?" Had he done something wrong? Everything was so hazy.

"You have to stop fighting the EMTs. They're taking you to the hospital. They're going to patch you up."

Patch him…Remy lost his train of thought. His veins seemed to have been pumped with ice. He knew that feeling—he'd experienced it before. After he'd been shot and the docs had given him morphine.

"Just relax," a voice said to his left. "I'm going to help you, but you've got to stay still. You're losing way too much blood."

His eyes began to sag closed.

Kennedy's fingers tightened on his. "Don't you dare die on me."

He'd been shot by…Henry? How many times? "You're…okay?" Had he already asked her that?

"Yes, dammit, don't worry about me. You are the one who has to get better. You are the one—"

He couldn't keep his eyes open. A siren was screaming. Wailing. Kennedy still had his hand, or at least, he thought she was holding his hand. And that was good. Kennedy was safe. She was alive.

"Stay…" Remy managed. He'd meant to say…*Stay with me. Forever. Please, stay with me.* Because he needed her with him. His life was better when Kennedy was with him. He had to prove that to her. Had to prove that they had a real shot at being happy together. They could have it all.

The house with the picket fence. The Friday night football games. The kids.

Or…shit, they could have none of that. If Kennedy wanted, they could travel around the country and live out of a freaking car. As long as he was with her, he didn't care.

He just…he had to be with her.

He needed to be with her. He wanted a chance.

He wasn't going to be a liar any longer. He wasn't a criminal. He wasn't going to deceive and trick. He was going to be real. He'd cook her breakfast and dinner. He'd hold her on cold nights.

If she wanted, maybe they could even have Christmas together. With her, it might be different. With her, everything could be different.

He just…*needed* her. A life with Kennedy.

So why did he feel like he was losing her? Why did he feel…

The cold was getting worse.

Was Kennedy still holding his hand? He didn't feel her.

"Love…"

I love you, Kennedy.

CHAPTER TWENTY-ONE

The morgue was cold. Icy. Joshua Morgan had never liked the place. How the hell the gorgeous coroner could handle it was totally beyond him, but Dr. Angela Crawford didn't seem to have any problems.

He stared at the body on the slab. Another victim. Another day, another death. He was getting tired of this shit. Maybe it was time for a new line of work.

"Death was instantaneous," Dr. Crawford said as she came to his side.

Yeah, well, considering the guy had taken a bullet to the brain, the death would have *needed* to be instantaneous. Connor Wise was on the table, a toe tag on his foot, his body hard and cold.

To think, they'd had the guy in the interrogation room such a short time ago...

Joshua cleared his throat. "How long is it going to take you on the others?"

"You don't want to know."

He dragged his gaze to her.

Dr. Crawford sadly shook her head. "We are understaffed and underfunded, and you pulled ten bodies out of the water. The decomposition rates are going to make their cases hell. If the FBI has some resources they want to throw my way, they'd sure be appreciated. Otherwise, we could be looking at months of work."

"I'll see what I can do." Those women—and the vics had all been women—they deserved justice. The Broken Doll Killer had been hurting his victims for too long.

Far longer than the FBI had realized. He'd been killing for years and dumping his vics in the lake as he'd become the perfect killing machine.

He'd turned that pit at the lake house into his own personal torture chamber. He'd kept his vics imprisoned there. The FBI had ripped the basement apart and finally found the mechanism the guy had used to open and close the floor slats. Tricky sonofabitch. With Connor never visiting the lake house, Henry Marshall had the perfect set-up.

Joshua's stare focused on the next exam table. On the next body.

You're not hurting anyone now, are you, bastard?

A sheet covered Henry Marshall. He'd died at the scene. Killed by Kennedy Clarke.

"I'm not supposed to be glad that anyone is dead." The coroner's voice was softer. "But this time, I am."

"So am I." Because all of those women in the lake — all of the women Henry had killed — they deserved justice.

She swallowed. "How are the others doing?"

Not as good as he would have liked. "Kyle Clarke was hit in the shoulder. He got stitched up, and he's staying in the hospital for observation." Joshua thought the bullet's location had been deliberate. Henry hadn't been aiming to kill Kyle.

When he'd fired straight at Connor Wise's head…yeah, Henry had meant for that man to go down and stay down.

"What about Remy St. Clair?"

Remy. The guy's blood had soaked the scene. But…

"He's gonna pull through." Joshua turned away from the dead men. Sometimes, the bad guys didn't win. "I think he has a lot to live for."

***

She was at his side. The minute that Remy opened his eyes, he saw her. Kennedy sat in the chair near his hospital bed. Her fingers were twined with his. Her gaze was directed out the window, and she looked so incredibly beautiful.

"Love…" Jesus, his voice sounded terrible. Like rusty nails. "You."

Her head turned toward him. A wide smile curved her gorgeous lips as she leaned toward him. "You're back?" Her eyes searched his. "Really back? Like, you know my name this time?"

"Kennedy Clarke." Again…rusty nails. Had a tube been shoved down his throat? It ached.

"And you know what happened?"

He had a flash of…a gunshot. Bleeding. "Henry." Machines near him started to beep fast and hard.

"It's okay. He's dead."

Remy's lashes flickered. "You?" He remembered—

She nodded. "I wasn't going to let him hurt you again. Not you and not Kyle."

Her brother. He tried to sit up. The machines went even crazier.

"Stop it!" She pushed him back down. "You'll tear your stitches! This is the first time in *two days* that we've had a real conversation. Don't you dare do anything to jeopardize yourself now that you're finally back with me!" Her stare fired fury at him. "You're going to heal and recover and not do anything else."

She was so insanely perfect. He'd never seen a more stunning woman. "Yes, ma'am."

Her eyes narrowed.

"Your brother…he's okay?"

"Yes, he's okay. The two of you sound just alike." Sympathy flashed on her face as she hurriedly grabbed a glass and a straw from a nearby table. "The nurse said this would help."

He sipped and, hell, yes, that helped. The fire in his throat settled some.

"You were bad." She kept holding the straw. He saw the fear flash in her eyes. "When I was in the ambulance with you, your whole body went slack. There was so much blood, and they couldn't seem to get the bleeding stopped. Then you were back in surgery for hours and hours, and I couldn't get anywhere near you because I wasn't family—"

"Let's change that."

"What?"

"I...think you are my family." She was the only one who mattered to him. "Be...my family? Marry—" He didn't get to say anything else.

She leaned down and kissed him. A soft, tender kiss. "This had better not be the drugs talking."

Was he on drugs?

"I love you," Kennedy whispered the words against his mouth. "I want a life with you. I want everything that we can possibly get, Remy. I want it all."

The machines were beeping fast again.

He ignored them.

He wanted her to kiss him once more. Or a thousand times more, whatever.

But she swallowed and eased back. "I thought I could count on Henry. I never saw him for what he was. He—he killed my parents. He confessed that to me. He killed them and so many other people, and I never knew. I let him into my life. I lived with him day after day. He lied and killed, and I never knew." Her hand rose to press to her heart. "I killed him, and when he took his last breath, I hurt because I loved him, too."

She'd loved the man she *thought* Henry had been.

"If Henry had killed you, if he had killed Kyle…" Her gaze cut away from him. "He *did* kill Connor. And Detective Amanda Jackson. And so many more people. I wish I'd known. I wish that I could have stopped him. I wish that it all could have been different."

He reached for her hand. He needed to touch her. Needed to be close.

"Connor had plenty of secrets, too. Remember when that car almost ran me down after the gala? Your partner Joshua found out that Connor paid the driver. Connor also paid someone to put that stupid doll in my house. Joshua thinks Connor wanted to scare me so that he could swoop in and be my protector."

Fucking asshole.

"Joshua found photos of me at Connor's place on Prytania. He'd been watching me. Kyle told me...said that Connor had been, um, *off*. Kyle is the one who got Connor sent out of my life. He was trying to protect me." Sadly, she shook her head. "I guess I can't see the men in life for what they really are."

"You see me." He didn't want her lumping him with the others. "I made mistakes, baby, and I'm so fucking sorry. I will always be sorry for the lies. I want to be different. I want to make you so happy. Please, give me a chance." His heart seemed to stop as he waited for her response.

"There has been too much loss. Too much pain. I don't want any more." She shook her head. "Joshua got permission for me to be in this room. When the doctors and nurses finally let me get close to you, I swore there wouldn't be any pain again. I want joy. I want happiness. And I want it all with you."

Didn't she get it? The woman was his joy. Without her, hell, he was just a man lost.

It was time to change. Time to grab for what he wanted. Time to leave the shadows and start living. "I love you, Kennedy Clarke."

Her smile warmed his heart. "And I love you, Remy."

***

One Week Later…

Christmas Eve had finally arrived. Kennedy hurried toward the front of Remy's place…a bag of packages gripped in her hand. She had a surprise for him, and she didn't know how he was going to react. They hadn't talked about presents. She knew how he felt about the holidays, and she didn't want to stress him. But she'd wanted to do something to make him happy. He made her so happy and she just —

The front door opened. Remy stood there, dressed in jeans and a green shirt. He smiled at her, the killer grin that could make her lose her breath. "Perfect timing. Your brother and Joshua will be here in less than an hour."

Wait…they were coming over?

He took the bag from her, frowning down at the brightly wrapped packages. A knot formed in her stomach. Maybe the presents had been a bad idea. Kennedy hoped she hadn't just screwed things up. He'd told her, though, that he wanted to try the whole Christmas routine again. That he wanted them to *try* making memories, so when she'd been out, she'd just —

He looked up at her, a huge smile on his face. "I love you."

"Uh, Remy —"

He caught her hand, pulled her inside and — there was a Christmas tree waiting. A completely naked, maybe a wee bit small Christmas tree. Just sitting in the middle of the den. "I didn't want to decorate without you," he said quickly. "I thought...I thought this could be something we do together. You know, our tradition and—"

"You're putting up a tree." She couldn't look away from it.

"*We're* putting it up. Remember? I said that I wanted to try Christmas. With you."

"But—" Now her stare jerked to him.

"I can't live in the past. And I know you don't want to live there, either." His fingers tightened on hers. "I met you during the Christmas season, Kennedy. You walked into that ball, wearing your beautiful red gown. My Cinderella, running away through the Christmas lights. I took one look, and I'm pretty sure that's when I started to lose my heart to you."

"Remy..." For a tough, ex-undercover FBI agent, the man could say the sweetest things.

"I want to celebrate. I want the holidays to be happy for us. For our kids. I want to do *everything* with you." His smile came and went. "But just so you know..." Now he seemed uncomfortable. "Finding a tree on Christmas Eve is not an easy task. I had to call in a favor from Kace Quick to get this thing."

She smiled at him. And told a small lie. "It's the most amazing tree I've ever seen in my life."

He laughed. Brought her in close. Kissed her lips so carefully. "Baby, you are a terrible liar, but

I love you." He put his forehead against hers. "Christmas will be different this year. It will be the start of our tradition together. Our life."

Time to let go of the past and the pain—for both of them.

He eased away from her. "I bought all of the ornaments that were left at the store. I thought you could choose what you wanted. There were only two sets of lights left, but I believe they'll work."

One set would easily work on their tiny tree.

"And I...I got presents for you."

"I got a few things for you, too." Some of the items were sexy pieces of lingerie that she'd picked up. Kennedy had thought that they could heat up the night together, and she definitely planned to still do that. But some of the other items...

They were just because.

Because I love him.

Remy. Alive. Safe. He was her best present—the only present she wanted. He'd helped her to get her brother back. They'd stopped the killer. The nightmares could end.

It was time for the real living to begin.

She cleared her throat. Focused on the here and now. The moment that mattered. Kennedy gazed tenderly at Remy. "Shall we start on the tree?"

Excitement lit his eyes. Joy. He was happy. And she saw the real man who'd been hiding inside. A man who wanted love, and magic, and everything else he could get in life.

Good. She was going to give him all of those things.

Just as he would give them to her.

The End

A NOTE FROM THE AUTHOR

Thank you for reading DON'T LOVE A LIAR.

I loved returning to New Orleans and catching up with some of the characters who had appeared in DON'T TRUST A KILLER. And now that I've written this story, I have to confess…I'm really thinking that Kennedy's twin brother may need a future story, too. What do you think? Should Kyle get a book?

If you enjoyed this story, please consider leaving a review. Reviews help new readers to find new books!

https://cynthiaeden.com/newsletter/

Again, thank you for reading DON'T LOVE A LIAR. Happy Holidays!

Best,
Cynthia Eden
cynthiaeden.com

ABOUT THE AUTHOR

Award-winning author Cynthia Eden writes dark tales of paranormal romance and romantic suspense. She is a New York Times, USA Today, Digital Book World, and IndieReader best-seller. Cynthia is also a three-time finalist for the RITA® award. Since she began writing full-time in 2005, Cynthia has written over eighty novels and novellas.

For More Information

- *cynthiaeden.com*
- *http://www.facebook.com/cynthiaedenfanpage*
- *http://www.twitter.com/cynthiaeden*

HER OTHER WORKS

Romantic Suspense

- Secret Admirer
- Don't Trust A Killer
- Don't Love A Liar

Lazarus Rising

- Never Let Go (Book One, Lazarus Rising)
- Keep Me Close (Book Two, Lazarus Rising)
- Stay With Me (Book Three, Lazarus Rising)
- Run To Me (Book Four, Lazarus Rising)
- Lie Close To Me (Book Five, Lazarus Rising)
- Hold On Tight (Book Six, Lazarus Rising)

Dark Obsession Series

- Watch Me (Dark Obsession, Book 1)
- Want Me (Dark Obsession, Book 2)

- Need Me (Dark Obsession, Book 3)
- Beware Of Me (Dark Obsession, Book 4)
- Only For Me (Dark Obsession, Books 1 to 4)

Mine Series

- Mine To Take (Mine, Book 1)
- Mine To Keep (Mine, Book 2)
- Mine To Hold (Mine, Book 3)
- Mine To Crave (Mine, Book 4)
- Mine To Have (Mine, Book 5)
- Mine To Protect (Mine, Book 6)
- Mine Series Box Set Volume 1 (Mine, Books 1-3)
- Mine Series Box Set Volume 2 (Mine, Books 4-6)

Other Romantic Suspense

- First Taste of Darkness
- Sinful Secrets
- Until Death
- Christmas With A Spy

Paranormal Romance
Bad Things

- The Devil In Disguise (Bad Things, Book 1)
- On The Prowl (Bad Things, Book 2)
- Undead Or Alive (Bad Things, Book 3)

- Broken Angel (Bad Things, Book 4)
- Heart Of Stone (Bad Things, Book 5)
- Tempted By Fate (Bad Things, Book 6)
- Bad Things Volume One (Books 1 to 3)
- Bad Things Volume Two (Books 4 to 6)
- Bad Things Deluxe Box Set (Books 1 to 6)
- Wicked And Wild (Bad Things, Book 7)
- Saint Or Sinner (Bad Things, Book 8)

Bite Series

- Forbidden Bite (Bite Book 1)
- Mating Bite (Bite Book 2)

Blood and Moonlight Series

- Bite The Dust (Blood and Moonlight, Book 1)
- Better Off Undead (Blood and Moonlight, Book 2)
- Bitter Blood (Blood and Moonlight, Book 3)
- Blood and Moonlight (The Complete Series)

Purgatory Series

- The Wolf Within (Purgatory, Book 1)
- Marked By The Vampire (Purgatory, Book 2)
- Charming The Beast (Purgatory, Book 3)
- Deal with the Devil (Purgatory, Book 4)

- The Beasts Inside (Purgatory, Books 1 to 4)

Bound Series

- Bound By Blood (Bound Book 1)
- Bound In Darkness (Bound Book 2)
- Bound In Sin (Bound Book 3)
- Bound By The Night (Bound Book 4)
- Forever Bound (Bound, Books 1 to 4)
- Bound in Death (Bound Book 5)

Made in the USA
Lexington, KY
11 February 2019